S
Leguin

Le Guin, Ursula K.,
1929-

The other wind.

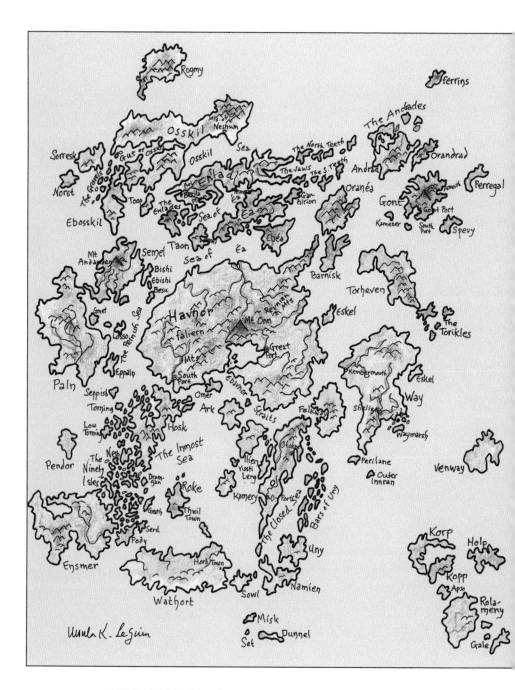

THE INNER LANDS OF EARTHSEA

The
Other Wind

THE BOOKS OF EARTHSEA
BY URSULA K. LE GUIN

A Wizard of Earthsea

The Tombs of Atuan

The Farthest Shore

Tehanu

Tales from Earthsea

Ursula K. Le Guin

The Other Wind

Harcourt, Inc.

New York   San Diego   London

www.harcourt.com

Library of Congress Cataloging-in-Publication Data
Le Guin, Ursula K., 1929–
The other wind/by Ursula K. Le Guin—1st ed.
p.   cm.
ISBN 0-15-100684-9
I. Title.
PS3562.E42 O84 2001
813'.54—dc21   2001024632

Text set in Adobe Caslon
Designed by Linda Lockowitz

First edition
B D F H J K I G E C A

Printed in the United States of America

Farther west than west
beyond the land
my people are dancing
on the other wind.

—The Song of the Woman of Kemay

Contents

The
Other Wind

CHAPTER I

Mending the Green Pitcher

S AILS LONG AND WHITE as swan's wings carried the ship *Farflyer* through summer air down the bay from the Armed Cliffs toward Gont Port. She glided into the still water landward of the jetty, so sure and graceful a creature of the wind that a couple of townsmen fishing off the old quay cheered her in, waving to the crewmen and the one passenger standing in the prow.

He was a thin man with a thin pack and an old black cloak, probably a sorcerer or small tradesman, nobody important. The two fishermen watched the bustle on the dock and the ship's deck as she made ready to unload her cargo, and only glanced at the passenger with a bit of curiosity when as he left the ship one of the sailors made a gesture behind his back, thumb and first and last finger of the left hand all pointed at him: *May you never come back!*

He hesitated on the pier, shouldered his pack, and set off into the streets of Gont Port. They were busy streets, and he got at once into the Fish Market, abrawl with hawkers and hagglers, paving stones glittering with fish scales and brine. If he had a way, he soon lost it among the carts and stalls and crowds and the cold stares of dead fish.

A tall old woman turned from the stall where she had been insulting the freshness of the herring and the veracity of the fishwife. Seeing her glaring at him, the stranger said unwisely, "Would you have the kindness to tell me the way I should go for Re Albi?"

"Why, go drown yourself in pig slop for a start," said the tall woman and strode off, leaving the stranger wilted and dismayed. But the fishwife, seeing a chance to seize the high moral ground, blared out, "Re Albi is it? Re Albi you want, man? Speak up then! The Old Mage's house, that would be what you'd want at Re Albi. Yes it would. So you go out by the corner there, and up Elvers Lane there, see, till you reach the tower . . ."

Once he was out of the market, broad streets led him uphill and past the massive watchtower to a town gate. Two stone dragons large as life guarded it, teeth the length of his forearm, stone eyes glaring blindly out over the town and the bay. A lounging guard told him just turn left at the top of the road and he'd be in Re Albi. "And keep on through the village for the Old Mage's house," the guard said.

So he went trudging up the road, which was pretty steep, looking up as he went to the steeper slopes and far peak of Gont Mountain that overhung its island like a cloud.

It was a long road and a hot day. He soon had his black cloak off and went on bareheaded in his shirtsleeves, but he had not thought to find water or buy food in the town, or had been too shy to, maybe, for he was not a man familiar with cities or at ease with strangers.

After several long miles he caught up to a cart which he had seen far up the dusty way for a long time as a dark blot in a white blot of dust. It creaked and screaked along at the pace of a pair of small oxen that looked as old, wrinkled, and unhopeful as tortoises. He greeted the carter, who resembled the oxen. The carter said nothing, but blinked.

"Might there be a spring of water up the road?" the stranger asked.

The carter slowly shook his head. After a long time he said, "No." A while later he said, "There ain't."

They all plodded along. Discouraged, the stranger found it hard to go any faster than the oxen, about a mile an hour, maybe.

He became aware that the carter was wordlessly reaching something out to him: a big clay jug wrapped round with wicker. He took it, and finding it very heavy, drank his fill of the water, leaving it scarcely lighter when he passed it back with his thanks.

"Climb on," said the carter after a while.

"Thanks. I'll walk. How far might it be to Re Albi?"

The wheels creaked. The oxen heaved deep sighs, first one, then the other. Their dusty hides smelled sweet in the hot sunlight.

"Ten mile," the carter said. He thought, and said, "Or twelve." After a while he said, "No less."

"I'd better walk on, then," said the stranger.

Refreshed by the water, he was able to get ahead of the oxen, and they and the cart and the carter were a good way behind him when he heard the carter speak again. "Going to the Old Mage's house," he said. If it was a question, it seemed to need no answer. The traveler walked on.

When he started up the road it had still lain in the vast shadow of the mountain, but when he turned left to the little village he took to be Re Albi, the sun was blazing in the western sky and under it the sea lay white as steel.

There were scattered small houses, a small dusty square, a fountain with one thin stream of water falling. He made for that, drank from his hands again and again, put his head under the stream, rubbed cool water through his hair and let it run down his arms, and sat for a while on the stone rim of the fountain, observed in attentive silence by two dirty little boys and a dirty little girl.

"He ain't the farrier," one of the boys said.

The traveler combed his wet hair back with his fingers.

"He'll be going to the Old Mage's house," said the girl, "stupid."

"Yerraghh!" said the boy, drawing his face into a horrible lopsided grimace by pulling at it with one hand while he clawed the air with the other.

"You watch it, Stony," said the other boy.

"Take you there," said the girl to the traveler.

"Thanks," he said, and stood up wearily.

"Got no staff, see," said one boy, and the other said, "Never said he did." Both watched with sullen eyes as the stranger followed the girl out of the village to a path that led north through rocky pastures that dropped down steep to the left.

The sun glared on the sea. His eyes dazzled, and the

high horizon and the blowing wind made him dizzy. The child was a little hopping shadow ahead of him. He stopped.

"Come on," she said, but she too stopped. He came up to her on the path. "There," she said. He saw a wooden house near the cliff's edge, still some way ahead.

"I ain't afraid," the girl said. "I fetch their eggs lots of times for Stony's dad to carry to market. Once she gave me peaches. The old lady. Stony says I stole 'em but I never. Go on. She ain't there. Neither of 'em is."

She stood still, pointing to the house.

"Nobody's there?"

"The old man is. Old Hawk, he is."

The traveler went on. The child stood watching him till he went round the corner of the house.

Two goats stared down at the stranger from a steep fenced field. A scatter of hens and half-grown chicks pecked and conversed softly in long grass under peach and plum trees. A man was standing on a short ladder against the trunk of one of the trees; his head was in the leaves, and the traveler could see only his bare brown legs.

"Hello," the traveler said, and after a while said it again a bit louder.

The leaves shook and the man came briskly down the ladder. He carried a handful of plums, and when he got off the ladder he batted away a couple of bees drawn by the juice. He came forward, a short, straight-backed man, grey hair tied back from a handsome, timeworn face. He looked to be seventy or so. Old scars, four white seams, ran from his left cheekbone down to the jaw. His gaze was clear, direct, intense. "They're ripe," he said, "though they'll be even better tomorrow." He held out his handful of little yellow plums.

"Lord Sparrowhawk," the stranger said huskily. "Archmage."

The old man gave a curt nod of acknowledgment. "Come into the shade," he said.

The stranger followed him, and did what he was told: he sat down on a wooden bench in the shade of the gnarled tree nearest the house; he accepted the plums, now rinsed and served in a wicker basket; he ate one, then another, then a third. Questioned, he admitted that he had eaten nothing that day. He sat while the master of the house went into it, coming out presently with bread and cheese and half an onion. The guest ate the bread and cheese and onion and drank the cup of cold water his host brought him. The host ate plums to keep him company.

"You look tired. How far have you come?"

"From Roke."

The old man's expression was hard to read. He said only, "I wouldn't have guessed that."

"I'm from Taon, lord. I went from Taon to Roke. And there the Lord Patterner told me I should come here. To you."

"Why?"

It was a formidable gaze.

"Because you *walked across the dark land living...*" The stranger's husky voice died away.

The old man picked up the words: *"And came to the far shores of the day.* Yes. But that was spoken in prophecy of the coming of our King, Lebannen."

"You were with him, lord."

"I was. And he gained his kingdom there. But I left mine there. So don't call me by any title. Hawk, or Sparrowhawk, as you please. And how shall I call you?"

The man murmured his use-name: "Alder."

Food and drink and shade and sitting down had clearly eased him, but he still looked exhausted. He had a weary sadness in him; his face was full of it.

The old man had spoken to him with a hard edge in his voice, but that was gone when he said, "Let's put off talking for a bit. You've sailed near a thousand miles and walked fifteen uphill. And I've got to water the beans and the lettuce and all, since my wife and daughter left the garden in my charge. So rest a while. We can talk in the cool of the evening. Or the cool of the morning. There's seldom as much hurry as I used to think there was."

When he came back by half an hour later his guest was flat on his back asleep in the cool grass under the peach trees.

The man who had been Archmage of Earthsea stopped with a bucket in one hand and a hoe in the other and looked down at the sleeping stranger.

"Alder," he said under his breath. "What's the trouble you bring with you, Alder?"

It seemed to him that if he wanted to know the man's true name he would know it only by thinking, by putting his mind to it, as he might have done when he was a mage.

But he did not know it, and thinking would not give it to him, and he was not a mage.

He knew nothing about this Alder and must wait to be

told. "Never trouble trouble," he told himself, and went on to water the beans.

As soon as the sun's light was cut off by a low rock wall that ran along the top of the cliff near the house, the cool of the shadow roused the sleeper. He sat up with a shiver, then stood up, a bit stiff and bewildered, with grass seed in his hair. Seeing his host filling buckets at the well and lugging them to the garden, he went to help him.

"Three or four more ought to do it," said the ex-Archmage, doling out water to the roots of a row of young cabbages. The smell of wet dirt was pleasant in the dry, warm air. The westering light came golden and broken over the ground.

They sat on a long bench beside the house door to see the sun go down. Sparrowhawk had brought out a bottle and two squat, thick cups of greenish glass. "My wife's son's wine," he said. "From Oak Farm, in Middle Valley. A good year, seven years back." It was a flinty red wine that warmed Alder right through. The sun set in calm clarity. The wind was down. Birds in the orchard trees made a few closing remarks.

Alder had been amazed when he learned from the Master Patterner of Roke that the Archmage Sparrowhawk, that man of legend, who had brought the king home from the realm of death and then flown off on a dragon's back, was still alive. Alive, said the Patterner, and living on his home island, Gont. "I tell you what not many know," the Patterner had said, "for I think you need to know it. And I think you will keep his secret."

"But then he is still Archmage!" Alder had said, with a kind of joy: for it had been a puzzle and concern to all men of the art that the wise men of Roke Island, the school and center of magery in the Archipelago, had not in all the years of King Lebannen's rule named an Archmage to replace Sparrowhawk.

"No," the Patterner had said. "He is not a mage at all."

The Patterner had told him a little of how Sparrowhawk had lost his power, and why; and Alder had had time to ponder it all. But still, here, in the presence of this man who had spoken with dragons, and brought back the Ring of Erreth-Akbe, and crossed the kingdom of the dead, and ruled the Archipelago before the king, all those stories and songs were in his mind. Even as he saw him old, content with his garden, with no power in him or about him but that of a soul made by a long life of thought and action, he still saw a great mage. And so it troubled him considerably that Sparrowhawk had a wife.

A wife, a daughter, a stepson ... Mages had no family. A common sorcerer like Alder might marry or might not, but the men of true power were celibate. Alder could imagine this man riding a dragon, that was easy enough, but to think of him as a husband and father was another matter. He couldn't manage it. He tried. He asked, "Your—wife—She's with her son, then?"

Sparrowhawk came back from far away. His eyes had been on the western gulfs. "No," he said. "She's in Havnor. With the king."

After a while, coming all the way back, he added, "She went there with our daughter just after the Long Dance.

Lebannen sent for them, to take counsel. Maybe on the same matter that brings you here to me. We'll see…But the truth is, I'm tired this evening, and not much disposed to weighing heavy matters. And you look tired too. So a bowl of soup, maybe, and another glass of wine, and sleep? And we'll talk in the morning."

"All with pleasure, lord," Alder said, "but for the sleep. That's what I fear."

It took the old man a while to register this, but then he said, "You fear to sleep?"

"Dreams."

"Ah." A keen glance from the dark eyes under eyebrows grown tangled and half grey. "You had a good nap there in the grass, I think."

"The sweetest sleep I've had since I left Roke Island. I'm grateful to you for that boon, lord. Maybe it will return tonight. But if not, I struggle with my dream, and cry out, and wake, and am a burden to anyone near me. I'll sleep outside, if you permit."

Sparrowhawk nodded. "It'll be a pleasant night," he said.

It was a pleasant night, cool, the sea wind mild from the south, the stars of summer whitening all the sky except where the broad, dark summit of the mountain loomed. Alder put down the pallet and sheepskin his host gave him, in the grass where he had slept before.

Sparrowhawk lay in the little western alcove of the house. He had slept there as a boy, when it was Ogion's house and he was Ogion's prentice in wizardry. Tehanu had slept there these last fifteen years, since she had been his daughter. With her and Tenar gone, when he lay in his and

Tenar's bed in the dark back corner of the single room he felt his solitude, so he had taken to sleeping in the alcove. He liked the narrow cot built out from the thick house wall of timbers, right under the window. He slept well there. But this night he did not.

Before midnight, wakened by a cry, voices outside, he leapt up and went to the door. It was only Alder struggling with nightmare, amid sleepy protests from the henhouse. Alder shouted in the thick voice of dream and then woke, starting up in panic and distress. He begged his host's pardon and said he would sit up a while under the stars. Sparrowhawk went back to bed. He was not wakened again by Alder, but he had a bad dream of his own.

He was standing by a wall of stone near the top of a long hillside of dry grey grass that ran down from dimness into the dark. He knew he had been there before, had stood there before, but he did not know when, or what place it was. Someone was standing on the other side of the wall, the downhill side, not far away. He could not see the face, only that it was a tall man, cloaked. He knew that he knew him. The man spoke to him, using his true name. He said, "You will soon be here, Ged."

Cold to the bone, he sat up, staring to see the space of the house about him, to draw its reality around him like a blanket. He looked out the window at the stars. The cold came into his heart then. They were not the stars of summer, beloved, familiar, the Cart, the Falcon, the Dancers, the Heart of the Swan. They were other stars, the small, still stars of the dry land, that never rise or set. He had known their names, once, when he knew the names of things.

"Avert!" he said aloud and made the gesture to turn away misfortune that he had learned when he was ten years old. His gaze went to the open doorway of the house, the corner behind the door, where he thought to see darkness taking shape, clotting together and rising up.

But his gesture, though it had no power, woke him. The shadows behind the door were only shadows. The stars out the window were the stars of Earthsea, paling in the first reflection of the dawn.

He sat holding his sheepskin up round his shoulders, watching those stars fade as they dropped west, watching the growing brightness, the colors of light, the play and change of coming day. There was a grief in him, he did not know why, a pain and yearning as for something dear and lost, forever lost. He was used to that; he had held much dear, and lost much; but this sadness was so great it did not seem to be his own. He felt a sadness at the very heart of things, a grief even in the coming of the light. It clung to him from his dream, and stayed with him when he got up.

He lit a little fire in the big hearth and went to the peach trees and the henhouse to gather breakfast. Alder came in from the path that ran north along the cliff top; he had gone for a walk at first light, he said. He looked jaded, and Sparrowhawk was struck again by the sadness in his face, which echoed the deep aftermood of his own dream.

They had a cup of the warmed barley gruel the country people of Gont drink, a boiled egg, a peach; they ate by the hearth, for the morning air in the shadow of the mountain was too cold for sitting outdoors. Sparrowhawk looked after his livestock: fed the chickens, scattered grain for doves, let the goats into the pasture. When he came back they sat again on the bench in the dooryard. The sun was not over the mountain yet, but the air had grown dry and warm.

"Now tell me what brings you here, Alder. But since you came by Roke, tell me first if things are well in the Great House."

"I did not enter it, my lord."

"Ah." A neutral tone but a sharp glance.

"I was only in the Immanent Grove."

"Ah." A neutral tone, a neutral glance. "Is the Patterner well?"

"He told me, 'Carry my love and honor to my lord and say to him: I wish we walked in the Grove together as we used to do.'"

Sparrowhawk smiled a little sadly. After a while he said, "So. But he sent you to me with more to say than that, I think."

"I will try to be brief."

"Man, we have all day before us. And I like a story told from the beginning."

So Alder told him his story from the beginning.

He was a witch's son, born in the town of Elini on Taon, the Isle of the Harpers.

Taon is at the southern end of the Sea of Éa, not far from where Soléa lay before the sea whelmed it. That was the ancient heart of Earthsea. All those islands had states and cities, kings and wizards, when Havnor was a land of feuding tribesmen and Gont a wilderness ruled by bears. People born on Éa or Ebéa, Enlad or Taon, though they may be a ditchdigger's daughter or a witch's son, consider themselves

13

to be descendants of the Elder Mages, sharing the lineage of the warriors who died in the dark years for Queen Elfarran. Therefore they often have a fine courtesy of manner, though sometimes an undue haughtiness, and a generous, uncalculating turn of mind and speech, a way of soaring above mere fact and prose, which those whose minds stay close to merchandise distrust. "Kites without strings," say the rich men of Havnor of such people. But they do not say it in the hearing of the king, Lebannen of the House of Enlad.

The best harps in Earthsea are made on Taon, and there are schools of music there, and many famous singers of the Lays and Deeds were born or learned their art there. Elini, however, is just a market town in the hills, with no music about it, Alder said; and his mother was a poor woman, though not, as he put it, hungry poor. She had a birthmark, a red stain from the right eyebrow and ear clear down over her shoulder. Many women and men with such a blemish or difference about them become witches or sorcerers perforce, "marked for it," people say. Blackberry learned spells and could do the most ordinary kind of witchery; she had no real gift for it, but she had a way about her that was almost as good as the gift itself. She made a living, and trained her son as well as she could, and saved enough to prentice him to the sorcerer who gave him his true name.

Of his father Alder said nothing. He knew nothing. Blackberry had never spoken of him. Though seldom celibate, witches seldom kept company more than a night or two with any man, and it was a rare thing for a witch to marry a man. Far more often two of them lived their lives together, and that was called witch marriage or she-troth. A witch's child, then, had a mother or two mothers, but no father. That went without saying, and Sparrowhawk asked nothing on that score; but he asked about Alder's training.

The sorcerer Gannet had taught Alder the few words he knew of the True Speech, and some spells of finding and illusion, at which Alder had shown, he said, no talent at all. But Gannet took enough interest in the boy to discover his true gift. Alder was a mender. He could rejoin. He could make whole. A broken tool, a knife blade or an axle snapped, a pottery bowl shattered: he could bring the fragments back together without joint or seam or weakness. So his master sent him about seeking various spells of mending, which he found mostly among witches of the island, and he worked with them and by himself to learn to mend.

"That is a kind of healing," Sparrowhawk said. "No small gift, nor easy craft."

"It was a joy to me," Alder said, with a shadow of a smile in his face. "Working out the spells, and finding sometimes how to use one of the True Words in the work... To put back together a barrel that's dried, the staves all fallen in from the hoops—that's a real pleasure, seeing it build up again, and swell out in the right curve, and stand there on its bottom ready for the wine... There was a harper from Meoni, a great harper, oh, he played like a storm on the high hills, like a tempest on the sea. He was hard on the harp strings, twanging and pulling them in the passion of his art, so they'd break at the very height and flight of the music. And so he hired me to be there near him when he played, and when he broke a string I'd mend it quick as the note itself, and he'd play on."

Sparrowhawk nodded with the warmth of a fellow professional talking shop. "Have you mended glass?" he asked.

"I have, but it's a long, nasty job," Alder said, "with all the tiny little bits and speckles glass goes to."

"But a big hole in the heel of a stocking can be worse," Sparrowhawk said, and they discussed mending for a while longer, before Alder returned to his story.

He had become a mender, then, a sorcerer with a modest practice and a local reputation for his gift. When he was about thirty, he went to the principal city of the island, Meoni, with the harper, who was playing for a wedding there. A woman sought him out in their lodging, a young woman, not trained as a witch; but she had a gift, she said, the same as his, and wanted him to teach her. And indeed she had a greater gift than his. Though she knew not a word of the Old Speech, she could put a smashed jug back together or mend a frayed-out rope just with the movements of her hands and a wordless song she sang under her breath, and she had healed broken limbs of animals and people, which Alder had never dared try to do.

So rather than his teaching her, they put their skills together and taught each other more than either had ever known. She came back to Elini and lived with Alder's mother Blackberry, who taught her various useful appearances and effects and ways of impressing customers, if not much actual witch knowledge. Lily was her name; and Lily and Alder worked together there and in all the hill towns nearby, as their reputation grew.

"And I came to love her," Alder said. His voice had changed when he began to speak of her, losing its hesitancy, growing urgent and musical.

"Her hair was dark, but with a shining of red gold in it," he said.

There was no way he could hide his love from her, and she knew it and returned it. Whether she was a witch now or not, she said she did not care; she said the two of them were born to be together, in their work and in their life; she loved him and would be married to him.

So they were married, and lived in very great happiness for a year, and half a second year.

"Nothing was wrong at all until the time came for the child to be born," Alder said. "But it was late, and then very late. The midwives tried to bring on the birth with herbs and spells, but it was as if the child would not let her bear it. It would not be separated from her. It would not be born. And it was not born. It took her with it."

After a while he said, "We had great joy."

"I see that."

"And my sorrow was in that degree."

The old man nodded.

"I could bear it," Alder said. "You know how it is. There was not much reason to be living that I could see, but I could bear it."

"Yes."

"But in the winter. Two months after her death. There was a dream came to me. She was in the dream."

"Tell it."

"I stood on a hillside. Along the top of the hill and

running down the slope was a wall, low, like a boundary wall between sheep pastures. She was standing across the wall from me, below it. It was darker there."

Sparrowhawk nodded once. His face had gone rock hard.

"She was calling to me. I heard her voice saying my name, and I went to her. I knew she was dead, I knew it in the dream, but I was glad to go. I couldn't see her clear, and I went to her to see her, to be with her. And she reached out across the wall. It was no higher than my heart. I had thought she might have the child with her, but she did not. She was reaching her hands out to me, and so I reached out to her, and we took each other's hands."

"You touched?"

"I wanted to go to her, but I could not cross the wall. My legs would not move. I tried to draw her to me, and she wanted to come, it seemed as if she could, but the wall was there between us. We couldn't get over it. So she leaned across to me and kissed my mouth and said my name. And she said, 'Set me free!'

"I thought if I called her by her true name maybe I could free her, bring her across that wall, and I said, 'Come with me, Mevre!' But she said, 'That's not my name, Hara, that's not my name any more.' And she let go my hands, though I tried to hold her. She cried, 'Set me free, Hara!' But she was going down into the dark. It was all dark down that hillside below the wall. I called her name and her use-name and all the dear names I had had for her, but she went on away. So then I woke."

Sparrowhawk gazed long and keenly at his visitor. "You gave me your name, Hara," he said.

18

Alder looked a little stunned, and took a couple of long breaths, but he looked up with desolate courage. "Who could I better trust it with?" he said.

Sparrowhawk thanked him gravely. "I will try to deserve your trust," he said. "Tell me, do you know what that place is—that wall?"

"I did not know it then. Now I know you have crossed it."

"Yes. I've been on that hill. And crossed the wall, by the power and art I used to have. And I've gone down to the cities of the dead, and spoken to men I had known living, and sometimes they answered me. But Hara, you are the first man I ever knew or heard of, among all the great mages in the lore of Roke or Paln or the Enlades, who ever touched, who ever kissed his love across that wall."

Alder sat with his head bowed and his hands clenched.

"Will you tell me: what was her touch like? Were her hands warm? Was she cold air and shadow, or like a living woman? Forgive my questions."

"I wish I could answer them, my lord. On Roke the Summoner asked the same. But I can't answer truly. My longing for her was so great, I wished so much—it could be I wished her to be as she was in life. But I don't know. In dream not all things are clear."

"In dream, no. But I never heard of any man coming to the wall in dream. It is a place a wizard may seek to come to, if he must, if he's learned the way and has the power. But without the knowledge and the power, only the dying can—"

And then he broke off, remembering his dream of the night before.

"I took it for a dream," Alder said. "It troubled me, but I

cherished it. It was like a harrow on my heart's ground to think of it, and yet I held to that pain, held it close to me. I wanted it. I hoped to dream again."

"Did you?"

"Yes. I dreamed again."

He looked unseeing into the blue gulf of air and ocean west of where they sat. Low and faint across the tranquil sea lay the sunlit hills of Kameber. Behind them the sun was breaking bright over the mountain's northern shoulder.

"It was nine days after the first dream. I was in that same place, but high up on the hill. I saw the wall below me across the slope. And I ran down the hill, calling out her name, sure of seeing her. There was someone there. But when I came close, I saw it wasn't Lily. It was a man, and he was stooping at the wall, as if he was repairing it. I said to him, 'Where is she, where is Lily?' He didn't answer or look up. I saw what he was doing. He wasn't working to mend the wall but to unbuild it, prying with his fingers at a great stone. The stone never moved, and he said, 'Help me, Hara!' Then I saw that it was my teacher, Gannet, who named me. He has been dead these five years. He kept prying and straining at the stone with his fingers, and said my name again—'Help me, set me free.' And he stood up and reached out to me across the wall, as she had done, and caught my hand. But his hand burned, with fire or with cold, I don't know, but the touch of it burned me so that I pulled away, and the pain and fear of it woke me from the dream."

He held his hand out as he spoke, showing a darkness on the back and palm like an old bruise.

"I've learned not to let them touch me," he said in a low voice.

Ged looked at Alder's mouth. There was a darkening across his lips too.

"Hara, you've been in mortal danger," he said, also softly. "There is more."

Forcing his voice against silence, Alder went on with his story.

The next night when he slept again he found himself on that dim hill and saw the wall that dropped down from the hilltop across the slope. He went down towards it, hoping to find his wife there. "I didn't care if she couldn't cross it, if I couldn't, so long as I could see her and talk to her," he said. But if she was there he never saw her among all the others: for as he came closer to the wall he saw a crowd of shadowy people on the other side, some clear and some dim, some he seemed to know and others he did not know, and all of them reached out their hands to him as he approached and called him by his name: "Hara! let us come with you! Hara, set us free!"

"It's a terrible thing to hear one's true name called by strangers," Alder said, "and it's a terrible thing to be called by the dead."

He tried to turn and climb back up the hill, away from the wall; but his legs had the awful weakness of dream and would not carry him. He fell to his knees to keep himself from being drawn down to the wall, and called out for help, though there was no one to help him; and so he woke in terror.

Since then, every night that he slept deeply, he found

himself standing on the hill in the dry grey grass above the wall, and the dead would crowd thick and shadowy below it, pleading and crying to him, calling his name.

"I wake," he said, "and I'm in my own room. I'm not there, on that hillside. But I know they are. And I have to sleep. I try to wake often, and to sleep in daylight when I can, but I have to sleep at last. And then I am there, and they are there. And I can't go up the hill. If I move it's always downhill, towards the wall. Sometimes I can turn my back to them, but then I think I hear Lily among them, crying to me. And I turn to look for her. And they reach out to me."

He looked down at his hands gripping each other.

"What am I to do?" he said.

Sparrowhawk said nothing.

After a long time Alder said, "The harper I told you of was a good friend to me. After a while he saw there was something amiss, and when I told him that I couldn't sleep for fear of my dreams of the dead, he urged me and helped me to take ship's passage to Éa, to speak to a grey wizard there." He meant a man trained in the School on Roke. "As soon as that wizard heard what my dreams were he said I must go to Roke."

"What is his name?"

"Beryl. He serves the Prince of Éa, who is Lord of the Isle of Taon."

The old man nodded.

"He had no help to give me, he said, but his word was as good as gold to the ship's master. So I went on the water again. That was a long journey, coasting clear round Havnor and down the Inmost Sea. I thought maybe being on the water, far from Taon, always farther, I might leave the dream behind me. The wizard on Éa called that place in my dream *the dry land,* and I thought maybe I'd be going away from it, going on the sea. But every night I was there on the hillside. And more than once in the night, as time went on. Twice, or three times, or every time my eyes close, I'm on the hill, and the wall below me, and the voices calling me. So I'm like a man crazy with the pain of a wound who can find peace only in sleep, but the sleep is my torment, with the pain and anguish of the wretched dead all crowding at the wall, and my fear of them."

The sailors soon began to shun him, he said, at night because he cried out and woke them with his miserable wakenings, and in daylight because they thought there was a curse on him or a gebbeth in him.

"And no relief for you on Roke?"

"In the Grove," Alder said, and his face changed entirely when he said the word.

Sparrowhawk's face had the same look for a moment.

"The Master Patterner took me there, under those trees, and I could sleep. Even at night I could sleep. In daylight, if the sun's on me—it was like that in the afternoon, yesterday, here—if the warmth of the sun's on me and the red of the sun shines through my eyelids, I don't fear to dream. But in the Grove there was no fear at all, and I could love the night again."

"Tell me how it was when you came to Roke."

Though hampered by weariness, anguish, and awe, Alder had the silver tongue of his island; and what he left out for fear of going on too long or telling the Archmage what he already knew, his listener could well imagine, remembering when he himself first came to the Isle of the Wise as a boy of fifteen.

When Alder left the ship at the docks at Thwil Town, one of the sailors had drawn the rune of the Closed Door on the top of the gangplank to prevent his ever coming back aboard. Alder noticed it, but he thought the sailor had good cause. He felt himself ill-omened; he felt he bore darkness in him. That made him shyer than he would have been in any case in a strange town. And Thwil was a very strange town.

"The streets lead you awry," Sparrowhawk said.

"They do that, my lord!—I'm sorry, my tongue will obey my heart, and not you—"

"Never mind. I was used to it once. I can be Lord Goatherd again, if it eases your speech. Go on."

Misdirected by those he asked, or misunderstanding the directions, Alder wandered about the hilly little labyrinth of Thwil Town with the School always in sight and never able to get to it, until, having reached despair, he came to a plain door in a bare wall on a dull square. After staring at it a while he recognised the wall was the one he had been trying to get to. He knocked, and a man with a quiet face and quiet eyes opened the door.

Alder was ready to say that he had been sent by the wizard Beryl of Éa with a message for the Master Summoner, but he didn't have a chance to speak. The Doorkeeper gazed at him a moment and said mildly, "You cannot bring them into this house, friend."

Alder did not ask who it was he could not bring with him. He knew. He had slept scarcely at all the past nights, snatching fragments of sleep and waking in terror, dozing off in the daylight, seeing the dry grass sloping down through the sunlit deck of the ship, the wall of stones across the waves of the sea. And waking, the dream was in him, with him, around him, veiled, and he could hear, always, faintly, through all the noises of wind and sea, the voices that cried his name. He did not know if he was awake now or asleep. He was crazy with pain and fear and weariness.

"Keep them out," he said, "and let me in, for pity's sake let me in!"

"Wait here," the man said, as gently as before. "There's a bench," pointing. And he closed the door.

Alder went and sat down on the stone bench. He remembered that, and he remembered some boys of fifteen or so looking curiously at him as they went by and entered that door, but what happened for some while after he could recall only in fragments.

The Doorkeeper came back with a young man with the staff and cloak of a Roke wizard. Then Alder was in a room, which he understood was in a lodging house. There the Master Summoner came and tried to talk with him. But Alder by then was not able to talk. Between sleep and waking, between the sunlit room and the dim grey hill, between the Summoner's voice speaking to him and the voices calling him across the wall, he could not think and he could not move, in the living world. But in the dim world where the voices called, he thought it would be easy to walk on down those few steps to the wall and let the reaching hands take him and hold him. If he was one of them they would let him be, he thought.

Then, as he remembered, the sunlit room was altogether gone, and he was on the grey hill. But with him stood the Summoner of Roke: a big, broad, dark-skinned man, with a great staff of yew wood that shimmered in the dim place.

The voices had ceased calling. The people, the crowding figures at the wall, were gone. He could hear a distant rustle and a kind of sobbing as they went down into the darkness, went away.

The Summoner stepped to the wall and put his hands on it.

The stones had been loosened here and there. A few had fallen and lay on the dry grass. Alder felt that he should pick them up and replace them, mend the wall, but he did not.

The Summoner turned to him and asked, "Who brought you here?"

"My wife, Mevre."

"Summon her here."

Alder stood dumb. At last he opened his mouth, but it was not his wife's true name that he spoke but her use-name, the name he had called her in life. He said it aloud, "Lily..." The sound of it was not like a white flower, but like a pebble dropping on dust.

No sound. Stars shone small and steady in the black sky. Alder had never looked up at the sky in this place before. He did not recognise the stars.

"Mevre!" said the Summoner, and in his deep voice spoke some words in the Old Speech.

Alder felt the breath go out of him and could barely stand. But nothing stirred on the long slope that led down to formless dark.

Then there was some movement, something lighter, coming up the hill, coming slowly nearer. Alder shook with fear and yearning, and whispered, "Oh my dear love."

But the figure as it came closer was too small to be Lily. He saw it was a child of twelve or so, girl or boy he could not tell. It paid no heed to him or the Summoner and never looked across the wall, but settled down just under it. When Alder came closer and looked down he saw the child was prying and pulling at the stones, trying to loosen one, then another.

The Summoner was whispering in the Old Speech. The child glanced up once indifferently and went on tugging at the stones with its thin fingers that seemed to have no strength in them.

This was so horrible to Alder that his head spun; he tried to turn away, and beyond that he could remember nothing till he woke in the sunny room, lying in bed, weak and sick and cold.

People looked after him: the aloof, smiling woman who kept the lodging house, and a brown-skinned, stocky old man who came with the Doorkeeper. Alder took him for a physician-sorcerer. Only after he had seen him with his staff of olive wood did he understand that he was the Herbal, the master of healing of the School on Roke.

His presence brought solace, and he was able to give Alder sleep. He brewed up a tea and had Alder drink it, and lighted some herb that burned slowly with a smell like the dark earth under pine woods, and sitting nearby began a long, soft chant. "But I must not sleep," Alder protested, feeling sleep coming into him like a great dark tide. The healer laid his warm hand on Alder's hand. Then peace came into Alder, and he slipped into sleep without fear. So long as the healer's hand was on his, or on his shoulder, it kept him from the dark hillside and the wall of stones.

He woke to eat a little, and soon the Master Herbal was there again with the tepid, insipid tea and the earth-smelling smoke and the dull untuneful chant and the touch of his hand; and Alder could have rest.

The healer had all his duties at the School, so could be there only some hours of the night. Alder got enough rest in three nights that he could eat and walk about the town a little in the day and think and talk coherently. On the fourth morning the three masters, the Herbal, the Doorkeeper, and the Summoner, came to his room.

Alder bowed to the Summoner with dread, almost distrust, in his heart. The Herbal was also a great mage, but his art was not altogether different from Alder's own craft, so they had a kind of understanding; and there was the great kindness of his hand. The Summoner, though, dealt not with bodily things but with the spirit, with the minds and wills of men, with ghosts, with meanings. His art was arcane, dangerous, full of risk and threat. And he had stood beside Alder there, not in the body, on the boundary, at the wall. With him the darkness and the fear returned.

None of the three mages said anything at first. If they had one thing in common, it was a great capacity for silence.

So Alder spoke, trying to say what was in his heart, for nothing less would do.

"If I did some wrong that brought me to that place, or brought my wife to me there, or the other souls, if I can mend or undo what I did, I will. But I don't know what it is I did."

"Or what you are," the Summoner said.

Alder was mute.

"Not many of us know who or what we are," said the Doorkeeper. "A glimpse is all we get."

"Tell us how you first went to the wall of stones," the Summoner said.

And Alder told them.

The mages listened in silence and said nothing for a while after he was done. Then the Summoner asked, "Have you thought what it means to cross that wall?"

"I know I could not come back."

"Only mages can cross the wall living, and only at utmost need. The Herbal may go with a sufferer all the way to that wall, but if the sick man crosses it, he does not follow."

The Summoner was so tall and broad-bodied and dark that, looking at him, Alder thought of a bear.

"My art of Summoning empowers us to call the dead back across the wall for a brief time, a moment, if there is need to do so. I myself question if any need could justify so great a breach in the law and balance of the world. I have never made that spell. Nor have I crossed the wall. The Archmage did, and the King with him, to heal the wound in the world the wizard called Cob made."

"And when the Archmage did not return, Thorion, who was our Summoner then, went down into the dry land to seek him," the Herbal said. "He came back, but changed."

"There is no need to speak of that," the big man said.

"Maybe there is," said the Herbal. "Maybe Alder needs

29

to know it. Thorion trusted his strength too far, I think. He stayed there too long. He thought he could summon himself back into life, but what came back was only his skill, his power, his ambition—the will to live that gives no life. Yet we trusted him, because we had loved him. So he devoured us. Until Irian destroyed him."

Far from Roke, on the Isle of Gont, Alder's listener interrupted him— "What name was that?" Sparrowhawk asked.

"Irian, he said."

"Do you know that name?"

"No, my lord."

"Nor I." After a pause Sparrowhawk went on softly, as if unwillingly. "But I saw Thorion, there. In the dry land, where he had risked going to seek me. It grieved me to see him there. I said to him he might go back across the wall." His face went dark and grim. "That was ill spoken. All is spoken ill between the living and the dead. But I had loved him too."

They sat in silence. Sparrowhawk got up abruptly to stretch his arms and rub his thighs. They both moved about a bit. Alder got a drink of water from the well. Sparrowhawk fetched out a garden spade and the new handle to fit to it, and set to work smoothing the oaken shaft and tapering the end that would go in the socket.

He said, "Go on, Alder," and Alder went on with his story.

The two masters had been silent for a while after the Herbal spoke about Thorion. Alder got up the courage to ask them about a matter that had been much on his mind: how those who died came to the wall, and how the mages came there.

The Summoner answered promptly: "It is a spirit journey."

The old healer was more hesitant. "It's not in the body that we cross the wall, since the body of one who dies stays here. And if a mage goes there in vision, his sleeping body is still here, alive. And so we call that voyager...we call what makes that journey from the body, the soul, the spirit."

"But my wife took my hand," Alder said. He could not say again to them that she had kissed his mouth. "I felt her touch."

"So it seemed to you," the Summoner said.

"If they touched bodily, if a link was made," the Herbal said to the Summoner, "might that not be why the other dead can come to him, call to him, even touch him?"

"That is why he must resist them," said the Summoner, with a glance at Alder. His eyes were small, fiery.

Alder felt it as an accusation, and not a fair one. He said, "I try to resist them, my lord. I have tried. But there are so many of them—and she's with them—and they're suffering, crying out to me."

"They cannot suffer," the Summoner said. "Death ends all suffering."

"Maybe the shadow of pain is pain," said the Herbal. "There are mountains in that land, and they are called Pain."

The Doorkeeper had scarcely spoken until now. He said in his quiet, easy voice, "Alder is a mender, not a breaker. I don't think he can break that link."

"If he made it he can break it," the Summoner said.

"Did he make it?"

"I have no such art, my lord," Alder said, so frightened by what they were saying that he spoke angrily.

31

"Then I must go down among them," said the Summoner.

"No, my friend," said the Doorkeeper, and the old Herbal said, "You last of us all."

"But this is my art."

"And ours."

"Who then?"

The Doorkeeper said, "It seems Alder is our guide. Having come to us for help, maybe he can help us. Let us all go with him in his vision—to the wall, though not across it."

So that night, when late and fearfully Alder let sleep overcome him, and found himself on the grey hill, the others were with him: the Herbal, a warm presence in the chill; the Doorkeeper, elusive and silvery as starlight; and the massive Summoner, the bear, a dark strength.

This time they were standing not where the hill ran down into the dark, but on the near slope, looking up to the top. The wall in this place ran along the crest of the hill and was low, little more than knee height. Above it the sky with its few small stars was perfectly black.

Nothing moved.

It would be hard to walk uphill to the wall, Alder thought. Always before it had been below him.

But if he could go to it maybe Lily would be there, as she had been the first time. Maybe he could take her hand, and the mages would bring her back with him. Or he could step over the wall where it was so low and come to her.

He began to walk up the hill. It was easy, it was no trouble, he was almost there.

"Hara!"

The Summoner's deep voice called him back like a

noose round his neck, a jerked leash. He stumbled, staggered forward one step more, almost at the wall, dropped to his knees and reached out to the stones. He was crying, "Save me!" but to whom? To the mages, or to the shadows beyond the wall?

Then hands were on his shoulders, living hands, strong and warm, and he was in his room, with the healer's hands indeed on his shoulders, and the werelight burning white around them. And there were four men in the room with him, not three.

The old Herbal sat down on the bed with him and soothed him a while, for he was shaking, shuddering, sobbing. "I can't do it," he kept saying, but still he did not know if he was talking to the mages or to the dead.

When the fear and pain began to lessen, he felt tired beyond bearing, and looked almost without interest at the man who had come into the room. His eyes were the color of ice, his hair and skin were white. A far Northerner, from Enwas or Bereswek, Alder thought him.

This man said to the mages, "What are you doing, my friends?"

"Taking risks, Azver," said the old Herbal.

"Trouble at the border, Patterner," said the Summoner.

Alder could feel the respect they had for this man, their relief that he was there, as they told him briefly what the trouble was.

"If he'll come with me, will you let him go?" the Patterner asked when they were done, and turning to Alder, "You need not fear your dreams in the Immanent Grove. And so we need not fear your dreams."

They all assented. The Patterner nodded and vanished. He was not there.

He had not been there; he had been a sending, a presentment. It was the first time Alder had seen the great powers of these masters made manifest, and it would have unnerved him if he had not been past amazement and fear.

He followed the Doorkeeper out into the night, through the streets, past the walls of the School, across fields under a high round hill, and along a stream singing its water music softly in the darkness of its banks. Ahead of them was a high wood, the trees crowned with grey starlight.

The Master Patterner came along the path to meet them, looking just as he had in the room. He and the Doorkeeper spoke for a minute, and then Alder followed the Patterner into the Grove.

"The trees are dark," Alder said to Sparrowhawk, "but it isn't dark under them. There is a light—a lightness there."

His listener nodded, smiling a little.

"As soon as I came there, I knew I could sleep. I felt as if I'd been asleep all along, in an evil dream, and now, here, I was truly awake: so I could truly sleep. There was a place he took me to, in among the roots of a huge tree, all soft with the fallen leaves of the tree, and he told me I could lie there. And I did, and I slept. I cannot tell you the sweetness of it."

THE MIDDAY SUN had grown strong; they went indoors, and the host set out bread and cheese and a bit of dried meat. Alder looked round him as they ate. The house had only the one long room with its little western alcove, but it was large and darkly airy, strongly built, with wide boards and beams, a gleaming floor, a deep stone fireplace. "This is a noble house," Alder said.

"An old one. They call it the Old Mage's house. Not for me, nor for my master Aihal who lived here, but for his master Heleth, who with him stilled the great earthquake. It's a good house."

Alder slept a while again under the trees with the sun shining on him through the moving leaves. His host rested too, but not long; when Alder woke, there was a good-sized basket of the small golden plums under the tree, and Sparrowhawk was up in the goat pasture mending a fence. Alder went to help him, but the job was done. The goats, however, were long gone.

"Neither of 'em's in milk," Sparrowhawk grumbled as they returned to the house. "They've got nothing to do but find new ways through the fence. I keep them for exasperation... The first spell I ever learned was to call goats from wandering. My aunt taught me. It's no more use to me now than if I sang them a love song. I'd better go see if they've got into the widower's vegetables. You don't have the kind of sorcery to charm a goat to come, do you?"

The two brown nannies were indeed invading a cabbage patch on the outskirts of the village. Alder repeated the spell Sparrowhawk told him:

Noth hierth malk man,
hiolk han merth han!

The goats gazed at him with alert disdain and moved away a little. Shouting and a stick got them out of the cabbages onto the path, and there Sparrowhawk produced some plums

35

from his pocket. Promising, offering, and cajoling, he slowly led the truants back into their pasture.

"They're odd creatures," he said, latching the gate. "You never know where you are with a goat."

Alder thought that he never knew where he was with his host, but did not say it.

When they were sitting in the shade again, Sparrowhawk said, "The Patterner isn't a Northerner, he's a Karg. Like my wife. He was a warrior of Karego-At. The only man I know of who ever came from those lands to Roke. The Kargs have no wizards. They distrust all sorcery. But they've kept more knowledge of the Old Powers of the Earth than we have. This man, Azver, when he was young, he heard some tale of the Immanent Grove, and it came to him that the center of all the earth's powers must be there. So he left his gods and his native tongue behind him and made his way to Roke. He stood on our doorstep and said, 'Teach me to live in that forest!' And we taught him, till he began to teach us... So he became our Master Patterner. He's not a gentle man, but he is to be trusted."

"I never could fear him," Alder said. "It was easy to be with him. He'd take me far into the wood with him."

They were both silent, both thinking of the glades and aisles of that wood, the sunlight and starlight in its leaves.

"It is the heart of the world," Alder said.

Sparrowhawk looked up eastward at the slopes of Gont Mountain, dark with trees. "I'll go walking there," he said, "in the forest, come autumn."

After a while he said, "Tell me what counsel the Patterner had for you, and why he sent you here to me."

36

"He said, my lord, that you knew more of the...the dry land than any living man, and so maybe you would understand what it means that the souls there come to me as they do, begging me for freedom."

"Did he say how he thinks it came about?"

"Yes. He said that maybe my wife and I didn't know how to be parted, only how to be joined. That it was not my doing, but was maybe ours together, because we drew each to the other, like drops of quicksilver. But the Master Summoner didn't agree. He said that only a great power of magery could so transgress the order of the world. Because my old master Gannet also touched me across the wall, the Summoner said maybe it was a mage power in him which had been hidden or disguised in life, but now was revealed."

Sparrowhawk brooded a while. "When I lived on Roke," he said, "I might have seen it as the Summoner does. There I knew no power stronger than what we call magery. Not even the Old Powers of the Earth, I thought...If the Summoner you met is the man I think, he came as a boy to Roke. My old friend Vetch of Iffish sent him to study with us. And he never left. That's a difference between him and Azver the Patterner. Azver lived till he was grown as a warrior's son, a warrior himself, among men and women, in the thick of life. Matters that the walls of the School keep out, he knows in his flesh and blood. He knows that men and women love, make love, marry...Having lived these fifteen years outside the walls, I incline to think Azver might be on the better track. The bond between you and your wife is stronger than the division between life and death."

Alder hesitated. "I've thought it might be so. But it

37

seems...shameless to think it. We loved each other, more than I can say we loved each other, but was our love greater than any other before us? Was it greater than Morred's and Elfarran's?"

"Maybe not less."

"How can that be?"

Sparrowhawk looked at him as if saluting something, and answered him with a care that made Alder feel honored. "Well," he said slowly, "sometimes there's a passion that comes in its springtime to ill fate or death. And because it ends in its beauty, it's what the harpers sing of and the poets make stories of: the love that escapes the years. That was the love of the Young King and Elfarran. That was your love, Hara. It wasn't greater than Morred's, but was his greater than yours?"

Alder said nothing, pondering.

"There's no less or greater in an absolute thing," Sparrowhawk said. "All or nothing at all, the true lover says, and that's the truth of it. My love will never die, he says. He claims eternity. And rightly. How can it die when it's life itself? What do we know of eternity but the glimpse we get of it when we enter in that bond?"

He spoke softly but with fire and energy; then he leaned back, and after a minute said, with a half smile, "Every oaf of a farm boy sings that, every young girl that dreams of love knows it. But it's not a thing the Masters of Roke are familiar with. The Patterner maybe knew it early. I learned it late. Very late. Not quite too late." He looked at Alder, the fire still in his eyes, challenging. "You had that," he said.

"I did." Alder drew a deep breath. Presently he said,

"Maybe they're there together, in the dark land. Morred and Elfarran."

"No," Sparrowhawk said with bleak certainty.

"But if the bond is true, what can break it?"

"There are no lovers there."

"Then what are they, what do they do, there in that land? You've been there, you crossed the wall. You walked and spoke with them. Tell me!"

"I will." But Sparrowhawk said nothing for a while. "I don't like to think about it," he said. He rubbed his head and scowled. "You saw...You've seen those stars. Little, mean stars, that never move. No moon. No sunrise...There are roads, if you go down the hill. Roads and cities. On the hill there's grass, dead grass, but farther down there's only dust and rocks. Nothing grows. Dark cities. The multitudes of the dead stand in the streets, or walk on the roads to no end. They don't speak. They don't touch. They never touch." His voice was low and dry. "There Morred would pass Elfarran and never turn his head, and she wouldn't look at him... There's no rejoining there, Hara. No bond. The mother doesn't hold her child, there."

"But my wife came to me," Alder said, "she called my name, she kissed my mouth!"

"Yes. And since your love wasn't greater than any other mortal love, and since you and she aren't mighty wizards whose power might change the laws of life and death, therefore, therefore something else is in this. Something is happening, is changing. Though it happens through you and to you, you are its instrument and not its cause."

Sparrowhawk stood up and strode to the beginning of

the path along the cliff and back to Alder; he was charged, almost quivering with tense energy, like a hawk about to stoop down on its prey.

"Did your wife not say to you, when you called her by her true name, *That is not my name any more*—?"

"Yes," Alder whispered.

"But how is that? We who have true names keep them when we die, it's our use-name that is forgotten...This is a mystery to the learned, I can tell you, but as well as we understand it, a true name is a word in the True Speech. That's why only one with the gift can know a child's name and give it. And the name binds the being—alive or dead. All the art of the Summoner lies in that...Yet when the master summoned your wife to come by her true name, she didn't come to him. You called by her use-name, Lily, and she came to you. Did she come to you as to the one who knew her truly?"

He gazed at Alder keenly and yet as if he saw more than the man who sat with him. After a while he went on, "When my master Aihal died, my wife was here with him; and as he was dying he said to her, *It is changed, all changed.* He was looking across that wall. From which side I do not know.

"And since that time, indeed there have been changes— a king on Morred's throne, and no Archmage of Roke. But more than that, much more. I saw a child summon the dragon Kalessin, the Eldest: and Kalessin came to her, calling her daughter, as I do. What does that mean? What does it mean that dragons have been seen above the islands of the west? The king sent to us, sent a ship to Gont Port, asking my daughter Tehanu to come and take counsel with him concerning dragons. People fear that the old covenant is broken, that the dragons will come to burn fields and cities as they did before Erreth-Akbe fought with Orm Embar. And now, at the boundary of life and death, a soul refuses the bond of her name...I do not understand it. All I know is that it is changing. It is all changing."

There was no fear in his voice, only fierce exultation.

Alder could not share that. He had lost too much and was too worn out by his struggle against forces he could not control or comprehend. But his heart rose to that gallantry.

"May it change for the good, my lord," he said.

"Be it so," the old man said. "But change it must."

As THE HEAT WENT OUT of the day, Sparrowhawk said he had to walk to the village. He carried the basket of plums with a basket of eggs nested in it.

Alder walked with him and they talked. When Alder understood that Sparrowhawk bartered fruit and eggs and the other produce of the little farm for barley and wheat flour, that the wood he burned was gathered patiently up in the forest, that his goats' not giving milk meant he must eke out last year's cheese, Alder was amazed: how could it be that the Archmage of Earthsea lived from hand to mouth? Did his own people not honor him?

When he went with him to the village, he saw women shut their doors when they saw the old man coming. The marketer who took his eggs and fruit tallied the count on his wooden tablet without a word, his face sullen and his eyes lowered. Sparrowhawk spoke to him pleasantly, "A good day to you then, Iddi," but got no answer.

"My lord," Alder asked as they walked home, "do they know who you are?"

"No," said the ex-Archmage, with a dry sidelong look. "And yes."

"But—" Alder did not know how to speak his indignation.

"They know I have no power of sorcery, but there's something uncanny about me. They know I live with a foreigner, a Kargish woman. They know the girl we call our daughter is something like a witch, but worse, because her face and hand were burnt away by fire, and because she herself burnt up the Lord of Re Albi, or pushed him off the cliff, or killed him with the evil eye—their stories vary. They honor the house we live in, though, because it was Aihal's and Heleth's house, and dead wizards are good wizards... You're a townsman, Alder, of an isle of Morred's kingdom. A village on Gont is another matter."

"But why do you stay here, lord? Surely the king would do you proper honor—"

"I want no honor," the old man said, with a violence that silenced Alder entirely.

They walked on. As they came to the house built at the cliff's edge he spoke again. "This is my eyrie," he said.

They had a glass of the red wine with supper, and another sitting out to watch the sun set. They did not talk much. Fear of the night, of the dream, was coming into Alder.

"I'm no healer," his host said, "but perhaps I can do what the Master Herbal did to let you sleep."

Alder looked his question.

"I've been thinking about it, and it seems to me maybe it

was no spell at all that kept you away from that hillside, but just the touch of a living hand. If you like, we can try it."

Alder protested, but Sparrowhawk said, "I'm awake half most nights anyway." So the guest lay that night in the low bed in the back corner of the big room, and the host sat up beside him, watching the fire and dozing.

He watched Alder, too, and saw him fall asleep at last; and not long after that saw him start and shudder in his sleep. He put out his hand and laid it on Alder's shoulder as he lay half turned away. The sleeping man stirred a little, sighed, relaxed, and slept on.

It pleased Sparrowhawk that he could do this much. As good as a wizard, he told himself with mild sarcasm.

He was not sleepy; the tension was still in him. He thought about all Alder had told him, and what they had talked about in the afternoon. He saw Alder stand in the path by the cabbage patch saying the spell to call the goats, and the goats' haughty indifference to the powerless words. He remembered how he had used to speak the name of the sparrowhawk, the marsh hawk, the grey eagle, calling them down from the sky to him in a rush of wings to grasp his arm with iron talons and glare at him, eye to wrathful, golden eye . . . None of that any more. He could boast, calling this house his eyrie, but he had no wings.

But Tehanu did. The dragon's wings were hers to fly on.

The fire had burned out. He pulled his sheepskin over him more closely, leaning his head back against the wall, still keeping his hand on Alder's inert, warm shoulder. He liked the man and was sorry for him.

He must remember to ask him to mend the green pitcher, tomorrow.

The grass next to the wall was short, dry, dead. No wind blew to make it move or rustle.

He roused up with a start, half rising from the chair, and after a moment of bewilderment put his hand back on Alder's shoulder, grasping it a little, and whispered, "Hara! Come away, Hara." Alder shuddered, then relaxed. He sighed again, turned more onto his face and lay still.

Sparrowhawk sat with his hand on the sleeper's arm. How had he himself come there, to the wall of stones? He no longer had the power to go there. He had no way to find the way. As in the night before, Alder's dream or vision, Alder's voyaging soul had drawn him with it to the edge of the dark land.

He was wide awake now. He sat gazing at the greyish square of the west window, full of stars.

The grass under the wall . . . It did not grow farther down where the hill leveled out into the dim, dry land. He had said to Alder that down there was only dust, only rock. He saw that black dust, black rock. Dead stream beds where no water ever ran. No living thing. No bird, no field mouse cowering, no glitter and buzz of little insects, the creatures of the sun. Only the dead, with their empty eyes and silent faces.

But did birds not die?

A mouse, a gnat, a goat—a white-and-brown, clever-hoofed, yellow-eyed, shameless goat, Sippy who had been Tehanu's pet, and who had died last winter at a great age— where was Sippy?

Not in the dry land, the dark land. She was dead, but she was not there. She was where she belonged, in the dirt. In the dirt, in the light, in the wind, the leap of water from the rock, the yellow eye of the sun.

Then why, then why...

HE WATCHED ALDER mend the pitcher. Fat-bellied and jade green, it had been a favorite of Tenar's; she had carried it all the way from Oak Farm, years ago. It had slipped from his hands the other day as he took it from the shelf. He had picked up the two big pieces of it and the little fragments with some notion of gluing them back together so it could sit out for looks, if never for use again. Every time he saw the pieces, which he had put into a basket, his clumsiness had outraged him.

Now, fascinated, he watched Alder's hands. Slender, strong, deft, unhurried, they cradled the shape of the pitcher, stroking and fitting and settling the pieces of pottery, urging and caressing, the thumbs coaxing and guiding the smaller fragments into place, reuniting them, reassuring them. While he worked he murmured a two-word, tuneless chant. They were words of the Old Speech. Ged knew and did not know their meaning. Alder's face was serene, all stress and sorrow gone: a face so wholly absorbed in time and task that timeless calm shone through it.

His hands separated from the pitcher, opening out from it like the sheath of a flower opening. It stood on the oak table, whole.

He looked at it with quiet pleasure.

When Ged thanked him, he said, "It was no trouble at

all. The breaks were very clean. It's a well-made piece, and good clay. It's the shoddy work that costs to mend."

"I had a thought how you might find sleep," Ged said.

Alder had waked at first light and had got up, so that his host could go to his bed and sleep sound till broad day; but clearly the arrangement would not do for long.

"Come along with me," the old man said, and they set off inland on a path that skirted the goats' pasture and wound between knolls, little, half-tended fields, and inlets of the forest. Gont was a wild-looking place to Alder, ragged and random, the shaggy mountain always frowning and looming above.

"It seemed to me," Sparrowhawk said as they walked, "if I could do as well as the Master Herbal did, keeping you from the hill of the wall only by putting my hand on you, that there might be others who could help you. If you have no objection to animals."

"Animals?"

"You see," Sparrowhawk began, but got no further, interrupted by a strange creature bounding down the path towards them. It was bundled in skirts and shawls, feathers stuck out in all directions from its head, and it wore high leather boots. "O Mastawk, O Mastawk!" it shouted.

"Hello, then, Heather. Gently now," said Sparrowhawk. The woman stopped, rocking her body, her head-feathers waving, a large grin on her face. "She knowed you was a-coming!" she bawled. "She made that hawk's beak with her fingers like this, see, she did, and she told me go, go, with her hand! She knowed you was a-coming!"

"And so I am."

"To see us?"

"To see you. Heather, this is Master Alder."

"Mastalder," she whispered, quieting suddenly as she included Alder in her consciousness. She shrank, drew into herself, looked down at her feet.

She had no leather boots on. Her bare legs were coated from the knee down with smooth, brown, drying mud. Her skirts were bunched, caught up into the waistband.

"You've been frogging, have you, Heather?"

She nodded vacantly.

"I'll go tell Aunty," she said, beginning in a whisper and ending with a bellow, and bolted back the way she had come.

"She's a good soul," Sparrowhawk said. "She used to help my wife. She lives with our witch now and helps her. I don't think you'll object to entering a witch's house?"

"Never in the world, my lord."

"Many do. Nobles and common folk, wizards and sorcerers."

"Lily my wife was a witch."

Sparrowhawk bowed his head and walked in silence for a while. "How did she learn of her gift, Alder?"

"It was born in her. As a child she'd make a torn branch grow on the tree again, and other children brought her their broken toys to mend. But when her father saw her do that he would strike her hands. Her family were considerable persons in their town. Respectable persons," Alder said in his even, gentle voice. "They didn't want her consorting with witches. Since it would keep her from marriage with a respectable man. So she kept all her study to herself. And the witches of her town would have nothing to do with her, even when she sought to learn from them, for they were afraid of her father, you see. Then a rich man came to court her, for she was beautiful, as I told you, my lord. More beautiful than I could say. And her father told her she was to be married. She ran away that night. She lived by herself, wandering, for some years. A witch here and there took her in, but she kept herself by her skill."

"It's not a big island, Taon."

"Her father wouldn't seek her. He said no tinker witch was his daughter."

Again Sparrowhawk bowed his head. "So she heard of you, and came to you."

"But she taught me more than I could teach her," Alder said earnestly. "It was a great gift she had."

"I believe it."

They had come to a little house or big hut, set down in a dell, with witch hazel and broom in tangles about it, and a goat on the roof, and a flock of white-speckled black hens squawking away, and a lazy little sheepdog bitch standing up and thinking about barking and thinking better of it and waving her tail.

Sparrowhawk went to the low doorway, stooping to look in. "There you are, Aunty!" he said. "I've brought you a visitor. Alder, a man of sorcery from the Isle of Taon. His craft is mending, and he's a master, I can tell you, for I just watched him put back together Tenar's green pitcher, you know the one, that I like a clumsy old fool dropped and broke to pieces the other day."

He entered the hut, and Alder followed him. An old woman sat in a cushioned chair near the doorway where she could look out into the sunlight. Feathers stuck out of her wispy white hair. A speckled hen was settled in her lap. She smiled at Sparrowhawk with enchanting sweetness and nodded politely to the visitor. The hen woke, cackled, and departed.

"This is Moss," said Sparrowhawk, "a witch of many skills, the greatest of which is kindness."

So, Alder imagined, might the Archmage of Roke have introduced a great wizard to a great lady. He bowed. The old woman ducked her head and laughed a little.

She made a circling motion with her left hand, looking a query at Sparrowhawk.

"Tenar? Tehanu?" he said. "Still in Havnor with the king, so far as I know. They'll be having a fine time there, seeing all the sights of the great city and the palaces."

"I made us crowns," Heather shouted, bouncing out of the odorous, dark jumble farther inside the house. "Like kings and queens. See?" She preened the chicken feathers that stuck out of her thick hair at all angles. Aunty Moss, becoming aware of her own peculiar headdress, batted ineffectively at the feathers with her left hand and grimaced.

"Crowns are heavy," Sparrowhawk said. He gently plucked the feathers from the thin hair.

"Who's the queen, Mastawk?" Heather cried. "Who's the queen? Bannen's the king, who's the queen?"

"King Lebannen has no queen, Heather."

"Why not? He ought to. Why not?"

"Maybe he's looking for her."

"He'll marry Tehanu!" the woman shrieked, joyful. "He will!"

49

Alder saw Sparrowhawk's face change, close, become rock.

He said only, "I doubt it." He held the feathers he had taken from Moss's hair and stroked them softly. "I've come to you for a favor, as always, Aunty Moss," he said.

She reached her good hand out and took his hand with such tenderness that Alder was moved to the heart.

"I want to borrow one of your puppies."

Moss began to look sad. Heather, gawking beside her, puzzled it over for a minute and then shouted, "The puppies! Aunty Moss, the puppies! But they're all gone!"

The old woman nodded, looking forlorn, caressing Sparrowhawk's brown hand.

"Somebody wanted them?"

"The biggest one got out and maybe it ran up in the forest and some creature killed it for it never came back and then old Ramballs, he came and said he needs sheepdogs and he'd take both and train them and Aunty gave them to him because they chased the new chicks Snowflakes hatched and ate out house and home, they did, besides."

"Well, Rambles may have a bit of a job training them," Sparrowhawk said with a half smile. "I'm glad he's got them but sorry they're gone, since I wanted to borrow one for a night or two. They slept on your bed, didn't they, Moss?"

She nodded, still sad. Then, brightening a little, she looked up with her head to one side and mewed.

Sparrowhawk blinked, but Heather understood. "Oh! The kittens!" she shouted. "Little Grey had four, and Old Black he killed one before we could stop him, but there's still two or three somewhere round here, they sleep with Aunty and Biddy most every night now the little dogs are gone. Kitty! kitty! kitty! where are you, kitty, kitty?" And after a good deal of commotion and scrambling and piercing mews in the dark interior, she reappeared with a grey kitten clutched squirming and squealing in her hand. "Here's one!" she shouted, and threw it at Sparrowhawk. He caught it awkwardly. It instantly bit him.

"There, there now," he told it. "Calm down." A tiny, rumbling growl emerged from it, and it tried to bite him again. Moss gestured, and he set the little creature down in her lap. She stroked it with her slow heavy hand. It flattened out at once, stretched, looked up at her, and purred.

"May I borrow it for a while?"

The old witch raised her hand from the kitten in a royal gesture that said clearly: It is yours and welcome.

"Master Alder here is having troublesome dreams, you see, and I thought maybe having an animal with him nights might help to ease the trouble."

Moss nodded gravely and, looking up at Alder, slipped her hand under the kitten and lifted it towards him. Alder took it rather gingerly into his hands. It did not growl or bite. It scrambled up his arm and clung to his neck under his hair, which he wore loosely gathered at the nape.

As they walked back to the Old Mage's house, the kitten tucked inside Alder's shirt, Sparrowhawk explained. "Once, when I was new to the art, I was asked to heal a child with the redfever. I knew the boy was dying, but I couldn't bring myself to let him go. I tried to follow him. To bring him back. Across the wall of stones . . . And so, here in the body, I fell down by the bedside and lay like the dead myself.

There was a witch there who guessed what the matter was, and she had me taken to my house and laid abed there. And in my house was an animal that had befriended me when I was a boy on Roke, a wild creature that came to me of its own will and stayed with me. An otak. Do you know them? I think there are none in the North."

Alder hesitated. He said, "I know of them only from the Deed that tells of how . . . how the mage came to the Court of the Terrenon in Osskil. And the otak tried to warn him of a gebbeth that walked with him. And he won free of the gebbeth, but the little animal was caught and slain."

Sparrowhawk walked on without speaking for twenty paces or so. "Yes," he said. "So. Well, my otak also saved my life when I was caught by my own folly on the wrong side of the wall, my body lying here and my soul astray there. The otak came to me and washed me, the way they wash themselves and their young, the way cats do, with a dry tongue, patiently, touching me and bringing me back with its touch, bringing me back into my body. And the gift the animal gave me was not only life but a knowledge as great as I ever learned on Roke . . . But you see, I forget all my learning.

"A knowledge, I say, but it's rather a mystery. What's the difference between us and the animals? Speech? All the animals have some way of speaking, saying *come* and *beware* and much else; but they can't tell stories, and they can't tell lies. While we can . . .

"But the dragons speak: they speak the True Speech, the language of the Making, in which there are no lies, in which to tell the story is to make it be! Yet we call the dragons animals . . .

"So maybe the difference isn't language. Maybe it's this: animals do neither good nor evil. They do as they must do. We may call what they do harmful or useful, but good and evil belong to us, who chose to choose what we do. The dragons are dangerous, yes. They can do harm, yes. But they're not evil. They're beneath our morality, if you will, like any animal. Or beyond it. They have nothing to do with it.

"We must choose and choose again. The animals need only be and do. We're yoked, and they're free. So to be with an animal is to know a little freedom...

"Last night, I was thinking of how witches often have a companion, a familiar. My aunt had an old dog that never barked. She called him Gobefore. And the Archmage Nemmerle, when I first came to Roke Island, had a raven that went with him everywhere. And I thought of a young woman I knew once who wore a little dragon-lizard, a harekki, for her bracelet. And so at last I thought of my otak. Then I thought, if what Alder needs to keep him on this side of the wall is the warmth of a touch, why not an animal? Since they see life, not death. Maybe a dog or cat is as good as a Master of Roke..."

So it proved. The kitten, evidently happy to be away from the household of dogs and tomcats and roosters and the unpredictable Heather, tried hard to show that it was a reliable and diligent cat, patrolling the house for mice, riding on Alder's shoulder under his hair when permitted, and settling right down to sleep purring under his chin as soon as he lay down. Alder slept all night without any dream he remembered, and woke to find the kitten sitting on his chest, washing its ears with an air of quiet virtue.

When Sparrowhawk tried to determine its sex, however, it growled and struggled. "All right," he said, getting his hand out of danger quickly. "Have it your way. It's either a male or a female, Alder, I'm certain of that."

"I won't name it, in any case," Alder said. "They go out like candle flames, little cats. If you've named one you grieve more for it."

That day at Alder's suggestion they went fence mending, walking the goat-pasture fence, Sparrowhawk on the inside and Alder on the outside. Whenever one of them found a place where the palings showed the beginning of rot or the tie laths had been weakened, Alder would run his hands along the wood, thumbing and tugging and smoothing and strengthening, a half-articulate chant almost inaudible in his throat and chest, his face relaxed and intent.

Once Sparrowhawk, watching him, murmured, "And I used to take it all for granted!"

Alder, lost in his work, did not ask him what he meant.

"There," he said, "that'll hold." And they moved on, followed closely by the two inquisitive goats, who butted and pushed at the repaired sections of fence as if to test them.

"I've been thinking," Sparrowhawk said, "that you might do well to go to Havnor."

Alder looked at him in alarm. "Ah," he said. "I thought maybe, if I have a way now to keep away from . . . that place . . . I could go home to Taon." He was losing faith in what he said as he said it.

"You might, but I don't think it would be wise."

Alder said reluctantly, "It is a great deal to ask of a kitten, to defend a man against the armies of the dead."

"It is."

"But I—what should I do in Havnor?" And, with sudden hope, "Would you go with me?"

Sparrowhawk shook his head once. "I stay here."

"The Lord Patterner..."

"Sent you to me. And I send you to those who should hear your tale and find out what it means... I tell you, Alder, I think in his heart the Patterner believes I am what I was. He believes I'm merely hiding here in the forests of Gont and will come forth when the need is greatest." The old man looked down at his sweaty, patched clothes and dusty shoes, and laughed. "In all my glory," he said.

"Beh," said the brown goat behind him.

"But all the same, Alder, he was right to send you here, since she'd have been here, if she hadn't gone to Havnor."

"The Lady Tenar?"

"*Hama Gondun.* So the Patterner himself called her," Sparrowhawk said, looking across the fence at Alder, his eyes unfathomable. "A woman on Gont. The Woman of Gont. Tehanu."

CHAPTER II

Palaces

W HEN ALDER CAME DOWN to the docks, *Farflyer* was
still there, taking on a cargo of timbers; but he knew
he had worn out his welcome on that ship. He went to a
small shabby coaster tied up next to her, the *Pretty Rose*.

Sparrowhawk had given him a letter of passage signed by
the king and sealed with the Rune of Peace. "He sent it for
me to use if I changed my mind," the old man had said with
a snort. "It'll serve you." The ship's master, after getting his
purser to read it for him, became quite deferential and apologised for the cramped quarters and the length of the voyage. *Pretty Rose* was going to Havnor, sure enough, but she
was a coaster, trading small goods from port to port, and it
might take her a month to work clear round the southeast
coast of the Great Island to the King's City.

That was all right with him, Alder said. For if he dreaded
the voyage, he feared its ending more.

New moon to half moon, the sea voyage was a time of

peace for him. The grey kitten was a hardy traveler, busy mousing the ship all day but faithfully curling up under his chin or within hand's reach at night; and to his unceasing wonder, that little scrap of warm life kept him from the wall of stones and the voices calling him across it. Not wholly. Not so that he ever entirely forgot them. They were there, just through the veil of sleep in darkness, just through the brightness of the day. Sleeping out on deck those warm nights, he opened his eyes often to see that the stars moved, swinging to the rocking of the moored ship, following their courses through heaven to the west. He was still a haunted man. But for a half month of summer along the coasts of Kameber and Barnisk and the Great Island he could turn his back on his ghosts.

For days the kitten hunted a young rat nearly as big as it was. Seeing it proudly and laboriously hauling the carcass across the deck, one of the sailors called it Tug. Alder accepted the name for it.

They sailed down the Ebavnor Straits and in through the portals of Havnor Bay. Across the sunlit water little by little the white towers of the city at the center of the world resolved out of the haze of distance. Alder stood at the prow as they came in and looking up saw on the pinnacle of the highest tower a flash of silver light, the Sword of Erreth-Akbe.

Now he wished he could stay aboard and sail on and not go ashore into the great city among great people with a letter for the king. He knew he was no fit messenger. Why had such a burden been laid on him? How could it be that a village sorcerer who knew nothing of high matters and deep arts was called on to make these journeys from land to land, from mage to monarch, from the living to the dead?

He had said something like that to Sparrowhawk. "It's all beyond me," he had said. The old man looked at him a while and then, calling him by his true name, said, "The world's vast and strange, Hara, but no vaster and no stranger than our minds are. Think of that sometimes."

Behind the city the sky darkened with a thunderstorm inland. The towers burned white against purple-black, and gulls soared like drifting sparks of fire above them.

Pretty Rose was moored, the gangplank run out. This time the sailors wished him well as he shouldered his pack. He picked up the covered poultry basket in which Tug crouched patiently, and went ashore.

The streets were many and crowded, but the way to the palace was plain, and he had no idea what to do except go there and say that he carried a letter for the king from the Archmage Sparrowhawk.

And that he did, many times.

From guard to guard, from official to official, from the broad outer steps of the palace to high anterooms, staircases with gilded banisters, inner offices with tapestried walls, across floors of tile and marble and oak, under ceilings coffered, beamed, vaulted, painted, he went repeating his talisman: "I come from Sparrowhawk who was the Archmage with a letter for the king." He would not give his letter up. A retinue, a crowd of suspicious, semi-civil, patronising, temporising, obstructive guards and ushers and officials kept gathering and thickening around him and followed and impeded his slow way into the palace.

Suddenly they were all gone. A door had opened. It closed behind him.

He stood alone in a quiet room. A wide window looked out over the roofs northwestward. The thundercloud had cleared and the broad grey summit of Mount Onn hovered above far hills.

Another door opened. A man came in, dressed in black, about Alder's age, quick moving, with a fine, strong face as smooth as bronze. He came straight to Alder: "Master Alder, I am Lebannen."

He put out his right hand to touch Alder's hand, palm against palm, as the custom was in Éa and the Enlades. Alder responded automatically to the familiar gesture. Then he thought he ought to kneel, or bow at least, but the moment to do so seemed to have passed. He stood dumb.

"You came from my Lord Sparrowhawk? How is he? Is he well?"

"Yes, lord. He sends you—" Alder hurriedly groped inside his jacket for the letter, which he had intended to offer to the king kneeling, when they finally showed him to the throne room where the king would be sitting on his throne—"this letter, my lord."

The eyes watching him were alert, urbane, as implacably keen as Sparrowhawk's, but withholding even more of the mind within. As the king took the letter Alder offered him, his courtesy was perfect. "The bearer of any word from him has my heart's thanks and welcome. Will you forgive me?"

Alder finally managed a bow. The king walked over to the window to read the letter.

He read it twice at least, then refolded it. His face was as impassive as before. He went to the door and spoke to some-one outside it, then turned back to Alder. "Please," he said, "sit down with me. They'll bring us something to eat. You've been all afternoon in the palace, I know. If the gate captain had had the wits to send me word, I could have spared you hours of climbing the walls and swimming the moats they set around me . . . Did you stay with my Lord Sparrowhawk? In his house on the cliff's edge?"

"Yes."

"I envy you. I've never been there. I haven't seen him since we parted on Roke, half my lifetime ago. He wouldn't let me come to him on Gont. He wouldn't come to my crowning." Lebannen smiled as if nothing he said was of any moment. "He gave me my kingdom," he said.

Sitting down, he nodded to Alder to take the chair fac-ing him across a little table. Alder looked at the tabletop, in-laid with curling patterns of ivory and silver, leaves and blossoms of the rowan tree twined about slender swords.

"Did you have a good voyage?" the king asked, and made other small talk while they were served plates of cold meat and smoked trout and lettuces and cheese. He set Alder a welcome example by eating with a good appetite; and he poured them wine, the palest topaz, in goblets of crystal. He raised his glass. "To my lord and dear friend," he said.

Alder murmured, "To him," and drank.

The king spoke about Taon, which he had visited a few years before—Alder remembered the excitement of the is-land when the king was in Meoni. And he spoke of some musicians from Taon who were in the city now, harpers and singers come to make music for the court; it might be Alder knew some of them; and indeed the names he said were familiar. He was very skilled at putting his guest at ease, and food and wine were a considerable help too.

When they were done eating, the king poured them another half glass of wine and said, "The letter concerns you, mostly. Did you know that?" His tone had not changed much from the small talk, and Alder was fuddled for a moment.

"No," he said.

"Do you have an idea what it deals with?"

"What I dream, maybe," Alder said, speaking low, looking down.

The king studied him for a moment. There was nothing offensive in his gaze, but he was more open in that scrutiny than most men would have been. Then he took up the letter and held it out to Alder.

"My lord, I read very little."

Lebannen was not surprised—some sorcerers could read, some could not—but he clearly and sharply regretted putting his guest at a disadvantage. The gold-bronze skin of his face went dusky red. He said, "I'm sorry, Alder. May I read you what he says?"

"Please, my lord," Alder said. The king's embarrassment made him, for a moment, feel the king's equal, and he spoke for the first time naturally and with warmth.

Lebannen scanned the salutation and some lines of the letter and then read aloud:

"'Alder of Taon who bears this to you is one called in dream and not by his own will to that land you and I crossed once together. He will tell you of suffering where suffering is past and change where no thing changes. We closed the door

Cob opened. Now the wall itself maybe is to fall. He has been to Roke. Only Azver heard him. My Lord the King will hear and will act as wisdom instructs and need requires. Alder bears my lifelong honor and obedience to my Lord the King. Also my lifelong honor and regard to my lady Tenar. Also to my beloved daughter Tehanu a spoken message from me.' And he signs it with the rune of the Talon." Lebannen looked up from the letter into Alder's eyes and held his gaze. "Tell me what it is you dream," he said.

So once more Alder told his story.

He told it briefly and not very well. Though he had been in awe of Sparrowhawk, the ex-Archmage looked and dressed and lived like an old villager or farmer, a man of Alder's own kind and standing, and that simplicity had defeated all su-perficial timidity. But however kind and courteous the king might be, he looked like the king, he behaved like the king, he was the king, and to Alder the distance was insuperable. He hurried through as best he could and stopped with relief.

Lebannen asked a few questions. Lily and then Gannet had each touched Alder once: never since? And Gannet's touch had burned?

Alder held out his hand. The marks were almost invisible under a month's tan.

"I think the people at the wall would touch me if I came close to them," he said.

"But you keep away from them?"

"I have done so."

"And they are not people you knew in life?"

"Sometimes I think I know one or another."

"But never your wife?"

"There are so many of them, my lord. Sometimes I think she's there. But I can't see her."

To talk about it brought it near, too near. He felt the fear welling up in him again. He thought the walls of the room might melt away and the evening sky and the floating mountain-crown vanish like a curtain brushed aside, to leave him standing where he was always standing, on a dark hill by a wall of stones.

"Alder."

He looked up, shaken, his head swimming. The room seemed bright, the king's face hard and vivid.

"You'll stay here in the palace?"

It was an invitation, but Alder could only nod, accepting it as an order.

"Good. I'll arrange for you to give the message you bear to Mistress Tehanu tomorrow. And I know the White Lady will wish to talk with you."

He bowed. Lebannen turned away.

"My lord—"

Lebannen turned.

"May I have my cat with me?"

Not a flicker of a smile, no mockery. "Of course."

"My lord, I am sorry to my heart to bring news that troubles you!"

"Any word from the man who sent you is a grace to me and to its bearer. And I'd rather get bad news from an honest man than lies from a flatterer," Lebannen said, and Alder, hearing the true accent of his home islands in the words, was a little cheered.

The king went out, and at once a man looked in the door

Alder had entered by. "I will take you to your chamber, if you will follow me, sir," he said. He was dignified, elderly, and well dressed, and Alder followed him without any idea whether he was a nobleman or a servant, and therefore not daring to ask him about Tug. In the room before the room where he had met the king, the officials and guards and ushers had absolutely insisted that he leave his poultry basket with them. It had been eyed with suspicion and inspected with disapproval by ten or fifteen officials already. He had explained ten or fifteen times that he had the cat with him because he had nowhere in the city to leave it. The anteroom where he had been compelled to set it down was far behind him, he had not seen it there as they went through, he would never find it now, it was half a palace away, corridors, hall-ways, passages, doors . . .

His guide bowed and left him in a small, beautiful room, tapestried, carpeted, a chair with an embroidered seat, a window that looked out to the harbor, a table on which stood a bowl of summer fruit and a pitcher of water. And the poultry basket.

He opened it. Tug emerged in a leisurely manner indicating his familiarity with palaces. He stretched, sniffed Alder's fingers in greeting, and went about the room examining things. He discovered a curtained alcove with a bed in it and jumped up on the bed. A discreet knock at the door. A young man entered carrying a large, flat, heavy wooden box with no lid. He bowed to Alder, murmuring, "Sand, sir." He placed the box in the far corner of the alcove. He bowed again and left.

"Well," Alder said, sitting down on the bed. He was not

in the habit of talking to the kitten. Their relationship was one of silent, trustful touch. But he had to talk to somebody. "I met the king today," he said.

THE KING HAD ALL TOO MANY people to talk to before he could sit down on his bed. Chief among them were the emissaries of the High King of the Kargs. They were about to take their leave, having accomplished their mission to Havnor, to their own satisfaction if not at all to Lebannen's.

He had looked forward to the visit of these ambassadors as the culmination of years of patient overture, invitation, and negotiation. For the first ten years of his reign he had been able to accomplish nothing at all with the Kargs. The God-King in Awabath rejected his offers of treaties and trade and sent his envoys back unheard, declaring that gods do not parley with vile mortals, least of all with accursed sorcerers. But the God-King's proclamations of universal divine empire were not followed by the threatened fleets of a myriad ships bearing plumed warriors to overrun the godless West. Even the pirate raids that had plagued the eastern isles of the Archipelago for so long gradually ceased. The pirates had become contrabanders, seeking to trade whatever unlicensed goods they could smuggle out of Karego-At for Archipelagan iron and steel and bronze, for the Kargad Lands were poor in mines and metal.

It was from these illicit traders that news first came of the rise of the High King.

On Hur-at-Hur, the big, poor, easternmost island of the Kargad Lands, a warlord, Thol, claiming descent from Thoreg of Hupun and from the God Wuluah, had made himself High King of that land. Next he had conquered Atnini, and then, with a fleet and an invading army drawn from both Hur-at-Hur and Atnini, he had claimed dominion over the rich central island, Karego-At. While his warriors were fighting their way towards Awabath, the capital city, the people of the city rose up against the tyranny of the God-King. They slaughtered the high priests, drove the bureaucrats out of the temples, threw the gates wide, and welcomed King Thol to the throne of Thoreg with banners and dancing in the streets.

The God-King fled with a remnant of his guards and hierophants to the Place of the Tombs on Atuan. There in the desert, in his temple by the earthquake-shattered ruins of the shrine of the Nameless Ones, one of his priest-eunuchs cut the God-King's throat.

Thol proclaimed himself High King of the Four Kargad Lands. As soon as he got word of that, Lebannen sent ambassadors to greet his brother king and assure him of the friendly disposition of the Archipelago.

Five years of difficult and tiresome diplomacy had ensued. Thol was a violent man on a threatened throne. In the wreckage of the theocracy, all control in his realm was chancy, all authority questionable. Lesser kings constantly declared themselves and had to be bought or beaten into obedience to the High King. Sectarians issued from shrines and caverns crying "Woe to the mighty!" and foretelling earthquake, tidal wave, plague upon the deicides. Ruling a troubled, divided empire, Thol could scarcely place any trust in the powerful and wealthy Archipelagans.

It meant nothing to him that their king talked about

friendship, flourishing the Ring of Peace. Did not the Kargs have a claim to that ring? It had been made in ancient days in the West, but long ago, King Thoreg of Hupun had accepted it as a gift from the hero Erreth-Akbe, a sign of amity between the Kargad and Hardic lands. It had disappeared, and there had been war, not amity. But then the Hawk-Mage had found the ring and stolen it back, along with the Priestess of the Tombs of Atuan, and carried both off to Havnor. So much for the trustworthiness of the Archipelagans.

Through his envoys, Lebannen patiently and politely pointed out that the Ring of Peace had, to begin with, been Morred's gift to Elfarran, a cherished token of the Archipelago's most beloved king and queen. And a very sacred thing as well, for on it was the Bond rune, a mighty enchantment of blessing. Nearly four centuries ago, Erreth-Akbe had taken it to the Kargad Lands as a pledge of unbreakable peace. But the priests of Awabath had broken the pledge, and broken the Ring. Some forty years ago now, Sparrowhawk of Roke and Tenar of Atuan had healed the Ring. What, then, of the peace?

That had been the gist of his messages to King Thol.

And a month ago, just after the Long Dance of summer, a fleet of ships had come sailing straight down the Passage of Felkway, up the Ebavnor Straits, and in between the portals of Havnor Bay: long red ships with red sails, carrying plumed warriors, gorgeous-robed emissaries, and a few veiled women.

"Let the daughter of Thol the High King, who sits upon the Throne of Thoreg and whose ancestor was Wuluah, wear the Ring of Peace upon her arm, as Queen Elfarran of

Soléa wore it, and this will be the sign of everlasting peace between the Western and the Eastern Isles."

That was the High King's message to Lebannen. It was written out in big Hardic runes on a scroll, but before handing it to King Lebannen, Thol's ambassador read it out loud, in public, at the reception of the emissaries at the court in Havnor, with the whole court there to do the Kargish envoys honor. Perhaps it was because the ambassador did not actually read Hardic, but spoke the words loudly and slowly from memory, that they had the tone of an ultimatum.

The princess said nothing. She stood among the ten handmaidens or slave girls who had accompanied her to Havnor and the flock of court ladies who had been hastily assigned to look after her and do her honor. She was veiled, entirely veiled, as was, it appeared, the custom of well-born women in Hur-at-Hur. The veils, red with lines of gold embroidery, fell straight down from a flat-brimmed hat or headdress, so that the princess appeared to be a red column or pillar, cylindrical, featureless, motionless, silent.

"The High King Thol does us great honor," Lebannen said in his clear, quiet voice; and then he paused. The court and the emissaries waited. "You are welcome here, princess," he said to the veiled figure. It did not stir.

"Let the princess be lodged in the River House, and let all be as she desires," Lebannen said.

The River House was a beautiful small palace at the northern edge of the city, fitted into the old city wall, with terraces built out over the little River Serrenen. Queen Heru had built it, and it was often called the Queen's House.

When Lebannen came to the throne he had had it repaired and refurnished, along with the Palace of Maharion, called the New Palace, in which he held court. He used the River House only for summer festivities and sometimes as a retreat for himself for a few days.

A little rustle now went through his courtiers. The Queen's House?

After urbanities among the Kargish emissaries, Lebannen left the audience room. He went to his dressing room, where he could be as alone as a king can be, with his old servant, Oak, whom he had known all his life.

He slapped the gilded scroll down on a table. "Cheese in a rat trap," he said. He was shaking. He whipped the dagger he always wore out of its sheath and stabbed it straight down through the High King's message. "A pig in a poke," he said. "A piece of goods. The Ring on her arm and the collar round my neck."

Oak stared at him in blank dismay. Prince Arren of Enlad had never lost his temper. When he was a child he might have wept for a moment, one bitter sob, but that was all. He was too well trained, too well disciplined to give way to anger. And as king, a king who had earned his realm by crossing the land of the dead, he could be stern, but always, Oak thought, too proud, too strong for anger.

"They will not use me!" Lebannen said, stabbing the dagger down again, his face so black and blind with fury that the old man drew back from him in real fear.

Lebannen saw him. He always saw the people around him.

He sheathed his dagger. He said in a steadier voice, "Oak, by my name, I will destroy Thol and his kingdom before I let him use me as a footstool to his throne." Then he drew a long breath and sat down to let Oak lift the heavy, gold-weighted state robe from his shoulders.

Oak never breathed a word of this scene to anyone, but there was, of course, immediate and continuous speculation about the princess of the Kargs and what the king was going to do about her—or what, in fact, he had already done.

He had not said that he accepted the offer of the princess as his bride. For all agreed she had been offered to him as his bride; the language about Elfarran's Ring barely veiled the offer, or the bargain, or the threat. But he had not refused it, either. His response (endlessly analyzed) had been to say she was welcome, that all should be as she desired, and that she should live in the River House: the Queen's House. Surely that was significant? But on the other hand, why not in the New Palace? Why send her across the city?

Ever since Lebannen's coronation, ladies of noble houses and princesses of the old royal lineages of Enlad, Éa, and Shelieth had come to visit or to stay at the court. They had all been entertained most royally, and the king had danced at their weddings as, one by one, they settled for noblemen or wealthy commoners. It was well known that he liked the company of women and their counsel as well, that he would willingly flirt with a pretty girl and invite an intelligent woman to advise him, tease him, or console him. But no girl or woman had ever come near the rumor of a shadow of a chance of marrying him. And none had ever been lodged in the River House.

The king must have a queen, his advisors told him at regular intervals.

You really must marry, Arren, his mother had told him the last time he saw her alive.

The heir of Morred, will he have no heir? asked the common people.

To all of them he had said, in various words and ways: Give me time. I have the ruins of a kingdom to rebuild. Let me make a house worthy of a queen, a realm my child can rule. And because he was well loved and trusted, and still a young man, and for all his gravity a charming and persuasive one, he had escaped all the hopeful maidens. Until now.

What was under the stiff red veils? Who lived inside that unrevealing tent? The ladies assigned to the princess's entourage were besieged by questions. Was she pretty? Ugly? Was it true she was tall and thin, short and muscular, white as milk, pockmarked, one-eyed, yellow-haired, black-haired, forty-five years old, ten years old, a drooling cretin, a brilliant beauty?

Gradually the rumors began to run one way. She was young, though not a child; hair neither yellow nor black; pretty enough, said some of the ladies; coarse, said others. Spoke not a word of Hardic, they all said, and would not learn. Hid among her women, and when forced to leave her room, hid in her red tent-veils. The king had paid her a visit of courtesy. She had not bowed to him, or spoken, or made any sign, but stood there, said old Lady Iyesa in exasperation, "like a brick chimney."

He spoke to her through men who had served as his envoys in the Kargad Lands and through the Karg ambassador, who spoke fairly good Hardic. Laboriously he transmitted his compliments and queries as to her wishes and desires. The translators spoke to her women, whose veils were shorter and somewhat less impenetrable. Her women gathered round the motionless red pillar and mumbled and buzzed and returned to the translators, and the translators informed the king that the princess was content and required nothing.

She had been there a half month when Tenar and Tehanu arrived from Gont. Lebannen had sent a ship and a message begging them to come, shortly before the Kargad fleet brought the princess, and for reasons that had nothing to do with her or King Thol. But the first time he was alone with Tenar, he burst out, "What am I going to do with her? What can I do?"

"Tell me about it," Tenar said, looking somewhat amazed.

Lebannen had spent only a brief time with Tenar, though they had written a few letters over the years; he was not yet used to her hair being grey, and she seemed smaller than he remembered her; but with her he felt immediately, as he had fifteen years earlier, that he could say anything and she would understand.

"For five years I've built up trade and tried to keep on good terms with Thol, because he's a warlord and I don't want my kingdom pinched, as it was in Maharion's reign, between dragons in the west and warlords in the east. And because I rule in the Sign of Peace. And it went well enough, till this. Till he sends this girl out of the blue, saying if you want peace, give her Elfarran's Ring. Your Ring, Tenar! Yours and Ged's!"

Tenar hesitated a while. "She is his daughter, after all."

"What's a daughter to a barbarian king? Goods. A bargaining piece to buy advantage with. You know that! You were born there!"

It was unlike him to speak so, and he heard it himself. He knelt down suddenly, catching her hand and putting it over his eyes in sign of contrition. "Tenar, I'm sorry. This disturbs me beyond all reason. I can't see what to do."

"Well, so long as you do nothing, you have some leeway...Maybe the princess has some opinion of her own?"

"How can she? Hidden in that red sack? She won't talk, she won't look out, she might as well be a tent pole." He tried to laugh. His own uncontrollable resentment alarmed him and he tried to excuse it. "This came on just as I had troubling news from the west. It was for that that I asked you and Tehanu to come. Not to bother you with this foolishness."

"It isn't foolishness," Tenar said, but he brushed the topic away, dismissed it, and began to talk about dragons.

Since the news from the west had been troubling indeed, he had succeeded in not thinking about the princess at all, most of the time. He was aware that it was not his habit to handle matters of state by ignoring them. Manipulated, one manipulates others. Several days after their conversation, he asked Tenar to visit the princess, to try to get her to talk. After all, he said, they spoke the same language.

"Probably," Tenar said. "I never knew anybody from Hur-at-Hur. On Atuan, we called them barbarians."

He was chastised. But of course she did what he asked. Presently she reported that she and the princess spoke the same language, or nearly the same, and that the princess had not known that there were any other languages. She had thought all the people here, the courtiers and ladies, were malicious lunatics, mocking her by chattering and yapping like animals without human speech. As well as Tenar could tell, she had grown up in the desert, in King Thol's original domain on Hur-at-Hur, and had only been very briefly at the imperial court in Awabath before she was sent on to Havnor.

"She's frightened," Tenar said.

"So she hides in her tent. What does she think I am?"

"How could she know what you are?"

He scowled. "How old is she?"

"Young. But a woman."

"I can't marry her," he said, with sudden resolution. "I'll send her back."

"A returned bride is a dishonored woman. If you send her back, Thol might kill her to keep the dishonor from his house. He'll certainly consider that you intend to dishonor him."

The look of fury came into his face again.

Tenar forestalled him. "Barbarian customs," she said stiffly.

He strode up and down the room. "Very well. But I will not consider this girl as queen of the Kingdom of Morred. Can she be taught to speak Hardic? A few words, at least? Is she unteachable? I'll tell Thol that a Hardic king can't marry a woman who doesn't speak the language of the realm. I don't care if he doesn't like it, he needs the slap. And it buys me time."

"And you'll ask her to learn Hardic?"

"How can I ask her anything if she takes it all for gibberish? What possible use is there in my going to her? I thought perhaps you'd speak to her, Tenar... You must see what an imposition this is, using this girl to make Thol appear my equal, using the Ring—the Ring you brought us—as a trap! I cannot even seem to condone it. I'm willing to temporise, to delay, in order to keep the peace. Nothing more. Even that much deceit is vile. Tell the girl what you think best. I will have nothing to do with her."

And he went out in a righteous wrath, which cooled slowly into an uneasy feeling much resembling shame.

When the Kargish emissaries announced they would be leaving soon, Lebannen prepared a carefully worded message for King Thol. He expressed his appreciation of the honor of the princess's presence in Havnor and the pleasure he and his court would have in introducing her to the manners, customs, and language of his kingdom. He said nothing at all about the Ring, about marrying her, or about not marrying her.

It was in the evening after his conversation with the dream-troubled sorcerer from Taon that he met for the last time with the Kargs and gave them his letter to the High King. He read it aloud first, as the ambassador had read aloud Thol's letter to him.

The ambassador listened complacently. "The High King will be pleased," he said.

All the time he was talking amenities to the emissaries and displaying the gifts he was sending to Thol, Lebannen puzzled over this easy acceptance of his evasiveness. His thoughts all came to one conclusion: He knows I'm stuck with her. To which his mind made a passionate silent answer: Never.

He inquired whether the ambassador would be going by the River House to bid his princess farewell. The ambassador looked at him blankly, as if he had been asked if he was going to say goodbye to a package he had delivered. Lebannen felt the anger rising in his heart again. He saw the ambassador's face change a little, taking on a wary, placating look. He smiled and wished the emissaries a fair wind to the Kargad Lands. He went out of the audience chamber and to his own room.

Rites and ceremony hedged most of his acts, and as king he must be in public most of his life; but because he had come to a throne empty for centuries, a palace where there were no protocols, he had been able to have some things as he liked them. He had kept ceremony out of his bedroom. His nights were his own. He said good night to Oak, who would sleep in the anteroom, and shut the door. He sat down on his bed. He felt tired and angry and strangely desolate.

Around his neck he always wore a slight gold chain with a little pouch of cloth-of-gold on it. In the pouch was a pebble: a dull, black bit of rock, rough edged. He took it out and held it in his hand as he sat and thought.

He tried to turn his mind away from all this stupidity about the Kargish girl by thinking about the sorcerer Alder and his dreams. But all that came into his mind was a painful envy of Alder for having gone ashore on Gont, having talked with Ged, having stayed with him.

That was why he felt desolate. The man he called his lord, the man he had loved above all others, wouldn't let him come near, wouldn't come to him.

Did Ged believe that because he had lost his wizardly power, Lebannen must think less of him? must despise him?

Given the power that power had over the minds and

hearts of men, it was not an implausible thought. But surely Ged knew him better, or at least thought better of him.

Was it that, having been truly Lebannen's lord and guide, Ged could not bear to be his subject? That might indeed be hard for the old man to bear: the blunt, irrevocable reversal of their status.

But Lebannen remembered very clearly how Ged had knelt to him, down on both knees, on Roke Knoll, in the shadow of the dragon and in the sight of the masters whose master Ged had been. He had stood up and kissed Lebannen, telling him to rule well, calling him *my lord and dear companion.*

"He gave me my kingdom," Lebannen had said to Alder. That had been the moment he gave it. Wholly, freely.

And that was why Ged wouldn't come to Havnor, wouldn't let Lebannen come to take counsel with him. He had handed over the power—wholly, freely. He would not even seem to meddle, to cast his shadow across Lebannen's light.

"He has done with doing," the Doorkeeper had said.

But Alder's story had moved Ged to send the man here, to Lebannen, asking him to act as need required.

It was indeed strange, Alder's story; and Ged's saying that maybe the wall itself was going to fall was stranger yet. What could it mean? And why should one man's dreams bear so much weight?

He himself had dreamed of the outskirts of the dry land, long ago, when he and Ged the Archmage were traveling together, before they ever came to Selidor.

And on that westernmost of all the islands he had followed Ged into the dry land. Across the wall of stones. Down to dim cities where the shadows of the dead stood in doorways or walked without aim or purpose in streets lit only by the moveless stars. With Ged he had walked across all that country, a weary way to a dark valley of dust and stones at the foot of the mountains whose only name was Pain.

He opened his palm, looked down at the little black stone he held, closed his hand on it again.

From the valley of the dry river, having done what they came to do, they had climbed up into the mountains, because there was no turning back. They had gone up the road forbidden to the dead, climbing, clambering over rocks that scored and burned their hands, till Ged could go no farther. Lebannen had carried him as far as he could, then crawled on with him to the end of darkness, the hopeless cliff of night. And so had come back, with him, into the sunlight and the sound of the sea breaking on the shores of life.

It was a long time since he had thought so vividly of that terrible journey. But the bit of black stone from those mountains was always over his heart.

And it seemed to him now that the memory of that land, the darkness of it, the dust, was always in his mind just under the bright various play and movement of the days, although he always looked away from it. He looked away because he could not bear the knowledge that in the end that was where he would come again: come alone, uncompanioned, and forever. To stand empty-eyed, unspeaking, in the shadows of a shadow city. Never to see sunlight, or drink water, or touch a living hand.

He got up abruptly, shaking off these morbid thoughts.

He closed the stone in its pouch, made ready for bed, put out the lamp, and lay down. At once he saw it again: the dim grey land of dust and rock. It rose up far ahead into black, sharp peaks, but here it sloped away, always downward, to the right, into utter darkness. "What lies that way?" he had asked Ged as they walked on and on. His companion had said he did not know, that maybe that way there was no end.

Lebannen sat up, angered and alarmed by the relentless drift of his thought. His eyes sought the window. It looked north. He liked the view from Havnor across the hills to the tall, grey-headed mountain Onn. Farther north, unseen, across all the width of the Great Island and the Sea of Éa, was Enlad, his home.

Lying in bed he could see only the sky, a clear summer night sky, the Heart of the Swan riding high among lesser stars. His kingdom. The kingdom of light, of life, where the stars blossomed like white flowers in the east and drooped in their brightness to the west. He would not think of that other realm where the stars stayed still, where there was no power in a man's hand, and no right way to go because no way led anywhere.

Lying gazing at the stars, he turned his mind deliberately from those memories and from the thought of Ged. He thought of Tenar: the sound of her voice, the touch of her hand. Courtiers were ceremonious, cautious about how and when they touched the king. She was not. She laid her hand on his, laughing. She was bolder with him than his mother had been.

Rose, princess of the House of Enlad, had died of a fever two years ago, while he was on shipboard coming to make a royal visit to Berila on Enlad and the isles south of it. He had not known of her death till he came home to a city and a house in mourning.

His mother was there now in the dark country, the dry country. If he came there and passed her in the street she would not look at him. She would not speak to him.

He clenched his hands. He rearranged the cushions of his bed, tried to make himself easy, tried to set his mind away from there, to think of things that would keep him from going back there. To think of his mother living, her voice, her dark eyes under dark arched brows, her delicate hands.

Or to think of Tenar. He knew he had asked Tenar to come to Havnor not only to take counsel from her but because she was the mother that remained to him. He wanted that love, to give it and be given it. The ruthless love that makes no allowances, no conditions. Tenar's eyes were grey, not dark, but she looked right through him with a piercing tenderness undeceived by anything he said or did.

He knew he did well what he had been called to do. He knew he was good at playing king. But only with his mother and with Tenar had he ever known beyond any self-doubt what it was to be king.

TENAR HAD KNOWN HIM since he was a very young man, not yet crowned. She had loved him then and ever since, for his sake, for Ged's sake, and for her own. He was to her the son who never breaks your heart.

But she thought he might yet manage to, if he kept on being so rageful and dishonest about this poor girl from Hur-at-Hur.

She attended the final audience of the emissaries from Awabath. Lebannen had asked her to be there, and she was glad to come. Finding Kargs at the court when she came there at the beginning of summer, she had expected them to shun her or at least to eye her askance: the renegade priestess who with the thieving Hawk Mage had stolen the Ring of Erreth-Akbe from the treasury of the Tombs of Atuan and traitorously fled with it to Havnor. It was her doing that the Archipelago had a king again. The Kargs might well hold it against her.

And Thol of Hur-at-Hur had restored the worship of the Twin Gods and the Nameless Ones, whose greatest temple Tenar had despoiled. Her treason had been not only political but religious.

Yet that was long ago, forty years and more, almost the stuff of legend; and statesmen remember things selectively. Thol's ambassador had begged the honor of an audience with her and had greeted her with elaborately pious respect, some of which she thought was real. He called her Lady Arha, the Eaten One, the One Ever Reborn. She had not been called by those names for years, and they sounded very strange to her. But it gave her a keen, rueful pleasure to hear her native tongue and to find she could still speak it.

So she came to bid the ambassador and his company goodbye. She asked him to assure the High King of the Kargs that his daughter was well, and she looked admiringly a last time at the tall, rawboned men with their pale, braided hair, their plumed headdresses, their court armor of silver mesh interwoven with feathers. When she lived in the Kargad Lands she had seen few men of her own race. Only women and eunuchs had lived at the Place of the Tombs.

After the ceremony she escaped into the gardens of the palace. The summer night was warm and restless, flowering shrubs of the gardens stirring in the night wind. The sounds of the city outside the palace walls were like the murmur of a quiet sea. A couple of young courtiers were walking entwined under the arbors; not to disturb them, Tenar walked among the fountains and the roses at the other end of the garden.

Lebannen had left the audience scowling again. What was wrong with him? So far as she knew, he had never before rebelled against the obligations of his position. Certainly he knew that a king must marry and has little real choice as to whom he marries. He knew that a king who does not obey his people is a tyrant. He knew his people wanted a queen, wanted heirs to the throne. But he had done nothing about it. Women of the court had been happy to gossip to Tenar about his several mistresses, none of whom had lost anything by being known as the king's lover. He had certainly managed all that quite well, but he couldn't expect to do so forever. Why was he so enraged by King Thol's offering him a perfectly appropriate solution?

Imperfectly appropriate, perhaps. The princess was something of a problem.

Tenar was going to have to try to teach the girl Hardic. And to find ladies willing to instruct her in the manners of the Archipelago and the etiquette of the court—something she certainly wasn't capable of herself. She had more sympathy with the princess's ignorance than with the courtiers' sophistication.

She resented Lebannen's failure or inability to take the girl's point of view. Couldn't he imagine what it was like for her? Brought up in the women's quarters of a warlord's fortress in a remote desert land, where she probably had never seen any man but her father and uncles and some priests; suddenly carried off from that changeless poverty and rigidity of life, by strangers, on a long and frightening sea voyage; abandoned among people whom she knew of only as irreligious and bloodthirsty monsters who dwelt on the far edge of the world, not truly human at all because they were wizards who could turn into animals and birds— And she was to marry one of them!

Tenar had been able to leave her own people and come to live among the monsters and wizards of the West because she had been with Ged, whom she loved and trusted. Even so it had not been easy; often her courage had failed. For all the welcome the people of Havnor had given her, the crowds and cheering and flowers and praise, the sweet names they called her, the White Lady, the Peace Bringer, Tenar of the Ring—for all that, she had cowered in her room in the palace those nights long ago, in misery because she was so lonely, and nobody spoke her language, and she didn't know any of the things they all knew. As soon as the rejoicings were over and the Ring was in its place she had begged Ged to take her away, and he had kept his promise, slipping away with her to Gont. There she had lived in the Old Mage's house as Ogion's ward and pupil, learning how to be an

Archipelagan, till she saw the way she wanted to follow for herself as a woman grown.

She had been younger than this girl when she came to Havnor with the Ring. But she had not grown up powerless, as the princess had. Though her power as the One Priestess had been mostly ceremonial, nominal, she had taken real control of her fate when she broke with the grim ways of her upbringing and won freedom for her prisoner and herself. But the daughter of a warlord would have control over only trivial things. When her father made himself king she would be called princess, she would be given richer clothing, more slaves, more eunuchs, more jewelry, until she herself was given in marriage; but she would have no say in any of it. All she ever saw of the world outside the women's quarters would be through window slits in thick walls, through layers of red veiling.

Tenar counted herself lucky not to have been born on so backward and barbaric an island as Hur-at-Hur, never to have worn the *feyag*. But she knew what it was to grow up in the grip of an iron tradition. It behooved her to do what she could to help the princess, so long as she was in Havnor. But she didn't intend to stay here long.

Strolling in the garden, watching the fountains glimmer in starlight, she thought about how and when she could go home.

She did not mind the formalities of court life or the knowledge that under the civility simmered a stew of ambitions, rivalries, passions, complicities, collusions. She had grown up with rituals and hypocrisy and hidden politics, and none of it frightened or worried her. She was simply home-sick. She wanted to be back on Gont, with Ged, in their house.

She had come to Havnor because Lebannen sent for her and Tehanu, and Ged if he would come; but Ged wouldn't come, and Tehanu wouldn't come without her. That did frighten and worry her. Could her daughter not break free from her? It was Tehanu's counsel Lebannen needed, not hers. But her daughter clung to her, as ill at ease, as out of place in the court of Havnor as the girl from Hur-at-Hur was, and like her, silent, in hiding.

So Tenar must play nursemaid, tutor, and companion now to both of them, two scared girls who didn't know how to take hold of their power, while she wanted no power on earth except the freedom to go home where she belonged and help Ged with the garden.

She wished they could grow white roses like these, at home. Their scent was so sweet in the night air. But it was too windy on the Overfell, and the sun was too strong in summer. And probably the goats would eat the roses.

She went back indoors at last and made her way through the eastern wing to the suite of rooms she shared with Tehanu. Her daughter was asleep, for it was late. A flame no bigger than a pearl burned on the wick of a tiny alabaster lamp. The high rooms were soft, shadowy. She blew out the lamp, got into bed, and soon sank towards sleep.

She was walking along a narrow, high-vaulted corridor of stone. She carried the alabaster lamp. Its faint oval of light died away into darkness in front of her and behind her. She came to the door of a room that opened off the corridor. In-

86

side the room were people with the wings of birds. Some had the heads of birds, hawks and vultures. They stood or squatted motionless, not looking at her or at anything, with eyes encircled with white and red. Their wings were like huge black cloaks hanging down behind them. She knew they could not fly. They were so mournful, so hopeless, and the air in the room was so foul that she struggled to turn, to run away, but she could not move; and fighting that paralysis, she woke.

There were the warm shadows, the stars in the window, the scent of roses, the soft stir of the city, Tehanu's breathing as she slept.

Tenar sat up to shake off the remnants of the dream. It had been of the Painted Room in the Labyrinth of the Tombs, where she had first met Ged face to face, forty years ago. In the dream the paintings on the walls had come to life. Only it was not life. It was the endless, timeless unlife of those who died without rebirth: those accursed by the Nameless Ones: infidels, westerners, sorcerers.

After you died you were reborn. That was the sure knowledge in which she had been brought up. When as a child she was taken to the Tombs to be Arha, the Eaten One, they told her that she alone of all people had been and would be reborn as herself, life after life. Sometimes she had believed that, but not always, even when she was the priestess of the Tombs, and never since. But she knew what all the people of the Kargad Lands knew, that when they died they would return in a new body, the lamp that guttered out flickering up again that same instant elsewhere, in a woman's womb or the tiny egg of a minnow or a windborne seed of grass, coming back to be, forgetful of the old life, fresh for the new, life after life eternally.

Only those outcast by the earth itself, by the Old Powers, the dark sorcerers of the Hardic Lands, were not reborn. When they died—so said the Kargs—they did not rejoin the living world, but went to a dreary place of half being where, winged but flightless, neither bird nor human, they must endure without hope. How the priestess Kossil had relished telling her about the terrible fate of those boastful enemies of the God-King, their souls doomed to be cast out of the world of light forever!

But the afterlife Ged had told her of, where he said his people went, that changeless land of cold dust and shadow— was that any less dreary, any less terrible?

Unanswerable questions clamored in her mind: because she was no longer a Karg, because she had betrayed the sacred place, must she go to that dry land when she died? Must Ged go there? Would they pass each other there, uncaring? That was not possible. But what if he must go there, and she be reborn, so that their parting must be eternal?

She would not think about all that. It was clear enough why she had dreamed of the Painted Room, all these years after she had left all that behind her. It had to do with seeing the ambassadors, speaking Kargish again, of course. But still she lay upset, unnerved by the dream. She did not want to go back to the nightmares of her youth. She wanted to be back in the house on the Overfell, lying by Ged, hearing Tehanu's breath while she slept. When he slept Ged lay still as a stone; but the fire had left some damage in Tehanu's throat so there was a little harshness always in her breathing, and Tenar had listened to that, listened for it, night after night, year after year. That was life, that was life returning, that dear sound, that slight harsh breath.

Listening to it, she slept again at last. If she dreamed it was only of gulfs of air and the colors of morning moving in the sky.

ALDER WOKE VERY EARLY. His little companion had been restless all night, and so had he. He was glad to get up and go to the window and sit sleepily watching light come into the sky over the harbor, fishing boats set out and the sails of ships loom from a low mist in the great bay, and listening to the hum and bustle of the city making ready for the day. About the time he began to wonder if he should venture into the bewilderment of the palace to find what he was supposed to do, there was a knock on his door. A man brought in a tray of fresh fruit and bread, a jug of milk, and a small bowl of meat for the kitten. "I will come to conduct you to the king's presence when the fifth hour is told," he informed Alder solemnly, and then rather less formally told him how to get down into the palace gardens if he wanted a walk.

Alder knew of course that there were six hours from midnight to noon and six hours from noon to midnight, but had never heard the hours told, and wondered what the man meant.

He learned, presently, that here in Havnor four trumpeters went out on the high balcony from which rose the highest tower of the palace, the one that was topped with the slender steel blade of the hero's sword, and at the fourth and fifth hours before noon, and at noon, and at the first, second, and third hours after noon they blew their trumpets one to the west, one to the north, one to the east, one to the south. So the courtiers of the palace and the merchants and shippers of the city could arrange their doings and meet their appointments at the hour agreed. A boy he met walking in the gardens explained all this, a small, thin boy in a tunic that was too long for him. He explained that the trumpeters knew when to blow their trumpets because there were great sand clocks in the tower, as well as the Pendulum of Ath which hung down from high up in the tower and if set swinging just at the hour would cease to swing just as the next hour began. And he told Alder that the tunes the trumpeters played were all parts of the Lament for Erreth-Akbe that King Maharion wrote when he came back from Selidor, a different part for each hour, but only at noon did they play the whole tune through. And if you wanted to be somewhere at a certain hour, you should keep an eye on the balconies, because the trumpeters always came out a few minutes early, and if the sun was shining they held up their silver trumpets to flash and shine. The boy was called Rody and he had come with his father, the Lord of Metama on Ark, to stay a year in Havnor, and he went to school in the palace, and he was nine, and he missed his mother and his sister.

Alder was back in his room in time to meet his guide, less nervous than he might have been. The conversation with the child had reminded him that the sons of lords were children, that lords were men, and that it was not men he need fear.

His guide brought him through the palace corridors to a long, light room with windows all along one wall, looking out over Havnor's towers and fantastic bridges that arched over the canals and leapt from roof to roof and balcony to balcony across the streets. He half saw that panorama as he stood near the door, hesitant, not knowing if he should go forward to the group of people at the far end of the room.

The king saw him and came to him, greeted him kindly, led him to the others, and introduced them one by one.

There was a woman of fifty or so, small and very light-skinned, with greying hair and large grey eyes: Tenar, the king said smiling: Tenar of the Ring. She looked Alder in the eye and greeted him quietly.

There was a man of about the king's age, dressed in velvet and airy linens, with jewels on his belt and at his throat and a great ruby stud in his earlobe: Shipmaster Tosla, said the king. Tosla's face, dark as old oak wood, was keen and hard.

There was a middle-aged man, simply dressed, with a steady look that made Alder feel he could trust him: Prince Sege of the House of Havnor, said the king.

There was a man of forty or so who carried a wooden staff of his own height, by which Alder knew him as a wizard of the School on Roke. He had a rather worn face, fine hands, an aloof but courteous manner. Master Onyx, said the king.

There was a woman whom Alder took for a servant because she was very plainly dressed and stayed outside the group, turned half away as if looking out the windows. He saw the beautiful fall of her black hair, heavy and glossy as falling water, as Lebannen led her forward. "Tehanu of Gont," the king said, and his voice rang out like a challenge.

The woman looked straight at Alder for a moment. She was young; the left side of her face was smooth copper-rose, a dark bright eye under an arched eyebrow. The right side had been destroyed and was ridged, slabby scar, eyeless. Her right hand was like a raven's curled claw.

She put out her hand to Alder, in the manner of the people of Éa and the Enlades, as the others had done, but it was her left hand she held out. He touched his hand to hers, palm to palm. Hers was hot, fever hot. She looked at him again, an amazing glance from that one eye, bright, frowning, fierce. Then she looked down again and stood back as if she wished not to be one of them, wished not to be there.

"Master Alder bears a message for you from your father the Hawk of Gont," the king said, seeing the messenger stand wordless.

Tehanu did not lift her head. The glossy black hair almost hid the ruin of her face.

"My lady," Alder said, dry-mouthed and husky-voiced, "he bade me ask you two questions." He paused, only because he had to wet his lips and get his breath in a moment of panic that he had forgotten what he was to say; but the pause became a waiting silence.

Tehanu said, in a voice hoarser than his, "Ask them."

"He said to ask first: *Who are those who go to the dry land?* And as I took my leave of him, he said, 'Ask my daughter also: *Will a dragon cross the wall of stones?*'"

Tehanu nodded her head in acknowledgment and stepped back a little more, as if to carry her riddles away with her, away from them.

"The dry land," the king said, "and the dragons..."

92

His alert gaze went from face to face.

"Come," he said, "let's sit and talk."

"Perhaps we could talk down in the gardens?" said the little grey-eyed woman, Tenar. The king agreed at once. Alder heard Tenar say to him as they went, "She finds it hard to be indoors all day. She wants the sky."

Gardeners brought chairs for them in the shade of a huge old willow beside one of the pools. Tehanu went to stand by the pool, gazing down into the green water where a few big silver carp swam lazily. Clearly she wanted to think over her father's message, not to talk, though she could hear what they said.

When the others were all settled, the king had Alder tell his story yet again. Their silence as they listened was compassionate, and he was able to speak without constraint or hurry. When he was done, they remained silent a while, and then the wizard Onyx asked him one question: "Did you dream last night?"

Alder said he had had no dream he could recall.

"I did," Onyx said. "I dreamed of the Summoner who was my teacher in the School on Roke. They say of him that he died twice: because he came back from that country across the wall."

"I dreamed of the spirits that are not reborn," Tenar said, very low.

Prince Sege said, "All night I thought I heard voices down in the city streets, voices I knew from my childhood, calling as they used to do. But when I listened, it was only watchmen or drunken sailors shouting."

"I never dream," said Tosla.

"I didn't dream of that country," the king said. "I remembered it. And couldn't cease remembering it."

He looked at the silent woman, Tehanu, but she only looked down into the pond and did not speak.

No one else spoke; and Alder could not stand it. "If I am a plague bringer, you must send me away!" he said.

The wizard Onyx spoke, not imperiously but with finality. "If Roke sent you to Gont, and Gont sent you to Havnor, Havnor is where you should be."

"Many heads make light thinking," said Tosla, sardonic.

Lebannen said, "Let's put dreams aside for a while. Our guest needs to know what we were concerned about before he came—why I begged Tenar and Tehanu to come, earlier this summer, and summoned Tosla from his voyaging to take counsel with us. Will you tell Alder of this matter, Tosla?"

The dark-faced man nodded. The ruby in his ear gleamed like a drop of blood.

"The matter is dragons," he said. "In the West Reach for some years now they've come to farms and villages on Ully and Usidero, flying low, seizing the roofs of houses with their talons, shaking them, terrifying the people. In the Toringates they've come twice now at harvest time and set the fields burning with their breath, and burnt haystacks and set the thatch of houses afire. They haven't struck at people, but people have died in the fires. They haven't attacked the houses of the lords of those islands, seeking after treasure, the way they did in the Dark Years, but only the villages and the fields. The same word came from a merchantman who'd been southwest as far as Simly trading for grain: dragons had come and burnt the crop just as they were harvesting.

"Then, last winter in Semel, two dragons settled on the summit of the volcano, Mount Andanden."

"Ah," said Onyx, and at the king's inquiring glance: "The wizard Seppel of Paln tells me that mountain was a most sacred place to the dragons, where they came to drink fire from the earth in ancient days."

"Well, they're back," said Tosla. "And they come down harrying the herds and flocks that are the wealth of the people there, not hurting the beasts but frightening them so they break loose and run wild. The people say they're young dragons, black and thin, without much fire yet.

"And in Paln, there are dragons living now in the mountains of the north part of the island, wild country without farms. Hunters used to go there to hunt mountain sheep and catch falcons to tame, but they've been driven out by the dragons, and no one goes near the mountains now. Maybe your Pelnish wizard knows about them?"

Onyx nodded. "He says flights of them have been seen above the mountains like the flights of wild geese."

"Between Paln and Semel, and the Island of Havnor, is only the width of the Pelnish Sea," said Prince Sege.

Alder was thinking that it was less than a hundred miles from Semel to his own island, Taon.

"Tosla set out to the Dragons' Run in his ship the *Tern*," the king said.

"But got barely in sight of the easternmost of those isles before a swarm of the beasts came at me," Tosla said, with a hard grin. "They harried me as they do the cattle and sheep, swooping down to singe my sails, till I ran back where I came from. But that's nothing new."

Onyx nodded again. "Nobody but a dragonlord has ever sailed the Dragons' Run."

"I have," the king said, and suddenly smiled a broad, boyish smile. "But I was with a dragonlord... Now that's a time I've been thinking about. When I was in the West Reach with the Archmage, seeking Cob the necromancer, we passed Jessage, which lies even farther out than Simly, and we saw burned fields there. And in the Dragons' Run, we saw that they fought and killed one another like animals gone rabid."

After a time Prince Sege asked, "Could it be that some of those dragons did not recover from their madness in that evil time?"

"It's been fifteen years and more," Onyx said. "But dragons live very long. Maybe time passes differently for them."

Alder noticed that as the wizard spoke he glanced at Tehanu, standing apart from them by the pool.

"Yet only within the last year or two have they attacked people," said the prince.

"That they have not," Tosla said. "If a dragon wanted to destroy the people of a farm or village, who'd stop it? They've been after people's livelihood. Harvests, hayricks, farms, cattle. They're saying, *Begone—get out of the West!*"

"But why are they saying it with fire, with havoc?" the wizard demanded. "They can speak! They speak the Language of the Making. Morred and Erreth-Akbe talked with dragons. Our Archmage talked with them."

"Those we saw in the Dragons' Run," the king said, "had lost the power of speech. The breach Cob had made in the world was drawing their power from them, as it did from us.

Only the great dragon Orm Embar came to us and spoke to the Archmage, telling him to go to Selidor..." He paused, his eyes far away. "And even from Orm Embar speech was taken, before he died." Again he looked away from them, a strange light in his face. "It was for us Orm Embar died. He opened the way for us into the dark land."

They were all silent for a while. Tenar's quiet voice broke the silence. "Once Sparrowhawk said to me—let me see if I can remember how he said it: that the dragon and the dragon's speech are one thing, one being. That a dragon does not learn the Old Speech, but *is* it."

"As a tern is flight. As a fish is swimming," Onyx said slowly. "Yes."

Tehanu was listening, standing motionless by the pool. They all looked at her now. The look on her mother's face was eager, urgent. Tehanu turned her head away.

"How do you make a dragon talk to you?" the king said. He said it lightly, as if it were a pleasantry, but it was followed by another silence. "Well," he said, "that's something I hope we can learn. Now, Master Onyx, while we're speaking of dragons, will you tell us your story of the girl who came to the School on Roke, for none but me has heard it yet."

"A girl in the School!" said Tosla, with a scoffing grin. "Things have changed on Roke!"

"Indeed they have," the wizard said, with a long cool look at the sailor. "This was some eight years ago. She came from Way, disguised as a young man, wanting to study the art magic. Of course her poor disguise didn't fool the Door-keeper. Yet he let her in, and he took her part. At that time, the School was headed by the Master Summoner—the man," and he hesitated a moment, "the man of whom I told you I dreamed last night."

"Tell us something of that man, if you will, Master Onyx," the king said. "That was Thorion, who returned from death?"

"Yes. When the Archmage had been long gone and no word came, we feared he was dead. So the Summoner used his arts to go see if indeed he had crossed the wall. He stayed long there, so the masters feared for him too. But at last he woke, and said that the Archmage was there among the dead, and would not return himself but had bade Thorion return to govern Roke. Yet before long the dragon bore the Archmage Sparrowhawk living to us, with my lord Lebannen... Then when the Archmage had departed again, the Summoner fell down and lay as if life had gone out of him. The Master Herbal, with all his art, believed him dead. Yet as we made ready to bury him, he moved, and spoke, saying he had come back to life to do what must be done. So, since we were not able to choose a new Archmage, Thorion the Summoner governed the School." He paused. "When the girl came, though the Doorkeeper had admitted her, Thorion would not have her within the walls. He would have nothing to do with her. But the Master Patterner took her to the Grove, and she lived there some while at the edge of the trees, and walked with him among them. He and the Doorkeeper, and the Herbal, and Kurremkarmerruk the Namer, believed that there was a reason she had come to Roke, that she was a messenger or an agent of some great event, even if she herself didn't know it; and so they protected her. The other masters followed Thorion, who said she brought only dissension and ruin and should be driven out. I was a student then. It was a sore trouble to us to know that our masters, masterless, were quarreling."

"And over a girl," said Tosla.

Onyx's look at him this time was extremely cold. "Quite," he said. After a minute he took up his story. "To be brief, then, when Thorion sent a group of us to compel her to leave the island, she challenged him to meet her that evening on Roke Knoll. He came, and summoned her by her name to obey him: 'Irian,' he called her. But she said, 'I am not only Irian,' and speaking, she changed. She became—she took the form of a dragon. She touched Thorion and his body fell to dust. Then she climbed the hill, and watching her, we didn't know whether we saw a woman that burned like a fire, or a winged beast. But at the summit we saw her clearly, a dragon like a flame of red and gold. And she lifted up her wings and flew into the west."

His voice had grown soft and his face was full of the re-membered awe. Nobody spoke.

The wizard cleared his throat. "Before she went up the hill the Namer asked her, 'Who are you?' She said she did not know her other name. The Patterner spoke to her, ask-ing where she would go and whether she would come back. She said she was going beyond the west, to learn her name from her own people, but if he called her she would come."

In the silence, a hoarse, weak voice, like metal brushing on metal, spoke. Alder did not understand the words and yet they seemed familiar, as if he could almost remember what they meant.

Tehanu had come close to the wizard and was standing by him, bending to him, tense as a drawn bow. It was she who had spoken.

Startled and taken aback, the wizard stared up at her, got to his feet, backed off a step, and then controlling himself said, "Yes, those were her words: *My people, beyond the west.*"

"Call her. Oh, call her," Tehanu whispered, reaching out both her hands to him. Again he drew back involuntarily.

Tenar stood up and murmured to her daughter, "What is it, what is it, Tehanu?"

Tehanu stared round at them all. Alder felt as if he were a wraith she saw through. "Call her here," she said. She looked at the king. "Can you call her?"

"I have no such power. Perhaps the Patterner of Roke—perhaps you yourself—"

Tehanu shook her head violently. "No, no, no, no," she whispered. "I am not like her. I have no wings."

Lebannen looked at Tenar as if for guidance. Tenar looked miserably at her daughter.

Tehanu turned round and faced the king. "I'm sorry," she said, stiffly, in her weak, harsh voice. "I have to be alone, sir. I will think about what my father said. I will try to answer what he asked. But I have to be alone, please."

Lebannen bowed to her and glanced at Tenar, who went at once to her daughter and put an arm about her; and they went away on the sunny path by the pools and fountains.

The four men sat down again and said nothing for a few minutes.

Lebannen said, "You were right, Onyx," and to the others, "Master Onyx told me this tale of the woman-dragon

Irian after I told him something about Tehanu. How as a child Tehanu summoned the dragon Kalessin to Gont, and spoke with the dragon in the Old Speech, and Kalessin called her daughter."

"Sire, this is very strange, this is a strange time, when a dragon is a woman, and when an untaught girl speaks in the Language of the Making!" Onyx was deeply and obviously shaken, frightened. Alder saw that, and wondered why he himself felt no such fear. Probably, he thought, because he did not know enough to be afraid, or what to be afraid of.

"But there are old stories," Tosla said. "Haven't you heard them on Roke? Maybe your walls keep them out. They're only tales simple people tell. Songs, even. There's a sailors' song, 'The Lass of Belilo,' that tells how a sailor left a pretty girl weeping in every port, until one of the pretty girls flew after his boat on wings of brass and snatched him out of it and ate him."

Onyx looked at Tosla with disgust. But Lebannen smiled and said, "The Woman of Kemay... The Archmage's old master, Aihal, called Ogion, told Tenar about her. She was an old village woman, and lived as such. She invited Ogion into her cottage and served him fish soup. But she said mankind and dragonkind had once been one. She herself was a dragon as well as a woman. And being a mage, Ogion saw her as a dragon."

"As you saw Irian, Onyx," said Lebannen.

Speaking stiffly and addressing himself to the king only, Onyx said, "After Irian left Roke, the Master Namer showed us passages in the most ancient lore-books which had always been obscure, but which could be understood to speak of beings both human and dragon. And of a quarrel or great division among them. But none of this is clear to our understanding."

"I hoped that Tehanu might make it clear," Lebannen said. His voice was even, so that Alder did not know whether he had given up or still held that hope.

A man was hurrying down the path to them, a grey-headed soldier of the king's guards. Lebannen looked round, stood up, went to him. They conferred for a minute, low-voiced. The soldier strode off again; the king turned back to his companions. "Here is news," he said, the ring of challenge in his voice again. "Over the west of Havnor there have been great flights of dragons. They have set forests afire, and a coaster's crew say people fleeing down to South Port told them the town of Resbel is burning."

THAT NIGHT THE KING'S swiftest ship carried him and his party across the Bay of Havnor, running fast before the magewind Onyx raised. They came into the mouth of the Onneva River, under the shoulder of Mount Onn, at daybreak. With them eleven horses were disembarked, fine, strong, slender-legged creatures from the royal stables. Horses were rare on all the islands but Havnor and Semel. Tehanu knew donkeys well enough but had never seen a horse before. She had spent much of the night with them and their handlers, helping control and calm them. They were well-bred, mannerly horses but not used to sea voyages.

When it came time to mount them, there on the sands of the Onneva, Onyx was fairly daunted, and had to be coached and encouraged by the handlers, but Tehanu was up in the saddle as soon as the king. She put the reins in her crippled hand and did not use them, seeming to communicate with her mare by other means.

So the little caravan set off due west into the foothills of the Falierns, keeping up a good pace. It was the swiftest way to travel that Lebannen had at his disposal; to coast clear round South Havnor would take too long. They had the wizard Onyx with them to keep the weather favorable, clear the path of any obstacles, and defend them from any harm short of dragon fire. Against the dragons, if they encountered them, they had no defense at all, except perhaps Tehanu.

Taking counsel the evening before with his advisors and the officers of his guard, Lebannen had quickly concluded that there was no way to fight the dragons or protect the towns and fields from them: arrows were useless, shields were useless. Only the greatest mages had ever been able to defeat a dragon. He had no such mage in his service and knew of none now living, but he must defend his people as best he could, and he knew no way to do it but to try to parley with the dragons.

His majordomo had been shocked when he set off for the apartment where Tenar and Tehanu were: the king should send for those he wished to see, command them to come to him. "Not if he's going to beg from them," Lebannen said.

He told the startled maid who answered their door to ask if he might speak with the White Lady and the Woman of Gont. So they were known to the people of the palace and the city. That each bore her true name openly, as the king did, was so rare a matter, so defiant of rule and custom, of safety and propriety, that though people might know the name they were reluctant to say it and preferred to speak around it.

He was admitted, and having told them briefly the news he had received, said, "Tehanu, it may be that you alone in my kingdom can help me. If you can call to these dragons as you called to Kalessin, if you have any power over them, if you can speak to them and ask why they war on my people, will you do so?"

The young woman shrank from his words, turning towards her mother.

But Tenar did not offer her any shelter. She stood unmoving. After a while she said, "Tehanu, long ago I told you: when a king speaks to you, you answer. You were a child then, and didn't answer. You're not a child now."

Tehanu took a step back from them both. Like a child, she hung her head. "I can't call to them," she said in her faint, harsh voice. "I don't know them."

"Can you call Kalessin?" Lebannen asked.

She shook her head. "Too far away," she whispered. "I don't know where."

"But you are Kalessin's daughter," Tenar said. "Can you not speak to these dragons?"

She said wretchedly, "I don't know."

Lebannen said, "If there is any chance, Tehanu, that they'll talk to you, that you can talk to them, I beg you to take that chance. For I can't fight them, and don't know their language, and how can I find what they want of us from creatures who can destroy me with a breath, with a look? Will you speak for me, for us?"

She was silent. Then, so faintly he could barely hear it, she said, "Yes."

"Then make ready to travel with me. We leave by the fourth hour of the evening. My people will bring you to the ship. I thank you. And I thank you, Tenar!" he said, taking her hand a moment, but no longer, for he had much to see to before he went.

When he came down to the wharf, late and hurrying, there was the slender hooded figure. The last horse to be led aboard was snorting and bracing its feet, refusing to go up the gangplank. Tehanu seemed to be conferring with the handler. Presently she took the horse's bridle and talked to it a little, and they went up the gangplank quietly together.

Ships are small, crowded houses; Lebannen heard two of the hostlers talking softly on the afterdeck towards midnight. "She has the true hand," one said, and the other, a younger voice, "Aye, she does, but she's horrible to look at, ain't she?" The first one said, "If a horse don't mind it, why should you?" and the other, "I don't know, but I do."

Now, as they rode from the Onneva sands into the foothills, where the way widened, Tosla brought his horse up beside Lebannen's. "She's to be our interpreter, is she?" he asked.

"If she can."

"Well, she's braver than I'd have thought. If that happened to her the first time she talked with a dragon, it's likely to happen again."

"What do you mean?"

"She was half burnt to death."

"Not by a dragon."

"Who then?"

"The people she was born to."

"How was that?" Tosla asked with a grimace.

"Tramps, thieves. She was five or six years old. Whatever she did or they did, it ended in her being beaten unconscious and shoved into their campfire. Thinking, I suppose, she was dead or would die and it would be taken for an accident. They made off. Villagers found her, and Tenar took her in."

Tosla scratched his ear. "There's a pretty tale of human kindness. So she's no daughter of the old Archmage either? But then what do they mean saying she's a dragon's get?"

Lebannen had sailed with Tosla, had fought beside him years ago in the siege of Sorra, and knew him a brave, keen, coolheaded man. When Tosla's coarseness chafed him he blamed his own thin skin. "I don't know what they mean," he answered mildly. "All I know is, the dragon called her daughter."

"That Roke wizard of yours, that Onyx, is quick to say he's no use in this matter. But he can speak the Old Tongue, can't he?"

"Yes. He could wither you into ash with a few words of it. If he hasn't it's out of respect for me, not you, I think."

Tosla nodded. "I know that," he said.

They rode all that day at as quick a pace as the horses could keep, coming at nightfall to a little hill town where the horses could be fed and rested and the riders could sleep in variously uncomfortable beds. Those of them unused to riding now discovered they could barely walk. The people there had heard nothing about dragons, and were overwhelmed only by the terror and glory of a whole party of rich strangers riding in and wanting oats and beds and paying for them with silver and gold.

The riders set off again long before dawn. It was nearly a hundred miles from the sands of Onneva to Resbel. This second day would take them over the low pass of the Faliern Mountains and down the western side. Yenay, one of Lebannen's most trusted officers, rode well ahead of the others; Tosla was rear guard; Lebannen led the main group. He was jogging along half asleep in the dull quiet before dawn when hoofbeats coming towards him woke him. Yenay had come riding back. Lebannen looked up where the man was pointing.

They had just emerged from woods on the crest of an open hillside and could see through the clear half light all the way to the pass. The mountains to either side of it massed black against the dull reddish glow of a cloudy dawn.

But they were looking west.

"That's nearer than Resbel," Yenay said. "Fifteen miles, maybe."

Tehanu's mare, though small, was the finest of the lot, and had a strong conviction that she should lead the others. If Tehanu didn't hold her back she would keep sidling and overtaking till she was ahead of the line. The mare came up at once when Lebannen reined in his big horse, and so Tehanu was beside him now, looking where he looked.

"The forest is burning," he said to her.

He could see only the scarred side of her face, so she seemed to gaze blindly; but she saw, and her claw hand that held the reins was trembling. The burned child fears the fire, he thought.

What cruel, cowardly folly had possessed him to tell this girl, "Come talk to the dragons, save my skin!" and bring her straight into the fire?

"We will turn back," he said.

Tehanu raised her good hand, pointing. "Look," she said. "Look!"

A spark from a bonfire, a burning cinder rising over the black line of the pass, an eagle of flame soaring, a dragon flying straight at them.

Tehanu stood up in her stirrups and let out a piercing, scraping cry, like a sea bird's or a hawk's scream, but it was a word, one word: *"Medeu!"*

The great creature drew nearer with terrible speed, its long, thin wings beating almost lazily; it had lost the reflection of fire and looked black or bronze-colored in the growing light.

"Mind your horses," Tehanu said in her cracked voice, and just then Lebannen's grey gelding saw the dragon and started violently, tossing its head and backing. He could control it, but behind him one of the other horses let out a neigh of terror, and he heard them trampling and the handlers' voices. The wizard Onyx came running up and stood beside Lebannen's horse. Mounted or afoot, they stood and watched the dragon come.

Again Tehanu cried out that word. The dragon veered in its flight, slowed, came on, stopped and hovered in the air about fifty feet from them.

"Medeu!" Tehanu called, and the answer came like an echo prolonged: *"Me-de-uuu!"*

"What does it mean?" Lebannen asked, bending to Onyx.

"Sister, brother," the wizard whispered.

Tehanu was off her horse, had tossed the reins to Yenay, was walking forward down the slight slope to where the dragon hovered, its long wings beating quick and short like a hovering hawk's. But these wings were fifty feet from tip to tip, and as they beat they made a sound like kettledrums or rattles of brass. As she came closer to it, a little curl of fire escaped from the dragon's long, long-toothed, open mouth.

She held up her hand. Not the slender brown hand but the burned one, the claw. The scarring of her arm and shoulder kept her from raising it fully. She could reach barely as high as her head.

The dragon sank a little in the air, lowered its head, and touched her hand with its lean, flared, scaled snout. Like a dog, an animal greeting and sniffing, Lebannen thought; like a falcon stooping to the wrist; like a king bowing to a queen.

Tehanu spoke, the dragon spoke, both briefly, in their cymbal-shiver voices. Another exchange, a pause; the dragon spoke at length. Onyx listened intently. One more exchange of words. A wisp of smoke from the dragon's nostrils; a stiff, imperious gesture of the woman's crippled, withered hand. She spoke clearly two words.

"Bring her," the wizard translated in a whisper.

The dragon beat its wings hard, lowered its long head, and hissed, spoke again, then sprang up into the air, high over Tehanu, turned, wheeled once, and set off like an arrow to the west.

"It called her Daughter of the Eldest," the wizard whispered, as Tehanu stood motionless, watching the dragon go.

She turned around, looking small and fragile in that great sweep of hill and forest in the grey dawn light. Lebannen swung off his horse and hurried forward to her. He thought to find her drained and terrified, he put out his hand to help her walk, but she smiled at him. Her face, half terrible half beautiful, shone with the red light of the unrisen sun.

"They won't strike again. They will wait in the mountains," she said.

Then indeed she looked around as if she did not know where she was, and when Lebannen took her arm she let him do so; but the fire and the smile lingered in her face, and she walked lightly.

While the hostlers held the horses, already grazing on the dew-wet grass, Onyx, Tosla, and Yenay came round her, though they kept a respectful distance. Onyx said, "My Lady Tehanu, I have never seen so brave an act."

"Nor I," Tosla said.

"I was afraid," Tehanu said, in her voice that carried no emotion. "But I called him brother, and he called me sister."

"I could not understand all you said," the wizard said. "I have no such knowledge of the Old Speech as you. Will you tell us what passed between you?"

She spoke slowly, her eyes on the west where the dragon had flown. The dull red of the distant fire was paling as the east grew bright. "I said, 'Why are you burning the king's island?' And he said, 'It is time we have our own lands again.' And I said, 'Did the Eldest bid you take them with fire?'

Then he said that the Eldest, Kalessin, had gone with Orm Irian beyond the west to fly on the other wind. And he said the young dragons who remained here on the winds of the world say men are oath breakers who stole the dragons' lands. They tell one another that Kalessin will never return, and they will wait no longer, but will drive men out of all the western lands. But lately Orm Irian has returned, and is on Paln, he said. And I told him to ask her to come. And he said she would come to Kalessin's daughter."

CHAPTER III

The Dragon Council

⌒

FROM THE WINDOW OF HER room in the palace Tenar
had watched the ship sail, carrying Lebannen and her
daughter away into the night. She had not gone down to the
wharf with Tehanu. It had been hard, very hard to refuse to
come with her on this journey. Tehanu had begged, she who
never asked for anything. She never cried, could not cry, but
her breath had caught sobbing: "But I can't go, I *can't* go
alone! Come with me, mother!"

"My love, my heart, if I could spare you this fear I would,
don't you see I can't? I've done what I could do for you, my
flame of fire, my star. The king is right—only you, you
alone, can do this."

"But if you were just there, so I knew you were there—"

"I'm here, I'm always here. What could I do there but be
a burden? You must travel fast, it will be a hard journey. I'd
hold you back. And you might fear for me. You don't need

113

me. I'm no use to you. You must learn that. You must go, Tehanu."

And she had turned away from her child and begun sorting out the clothing Tehanu should take, home clothes, not the fancy things they wore here in the palace: her stout shoes, her good cloak. If she wept while she did it, she did not let her daughter see it.

Tehanu stood as if bewildered, paralysed with fear. When Tenar gave her clothes to change into, she obeyed. When the king's lieutenant, Yenay, knocked and asked if he might conduct Mistress Tehanu down to the wharf, she stared at him like a dumb animal.

"Go now," Tenar said. She embraced her and laid her hand on the great scar that was half her face. "You are Kalessin's daughter as well as mine."

The girl held her very tightly for a long moment, let go, turned away without a word, and followed Yenay out the door.

Tenar stood feeling the chill of the night air where the heat of Tehanu's body and arms had been.

She went over to the window. Lights down on the dock, the coming and going of men, the hoof clatter of horses being led down the steep streets above the water. A tall ship was at the pier, a ship she knew, the *Dolphin*. She watched from the window and saw Tehanu on the dock. She saw her go aboard at last, leading a horse that had been balking, and saw Lebannen follow her. She saw the mooring lines cast off, the docile movement of the ship following the oared tug that towed her clear, the sudden fall and flowering of the white sails in the darkness. The light of the stern lantern trembled on the dark water, shrank slowly to a tiny drop of brightness, and was gone.

Tenar went about the room folding up the clothes Tehanu had worn, the silken shift and overskirt; she picked up the light sandals and held them to her cheek a while before she put them away.

She lay awake in the wide bed and saw before her mind's eye over and over again the same scene: a road, and Tehanu walking on it alone. And a knot, a net, a black writhing coiling mass descending from the sky, dragons swarming, fire licking and streaming from them at her, her hair burning, her clothes burning— No, Tenar said, no! it will not happen! She would force her mind away from that scene, until she saw it again, the road, and Tehanu walking on it alone, and the black, burning knot in the sky, coming closer.

When the first light began to turn the room grey she slept at last, exhausted. She dreamed that she was in the Old Mage's house on the Overfell, her house, and she was glad beyond all words to be there. She took the broom from behind the door to sweep the shining oaken floor, for Ged had let it get dusty. But there was a door at the back of the house that had not been there before. When she opened it she found a small, low room with stone walls painted white. Ged was crouching in the room, squatting with his arms on his knees and his hands hanging limp. His head was not a man's head but small, black, and beaked, a vulture's head. He said in a faint, hoarse voice, "Tenar, I have no wings." And when he said that, such anger and terror rose up in her that she woke, gasping, to see sunlight on the high wall of her palace room and hear the sweet clear trumpets telling the fourth hour of morning.

Breakfast was brought. She ate a little and talked with Berry, the elderly servant whom she had chosen from all the retinue of maids and ladies of honor Lebannen had offered her. Berry was an intelligent, competent woman, born in a village in inland Havnor, with whom Tenar got on better than with most of the ladies of the court. They were civil and respectful, but they didn't know what to do with her, how to talk to a woman who was half Kargish priestess, half farmwife from Gont. She saw that it was easier for them to be kind to Tehanu in her fierce timidity. They could be sorry for her. They could not be sorry for Tenar.

Berry, however, could be and was, and she gave Tenar considerable comfort that morning. "The king will bring her back safe and sound," she said. "Why, do you think he'd take the girl into a danger he couldn't get her out of? Never! Not him!" It was false comfort, but Berry so passionately believed it to be true that Tenar had to agree with her, which was a little solace in itself.

She needed something to do, for Tehanu's absence was everywhere. She resolved to go talk to the Kargish princess, to see if the girl was willing to learn a word of Hardic, or at least to tell Tenar her name.

In the Kargad Lands people did not have a true name that they kept secret, as the speakers of Hardic did. Like use-names here, Kargish names often had some meaning— Rose, Alder, Honor, Hope; or they were traditional, often the name of an ancestor. People spoke them openly and were

proud of the antiquity of a name passed down from generation to generation. She had been taken too young from her
parents to know why they had called her Tenar, but thought
it might be for a grandmother or great-grandmother. That
name had been taken from her when she was recognised as
Arha, the Nameless One reborn, and she had forgotten it till
Ged gave it back to her. To her, as to him, it was her true
name; but it was not a word of the Old Speech; it gave no
one any power over her, and she had never concealed it.

She was puzzled now why the princess did so. Her bondwomen called her only Princess, or Lady, or Mistress; the
ambassadors had talked about her as the High Princess,
Daughter of Thol, Lady of Hur-at-Hur, and so on. If all the
poor girl had was titles, it was time she had a name.

Tenar knew it was not fitting for a guest of the king to go
alone through the streets of Havnor, and she knew Berry had
duties in the palace, so she asked for a servant to accompany
her. She was provided with a charming footman, or footboy,
for he was only about fifteen, who looked after her at the
street crossings as if she were a doddering crone. She liked
walking in the city. She had already found and admitted to
herself, going to the River House, that it was easier without
Tehanu beside her. People would look at Tehanu and look
away, and Tehanu walked in stiff, suffering pride, hating
their looks and their looking away, and Tenar suffered with
her, maybe more than she herself did.

Now she was able to loiter and watch the street shows,
the market booths, the various faces and clothing from all
over the Archipelago, to go out of the direct way to let her
footboy show her a street where the painted bridges from

rooftop to rooftop made a kind of airy vaulted ceiling high above them, from which red-flowering vines looped down in festoons, and people put birdcages out the windows on gilt poles among the flowers, so that it all seemed a garden in the middle of the air. "Oh, I wish Tehanu could see this," she thought. But she could not think of Tehanu, of where she might be.

The River House, like the New Palace, dated from the reign of Queen Heru, five centuries ago. It had been in ruins when Lebannen came to the throne; he had rebuilt it with much care, and it was a lovely, peaceful place, sparsely furnished, with dark, polished, uncarpeted floors. Ranks of narrow door-windows slid aside to open up the whole side of a room to a view of the willows and the river, and one could walk out onto deep wooden balconies built over the water. Court ladies had told Tenar that it had been the place the king liked best to slip away to for a night of solitude or a night with a lover, which lent even more significance, they hinted, to his housing the princess there. Her own suspicion was that he had not wanted the princess under the same roof with him and had simply named the only other possible place for her, but maybe the court ladies were right.

Guards in their fine harness recognised and let her pass, footmen announced her and went off with her footboy to crack nuts and gossip, which seemed to be the principal occupation of footmen, and ladies-in-waiting came to greet her, grateful for any new face and gasping for more news of the king's expedition against the dragons. Having run the whole gamut she was admitted at last to the apartments of the princess.

On her two previous visits she had been kept waiting some while in an anteroom, and then the veiled bondwomen had brought her into an inner room, the only dim room in the whole airy house, where the princess had stood in her round-brimmed hat with the red veil hanging down all round it to the floor, looking permanently fixed there, built in, exactly as if she were a brick chimney, as Lady Iyesa had said.

This time it was different. As soon as she came into the anteroom there was shrieking within and the sound of people running in various directions. The princess burst through the door and with a wild cry flung her arms around Tenar. Tenar was small, and the princess, a tall, vigorous young woman full of emotion, knocked her right off her feet, but held her up in strong arms. "Oh Lady Arha, Lady Arha, save me, save me!" she was crying.

"Princess! What's wrong?"

The princess was in tears of terror or relief or both at once, and all Tenar could understand of her laments and pleas was a babble of dragons and sacrifice.

"There are no dragons near Havnor," she said sternly, disengaging herself from the girl, "and nobody is being sacrificed. What is all this about? What have you been told?"

"The women said the dragons were coming and they'd sacrifice a king's daughter and not a goat because they're sorcerers and I was afraid." The princess wiped her face, clenched her hands, and began trying to master the panic she had been in. It had been real, ungovernable terror, and Tenar was sorry for her. She did not let her pity show. The girl needed to learn to hold on to her dignity.

"Your women are ignorant and don't know enough Hardic to understand what people tell them. And you don't know any Hardic at all. If you did you'd know there's nothing to be afraid of. Do you see the people of the house here rushing about weeping and screaming?"

The princess stared at her. She wore no hat, no veils, and only a light shift-dress, for it was a hot day. It was the first time Tenar had seen her except as a dim form through the red veiling. Though the princess's eyes were swollen with tears and her face blotched, she was magnificent: tawny-haired, tawny-eyed, with round arms and full breasts and slender waist, a woman in her first full beauty and strength.

"But none of those people is going to be sacrificed," she said finally.

"Nobody is going to be sacrificed."

"Then why are the dragons coming?"

Tenar drew a deep breath. "Princess," she said, "there are a great many things we need to talk about. If you'll look at me as your friend—"

"I do," the princess said. She stepped forward and took Tenar's right arm in a very strong grasp. "You are my friend, I have no other friend, I will shed my blood for you."

Ridiculous as it was, Tenar knew it was true.

She returned the girl's grip as well as she could and said, "You are my friend. Tell me your name."

The princess's eyes got big. There was a little snot and blubber still on her upper lip. Her lower lip trembled. She said, with a deep breath, "Seserakh."

"Seserakh: my name is not Arha, but Tenar."

"Tenar," the girl said, and grasped her arm tighter.

"Now," Tenar said, trying to regain control of the situation, "I have walked a long way and I'm thirsty. Please let's sit down, and may I have some water to drink? And then we can talk."

"Yes," said the princess, and leapt out of the room like a hunting lioness. There were shouts and cries from the inner rooms, and more sounds of running. A bondwoman appeared, adjusting her veil shakily and gibbering something in such thick dialect Tenar could not understand her. "Speak in the accursed tongue!" shouted the princess from within, and the woman pitifully squeaked out in Hardic, "To sit? to drink? lady?"

Two chairs had been set in the middle of the dark, stuffy room, facing each other. Seserakh stood beside one of them.

"I should like to sit outside, in the shade, over the water," Tenar said. "If it please you, princess."

The princess shouted, the women scuttled, the chairs were carried out onto the deep balcony. They sat down side by side.

"That's better," Tenar said. It was still strange to her to be speaking Kargish. She had no difficulty with it at all, but she felt as if she were not herself, were somebody else speaking, an actor enjoying her role.

"You *like* the water?" the princess asked. Her face had returned to its normal color, that of heavy cream, and her eyes, no longer swollen, were bluish gold, or blue with gold flecks.

"Yes. You don't?"

"I hate it. There was no water where I lived."

"A desert? I lived in a desert too. Until I was sixteen. Then I crossed the sea and came west. I love the water, the sea, the rivers."

"Oh, the sea," Seserakh said, shrinking and putting her head in her hands. "Oh I hate it, I hate it. I vomited my soul out. Over and over and over. Days and days and days. I never want to see the sea again." She shot a quick glance through the willow boughs at the quiet, shallow stream below them. "This river is all right," she said distrustfully.

A woman brought a tray with a pitcher and cups, and Tenar had a long drink of cool water.

"Princess," she said, "we have a great deal to talk about. First: the dragons are still a long way away, in the west. The king and my daughter have gone to talk with them."

"To *talk* with them?"

"Yes." She had been going to say more, but she said, "Now please tell me about the dragons in Hur-at-Hur."

Tenar had been told as a child in Atuan that there were dragons in Hur-at-Hur. Dragons in the mountains, brigands in the deserts. Hur-at-Hur was poor and far away and nothing good came from it but opals and turquoises and cedar logs.

Seserakh heaved a deep sigh. Tears came into her eyes. "It makes me cry to think about home," she said, with such pure simplicity of feeling that tears came into Tenar's eyes too. "Well, the dragons live up in the mountains. Two days, three days journey from Mesreth. It's all rocks up there and nobody bothers the dragons and they don't bother anybody. But once a year they come down, crawling down a certain way. It's a path, all smooth dust, made by their bellies crawling along it every year since time began. It's called the Drag-ons' Way." She saw that Tenar was listening with deep atten-tion, and went on. "It's taboo to cross the Dragons' Way. You mustn't set foot on it at all. You have to go clear round it, south of the Place of the Sacrifice. They start crawling down it late in spring. On the fourth day of the fifth month they've all arrived at the Place of the Sacrifice. None of them is ever late. And everybody from Mesreth and the villages is there waiting for them. And then, when they've all come down the Dragons' Way, the priests begin the sacrifice. And that's . . . Don't you have the spring sacrifice, in Atuan?"

Tenar shook her head.

"Well, that's why I got scared, you see, because it can be a human sacrifice. If things weren't going well, they'd sacri-fice a king's daughter. Otherwise it would just be some ordi-nary girl. But they haven't done even that for a long time. Not since I was little. Since my father defeated all the other kings. Since then, they've only sacrificed a she-goat and a ewe. And they catch the blood in bowls, and throw the fat into the sacred fire, and call to the dragons. And the dragons all come crawling up. They drink the blood and eat the fire." She shut her eyes for a moment; so did Tenar. "Then they go back up into the mountains, and we go back to Mesreth."

"How big are the dragons?"

Seserakh put her hands about a yard apart. "Sometimes bigger," she said.

"And they can't fly? Or speak?"

"Oh, no. Their wings are just little stubs. They make a kind of hissing. Animals can't talk. But they're sacred ani-mals. They're the sign of life, because fire is life, and they eat fire and spit out fire. And they're sacred because they come to the spring sacrifice. Even if no people came, the dragons would come and gather at that place. We come there because the dragons do. The priests always tell all about that before the sacrifice."

Tenar absorbed this for a while. "The dragons here in the west," she said, "are large. Huge. And they can fly. They're animals, but they can speak. And they are sacred. And dangerous."

"Well," the princess said, "dragons may be animals, but they're more like us than the accursed-sorcerers are."

She said "accursed-sorcerers" all as one word and without any particular emphasis. Tenar remembered that phrase from her childhood. It meant the Dark Folk, the Hardic people of the Archipelago.

"Why is that?"

"Because the dragons are reborn! Like all the animals. Like us." Seserakh looked at Tenar with frank curiosity. "I thought since you were a priestess at the Most Sacred Place of the Tombs you'd know a lot more about all that than I do."

"But we had no dragons there," Tenar said. "I didn't learn anything about them at all. Please, my friend, tell me."

"Well, let me see if I can tell the story about it. It's a winter story. I guess it's all right to tell it in summer here. Everything here is all wrong anyway." She sighed. "Well, in the beginning, you know, in the first time, we were all the same, all the people and the animals, we did the same things. And then we learned how to die. And so we learned how to be reborn. Maybe as one kind of being, maybe another. But it doesn't matter so much because anyhow you'll die again and get reborn again and get to be everything sooner or later."

Tenar nodded. So far, the story was familiar to her.

"But the best things to get reborn as are people and dragons, because those are the sacred beings. So you try not to break the taboos, and you try to observe the Precepts, so you have a better chance to be a person again, or anyhow a dragon...If dragons here can talk and are so big, I can see why that would be a reward. Being one of ours never seemed like much to look forward to.

"But the story is about the accursed-sorcerers discovering the Vedurnan. That was a thing, I don't know what it was, that told some people that if they'd agree never to die and never be reborn, they could learn how to do sorcery. So they chose that, they chose the Vedurnan. And they went off into the west with it. And it turned them dark. And they live here. All these people here—they're the ones who chose the Vedurnan. They live, and they can do their accursed sorceries, but they can't die. Only their bodies die. The rest of them stays in a dark place and never gets reborn. And they look like birds. But they can't fly."

"Yes," Tenar whispered.

"You didn't learn about that on Atuan?"

"No," Tenar said.

Her mind was recalling the story the Woman of Kemay told Ogion: in the beginning of time, mankind and the dragons had been one, but the dragons chose wildness and freedom, and mankind chose wealth and power. A choice, a separation. Was it the same story?

But the image in Tenar's heart was of Ged squatting in a stone room, his head small, black, beaked...

"The Vedurnan isn't that ring, is it, that they kept talking about, that I'm going to have to wear?"

Tenar tried to force her mind away from the Painted Room and from last night's dream to Seserakh's question. "Ring?"

"Urthakby's ring."

"Erreth-Akbe. No. That ring is the Ring of Peace. And you'll wear it only if and when you're King Lebannen's queen. And you'll be a lucky woman to be that."

Seserakh's expression was curious. It was not sullen or cynical. It was hopeless, half humorous, patient, the expression of a woman decades older. "There is no luck about it, dear friend Tenar," she said. "I have to marry him. And so I will be lost."

"Why are you lost if you marry him?"

"If I marry him I have to give him my name. If he speaks my name, he steals my soul. That's what the accursed-sorcerers do. So they always hide their names. But if he steals my soul, I won't be able to die. I'll have to live forever without my body, a bird that can't fly, and never be reborn."

"That's why you hid your name?"

"I gave it to you, my friend."

"I honor the gift, my friend," Tenar said energetically. "But you can say your name to anybody you want, here. They can't steal your soul with it. Believe me, Seserakh. And you can trust him. He doesn't—he won't do you any harm."

The girl had caught her hesitation. "But he wishes he could," she said. "Tenar my friend, I know what I am, here.

126

In that big city Awabath where my father is, I was a stupid ignorant desert woman. A *feyagat*. The city women sniggered and poked each other whenever they saw me, the barefaced whores. And here it's worse. I can't understand anybody and they can't understand me, and everything, everything is different! I don't even know what the food is, it's sorcerer food, it makes me dizzy. I don't know what the taboos are, there aren't any priests to ask, only sorcerer women, all black and barefaced. And I saw the way he looked at me. You can see out of the *feyag*, you know! I saw his face. He's very handsome, he looks like a warrior, but he's a black sorcerer and he hates me. Don't say he doesn't, because I know he does. And I think when he learns my name he'll send my soul to that place forever."

After a while, gazing into the moving branches of the willows over the softly moving water, feeling sad and weary, Tenar said, "What you need to do, then, princess, is learn how to make him like you. What else can you do?"

Seserakh shrugged mournfully.

"It would help if you understood what he said."

"Bagabba-bagabba. They all sound like that."

"And we sound like that to them. Come on, princess, how can he like you if all *you* can say to *him* is bagabba-bagabba? Look," and she held up her hand, pointed to it with the other, and said the word first in Kargish, then in Hardic.

Seserakh repeated both words in a dutiful tone. After a few more body parts she suddenly grasped the potentialities of translation. She sat up straighter. "How do sorcerers say 'king'?"

127

"Agni. It's a word of the Old Speech. My husband told me that."

She realised as she spoke that it was foolish to bring up the existence of yet a third language at this point; but that was not what caught the princess's attention.

"You have a husband?" Seserakh stared at her with luminous, leonine eyes, and laughed aloud. "Oh, how wonderful! I thought you were a priestess! Oh please, my friend, tell me about him! Is he a warrior? Is he handsome? Do you love him?"

AFTER THE KING WENT dragon hunting, Alder had no idea what to do; he felt utterly useless, unjustified in staying in the palace eating the king's food, guilty for the trouble he had brought with him. He could not sit all day in his room, so he went out into the streets, but the splendor and activity of the city were daunting to him, and having no money or purpose all he could do was walk till he was tired. He would come back to the Palace of Maharion wondering if the stern-faced guards would readmit him. The nearest he came to peace was in the palace gardens. He hoped to meet Rody there again, but the child did not appear, and perhaps that was as well. Alder thought that he should not talk with people. The hands that reached to him from death would reach out to them.

On the third day after the king's departure he went down to walk among the garden pools. The day had been very hot; the evening was still and sultry. He brought Tug with him and let the little cat loose to stalk insects under the bushes, while he sat on a bench near the big willow and watched the silver-green glimmer of fat carp in the water. He felt lonely and discouraged; he felt his defense against the voices and the reaching hands was breaking down. What was the good of being here, after all? Why not go into the dream once and for all, go down that hill, be done with it? Nobody in the world would grieve for him, and his death would spare them this sickness he had brought with him. Surely they had enough to do fighting dragons. Maybe if he went there he would see Lily.

If he was dead they could not touch each other. The wizards said they would not even want to. They said the dead forgot what it was to be alive. But Lily had reached to him. At first, for a little while, maybe they would remember life long enough to look at each other, to see each other, even if they did not touch.

"Alder."

He looked up slowly at the woman who stood near him. The small grey woman, Tenar. He saw the concern in her face, but did not know why she was troubled. Then he remembered that her daughter, the burned girl, had gone with the king. Maybe there had been bad news. Maybe they were all dead.

"Are you ill, Alder?" she asked.

He shook his head. It was hard to talk. He understood now how easy it would be, in that other land, not to speak. Not to meet people's eyes. Not to be troubled.

She sat down on the bench beside him. "You look troubled," she said.

He made a vague gesture—it's all right, it's no matter.

"You were on Gont. With my husband Sparrowhawk. How was he? Was he looking after himself?"

"Yes," Alder said. He tried to answer more adequately. "He was the kindest of hosts."

"I'm glad to hear that," she said. "I worry about him. He keeps house as well as I do, but still, I didn't like leaving him alone...Please, would you tell me what he was doing while you were there?"

He told her that Sparrowhawk had picked the plums and taken them to sell, that the two of them had mended the fence, that Sparrowhawk had helped him sleep.

She listened intently, seriously, as if these small matters were as weighty as the strange events they had talked about here three days ago—the dead calling to a living man, a girl becoming a dragon, dragons setting fire to the islands of the west.

Indeed he did not know what weighed more heavily after all, the great strange things or the small common ones.

"I wish I could go home," the woman said.

"I could wish the same thing, but it would be in vain. I think I'll never go home again." He did not know why he said it, but heard himself say it and thought it was true.

She looked at him a minute with her quiet grey eyes and asked no question.

"I could wish my daughter would go home with me," she said, "but it would be in vain, too. I know she must go on. I don't know where."

"Will you tell me what gift it is that she has, what

woman she is, that the king sent for her, and took her with him to meet the dragons?"

"Oh, if I knew what she is, I'd tell you," Tenar said, her voice full of grief and love and bitterness. "She's not my daughter born, as you may have guessed or known. She came to me a little child, saved from the fire, but only barely and not wholly saved... When Sparrowhawk came back to me she became his daughter too. And she kept both him and me from a cruel death, by summoning a dragon, Kalessin, called Eldest. And that dragon called her daughter. So she's the child of many and none, spared no pain yet spared from the fire. Who she is in truth I may never know. But I wish she were here now, safe with me!"

He wanted to reassure her, but his own heart was too low.

"Tell me a little more about your wife, Alder," she said.

"I cannot," he said at last into the silence that lay easily between them. "I would if I could, Lady Tenar. There's such a heaviness in me, and a dread and fear, tonight. I try to think of Lily, but there's only that dark desert going down and down, and I can't see her in it. All the memories I had of her, that were like water and breath to me, have gone into that dry place. I have nothing left."

"I am sorry," she whispered, and they sat again in silence. The dusk was deepening. It was windless, very warm. Lights in the palace shone through the carved window screens and the still, hanging foliage of the willows.

"Something is happening," Tenar said. "A great change in the world. Maybe nothing we knew will be left to us."

Alder looked up into the darkening sky. The towers of the palace stood clear against it, their pale marble and alabaster catching all the light left in the west. His eyes sought the sword blade mounted at the point of the highest tower and he saw it, faint silver. "Look," he said. At the sword's point, like a diamond or a drop of water, shone a star. As they watched the star moved free of the sword, rising straight above it.

There was a commotion, in the palace or outside the walls; voices; a horn sounded, a sharp imperative call.

"They've come back," Tenar said, and stood up. Excitement had come into the air, and Alder too stood up. Tenar hurried into the palace, from which the harbor could be seen. But before he took Tug back inside, Alder looked up again at the sword, now only a faint glimmer, and the star riding bright above it.

DOLPHIN CAME SAILING UP the harbor in that windless summer night, leaning forward, urgent, the magewind bellying out her sails. Nobody in the palace had looked for the king to return so soon, but nothing was out of order or unready when he came. The quay was instantly crowded with courtiers, off-duty soldiers, and townspeople ready to greet him, and song makers and harpers were waiting to hear how he had fought and defeated dragons so they could make ballads about it.

They were disappointed: the king and his party made straight for the palace, and the guards and sailors from the ship said only, "They went up into the country above Onneva Sands, and in two days they came back. The wizard sent out a message bird to us, for we were down at the Gates of the Bay by then, since we were going to meet them in South Port. We came back and there they were awaiting us at the river mouth, all unharmed. But we saw the smoke of forests afire over the South Falierns."

Tenar was in the crowd on the quay, and Tehanu went straight to her. They embraced fiercely. But as they walked up the street among the lights and the rejoicing voices, Tenar was still thinking, "It has changed. She has changed. She'll never come home."

Lebannen walked among his guards. Charged with tension and energy, he was regal, warlike, radiant. "Erreth-Akbe," people called out, seeing him, and "Son of Morred!" On the steps of the palace he turned and faced them all. He had a strong voice to use when he wanted it, and it rang out now silencing the tumult. "Listen, people of Havnor! The Woman of Gont has spoken for us with a chief among the dragons. They have pledged a truce. One of them will come to us. A dragon will come here, to the City of Havnor, to the Palace of Maharion. Not to destroy, but to parley. The time has come when men and dragons must meet and talk. So I tell you: when the dragon comes, do not fear it, do not fight it, do not flee it, but welcome it in the Sign of Peace. Greet it as you would greet a great lord come in peace from afar. And have no fear. For we are well protected by the Sword of Erreth-Akbe, by the Ring of Elfarran, and by the Name of Morred. And by my own name I promise you, so long as I live I will defend this city and this realm!"

They listened in a breathless hush. A burst of cheers and shouts followed on his words as he turned and strode into the palace. "I thought it best to give them some warning," he said in his usual quiet voice to Tehanu, and she nodded. He spoke to her as to a comrade, and she behaved as such. Tenar and the courtiers nearby saw this.

He ordered that his full Council meet in the morning at the fourth hour, and then they all dispersed, but he kept Tenar with him a minute while Tehanu went on. "It's she who protects us," he said.

"Alone?"

"Don't fear for her. She is the dragon's daughter, the dragon's sister. She goes where we can't go. Don't fear for her, Tenar."

She bowed her head in acceptance. "I thank you for bringing her safe back to me," she said. "For a while."

They were apart from other people, in the corridor that led to the western apartments of the palace. Tenar looked up at the king and said, "I've been talking about dragons with the princess."

"The princess," he said blankly.

"She has a name. I can't tell it to you, since she believes you might use it to destroy her soul."

He scowled.

"In Hur-at-Hur there are dragons. Small, she says, and wingless, and they don't speak. But they're sacred. The sacred sign and pledge of death and rebirth. She reminded me that my people don't go where your people do when they die. That dry land Alder tells of, it's not where we go. The princess, and I, and the dragons."

Lebannen's face changed from wary reserve to intense attention. "Ged's questions to Tehanu," he said in a low voice. "Are these the answers?"

"I know only what the princess told me, or reminded me. I'll speak with Tehanu about these things tonight."

He frowned, pondering; then his face cleared. He stooped and kissed Tenar's cheek, bidding her good night. He strode off and she watched him go. He melted her heart, he dazzled her, but she was not blinded. "He's still afraid of the princess," she thought.

THE THRONE ROOM WAS the oldest room in the Palace of Maharion. It had been the hall of Gemal Sea-Born, Prince of Ilien, who became king in Havnor and of whose lineage came Queen Heru and her son Maharion. The Havnorian Lay says:

> *A hundred warriors, a hundred women*
> *sat in the great hall of Gemal Sea-Born*
> *at the king's table, courtly in talk,*
> *handsome and generous gentry of Havnor,*
> *no warriors braver, no women more beautiful.*

Around this hall for over a century Gemal's heirs had built an ever larger palace, and lastly Heru and Maharion had raised above it the Tower of Alabaster, the Tower of the Queen, the Tower of the Sword.

These still stood; but though the people of Havnor had stoutly called it the New Palace all through the long centuries since Maharion's death, it was old and half in ruins when Lebannen came to the throne. He had rebuilt it almost entirely, and richly. The merchants of the Inner Isles, in their first joy at having a king and laws again to protect their trading, had set his revenue high and offered him yet more money for all such undertakings; for the first few years of his reign they had not even complained that taxation was destroying their business and would leave their children destitute. So he had been able to make the New Palace new again, and splendid. But the throne room, once the beamed ceiling was rebuilt, the stone walls replastered, the narrow, high-set windows reglazed, he left in its old starkness.

Through the brief false dynasties and the Dark Years of tyrants and usurpers and pirate lords, through all the insults of time and ambition, the throne of the kingdom had stood at the end of the long room: a wooden chair, high-backed, on a plain dais. It had once been sheathed in gold. That was long gone; the small golden nails had left rents in the wood where they had been torn out. Its silken cushions and hangings had been stolen or destroyed by moth and mouse and mold. Nothing showed it to be what it was but the place where it stood and a shallow carving on the back, a heron flying with a twig of rowan in its beak. That was the crest of the House of Enlad.

The kings of that house had come from Enlad to Havnor eight hundred years ago. Where Morred's High Seat is, they said, the kingdom is.

Lebannen had it cleaned, the decayed wood repaired and replaced, oiled and burnished back to dark satin, but left it unpainted, ungilt, bare. Some of the rich people who came to admire their expensive palace complained about the throne room and the throne. "It looks like a barn," they said, and, "Is it Morred's High Seat or an old farmer's chair?"

To which some said the king had replied, "What is a kingdom without the barns that feed it and the farmers to grow the grain?" Others said he had replied, "Is my kingdom gauds of gilt and velvet or does it stand by the strength of wood and stone?" Still others said he had said nothing except that he liked it the way it was. And it being his royal buttocks that sat on the uncushioned throne, his critics did not get the last word on the matter.

Into that stern and high-beamed hall, on a cool morning of late summer sea fog, filed the King's Council: ninety-one men and women, a hundred if all had been there. All had been chosen by the king, some to represent the great noble and princely houses of the Inner Isles, pledged vassals of the Crown; some to speak for the interests of other islands and parts of the Archipelago; some because the king had found them or hoped to find them useful and trustworthy counselors of state. There were merchants, shippers, and factors of Havnor and the other great port cities of the Sea of Éa and the Inmost Sea, splendid in their conscious gravity and their dark robes of heavy silk. There were masters from the workers' guilds, flexible and canny bargainers, notable among them a pale-eyed, hard-handed woman, the chief of the miners of Osskil. There were Roke wizards like Onyx, with grey cloaks and wooden staffs. There was also a Pelnish wizard, called Master Seppel, who carried no staff and of whom people mostly steered clear, though he seemed mild enough. There were noblewomen, young and old, from the kingdom's fiefs and principalities, some in silks of Lorbanery and pearls from the Isles of Sand, and two Islandwomen, stout, plain, and dignified, one from Iffish and one from Korp, to speak for the people of the East Reach. There were some poets, some learned people from the old colleges of Éa and the Enlades, and several captains of soldiery or of the king's ships.

All these councillors the king had chosen. At the end of two or three years he would ask them to serve again or send them home with thanks and in honor, and replace them. All laws and taxations, all judgments brought before the throne, he discussed with them, taking their counsel. They would then vote on his proposal, and only with the consent of the majority was it enacted. There were those who said the council was nothing but the king's pets and puppets, and so indeed it might have been. He mostly got his way if he argued for it. Often he expressed no opinion and let the council make the decision. Many councillors had found that if they had enough facts to support their opposition and made a good argument, they might sway the others and even persuade the king. So debates within the various divisions and special bodies of the council were often hotly contested, and even in full session the king had several times been opposed, argued with, and voted down. He was a good diplomat, but an indifferent politician.

He found his council served him well, and people of power had come to respect it. Common folk did not pay much attention to it. They centered their hopes and attention on the king's person. There were a thousand lays and ballads about the son of Morred, the prince who rode the dragon back from death to the shores of day, the hero of Sorra, wielder of the Sword of Serriadh, the Rowan Tree, the Tall Ash of Enlad, the well-loved king who ruled in the Sign of Peace. But it was hard going to make songs about councillors debating shipping taxes.

Unsung, then, they filed in and took their seats on the cushioned benches facing the uncushioned throne. They stood again as the king came in. With him came the Woman of Gont, whom most of them had seen before so that her appearance caused no stir, and a slight man in rusty black. "Looks like a village sorcerer," a merchant from Kamery said to a shipwright from Way, who answered, "No doubt," in a resigned, forgiving tone. The king was loved also by many of the councillors, or at least liked; he had after all put power in their hands, and even if they felt no obligation to be grateful to him, they respected his judgment.

The elderly Lady of Ebéa hurried in late, and Prince Sege, who presided over protocol, told the council to be seated. They all sat down. "Hear the king," Sege said, and they listened.

He told them, and for many it was the first real news of these matters, about the dragons' attacks on West Havnor, and how he had set out with the Woman of Gont, Tehanu, to parley with them.

He kept them in suspense while he spoke of the earlier attacks by dragons on the islands of the west, and told them briefly Onyx's tale of the girl who turned into a dragon on Roke Knoll, and reminded them that Tehanu was claimed as daughter by Tenar of the Ring, by the onetime Archmage of Roke, and by the dragon Kalessin, on whose back the king himself had been borne from Selidor.

Then finally he told them what had happened at the pass in the Faliern Mountains at dawn three days ago.

He ended by saying, "That dragon carried Tehanu's message to Orm Irian in Paln, who then must make the long flight here, three hundred miles or more. But dragons are swifter than any ship even with the magewind. We may look for Orm Irian at any time."

Prince Sege asked the first question, knowing the king would welcome it: "What do you hope to gain, my lord, by parley with a dragon?"

The answer was prompt: "More than we can ever gain by trying to fight it. It is a hard thing to say, but it is the truth: against the anger of these great creatures, if indeed they were to come against us in any number, we have no true defense. Our wise men tell us there is maybe one place that could stand against them, Roke Island. And on Roke there is maybe one man who could face the wrath of even a single dragon and not be destroyed. Therefore we must try to find out the cause of their anger and, by removing it, make peace with them."

"They are animals," said the old Lord of Felkway. "Men cannot reason with animals, make peace with them."

"Have we not the Sword of Erreth-Akbe, who slew the Great Dragon?" cried a young councillor.

He was answered at once by another: "And who slew Erreth-Akbe?"

Debate in the council tended to be tumultuous, though Prince Sege kept strict rule, not letting anyone interrupt another or speak for more than one turn of the two-minute sandglass. Babblers and droners were cut off by a crash of the prince's silver-tipped staff and his call to the next speaker. So they talked and shouted back and forth at a fast pace, and all the things that had to be said and many things that did not need to be said were said, and refuted, and said again. Mostly they argued that they should go to war, fight the dragons, defeat them.

"A band of archers on one of the king's warships could bring them down like ducks," cried a hot-blooded merchant from Wathort.

"Are we to grovel before mindless beasts? Are there no heroes left among us?" demanded the imperious Lady of O-tokne.

To that, Onyx made a sharp reply: "Mindless? They speak the Language of the Making, in the knowledge of which our art and power lies. They are beasts as we are beasts. Men are animals that speak."

A ship's captain, an old, far-traveled man, said, "Then isn't it you wizards who should be talking with them? Since you know their speech, and maybe share their powers? The king spoke of a young untaught girl who turned into a dragon. But mages can take that form at will. Couldn't the Masters of Roke speak with the dragons or fight with them, if need be, evenly matched?"

The wizard from Paln stood up. He was a short man with a soft voice. "To take the form is to be the being, captain," he said politely. "A mage can look like a dragon. But true Change is a risky art. Especially now. A small change in the midst of great changes is like a breath against the wind... But we have here among us one who need use no art, and yet can speak for us to dragons better than any man could do. If she will speak for us."

At that, Tehanu stood up from her bench at the foot of the dais. "I will," she said. And sat down again.

That brought a pause to the discussion for a minute, but soon they were all at it again.

The king listened and did not speak. He wanted to know the temper of his people.

The sweet silver trumpets high on the Tower of the Sword played all their tune four times, telling the sixth hour, noon. The king stood, and Prince Sege declared a recess until the first hour of the afternoon.

A lunch of fresh cheese and summer fruits and greens was set out in a room in Queen Heru's Tower. There Lebannen invited Tehanu and Tenar, Alder, Sege, and Onyx; and Onyx, with the king's permission, brought with him the Pelnish wizard Seppel. They sat and ate together, talking little and quietly. The windows looked over all the harbor and the north shoreline of the bay fading off into a bluish haze that might be either the remnants of the morning fog or smoke from the forest fires in the west of the island.

Alder remained bewildered at being included among the king's intimates and brought into his councils. What had he to do with dragons? He could neither fight with them nor talk with them. The idea of such mighty beings was great and strange to him. At moments the boasts and challenges of the councillors seemed to him like a yapping of dogs. He had seen a young dog once on a beach barking and barking at the ocean, rushing and snapping at the ebb wave, running back from the breaker with its wet tail between its legs.

But he was glad to be with Tenar, who put him at ease, and whom he liked for her kindness and courage, and he found now that he was also at ease with Tehanu.

Her disfigurement made it seem that she had two faces. He could not see them both at one time, only the one or the other. But he had got used to that and it did not disquiet him. His mother's face had been half masked by its wine-red birthmark. Tehanu's face reminded him of that.

She seemed less restless and troubled than she had been. She sat quietly, and a couple of times she spoke to Alder, sitting next to her, with a shy comradeliness. He felt that, like him, she was there not by choice but because she had forgone choice, driven to follow a way she did not understand. Maybe her way and his went together, for a while at least. The idea gave him courage. Knowing only that there was something he had to do, something begun that must be finished, he felt that whatever it might be, it would be better done with her than without her. Perhaps she was drawn to him out of the same loneliness.

But her conversation was not of such deep matters. "My father gave you a kitten," she said to him as they left the table. "Was it one of Aunty Moss's?"

He nodded, and she asked, "The grey one?"

"Yes."

"That was the best cat of the litter."

"She's getting fat, here."

Tehanu hesitated and then said timidly, "I think it's a he."

Alder found himself smiling. "He's a good companion. A sailor named him Tug."

"Tug," she said, and looked satisfied.

"Tehanu," the king said. He had sat down beside Tenar in the deep window seat. "I didn't call on you in council today to speak of the questions Lord Sparrowhawk asked you. It was not the time. Is it the place?"

Alder watched her. She considered before answering. She glanced once at her mother, who made no answering sign.

"I'd rather speak to you here," she said in her hoarse voice. "And maybe to the Princess of Hur-at-Hur."

After a brief pause the king said pleasantly, "Shall I send for her?"

"No, I can go see her. Afterward. I haven't much to say, really. My father asked, *Who goes to the dry land when they die?* And my mother and I talked about it. And we thought, people go there, but do the beasts? Do birds fly there? Are there trees, does the grass grow? Alder, you've seen it."

Taken by surprise, he could say only, "There...there's grass, on the hither side of the wall, but it seems dead. Beyond that I don't know."

Tehanu looked at the king. "You walked across that land, my lord."

"I saw no beast, or bird, or growing thing."

Alder spoke again: "Lord Sparrowhawk said: dust, rock."

"I think no beings go there at death but human beings," Tehanu said. "But not all of them." Again she looked at her mother, and did not look away.

Tenar spoke. "The Kargish people are like the animals." Her voice was dry and let no feeling be heard. "They die to be reborn."

"That is superstition," Onyx said. "Forgive me, Lady Tenar, but you yourself—" He paused.

"I no longer believe," Tenar said, "that I am or was, as they told me, Arha forever reborn, a single soul reincarnated

144

endlessly and so immortal. I do believe that when I die I will, like any mortal being, rejoin the greater being of the world. Like the grass, the trees, the animals. Men are only animals that speak, sir, as you said this morning."

"But we can speak the Language of the Making," the wizard protested. "By learning the words by which Segoy made the world, the very speech of life, we teach our souls to conquer death."

"That place where nothing is but dust and shadows, is that your conquest?" Her voice was not dry now, and her eyes flashed.

Onyx stood indignant but wordless.

The king intervened. "Lord Sparrowhawk asked a second question," he said. *"Can a dragon cross the wall of stones?"* He looked at Tehanu.

"It's answered in the first answer," she said, "if dragons are only animals that speak, and animals don't go there. Has a mage ever seen a dragon there? Or you, my lord?" She looked first at Onyx, then at Lebannen. Onyx pondered only a moment before he said, "No."

The king looked amazed. "How is it I never thought of that?" he said. "No, we saw none. I think there are no dragons there."

"My lord," Alder said, louder than he had ever said anything in the palace, "there is a dragon here." He was standing facing the window, and he pointed at it.

They all turned. In the sky above the Bay of Havnor they saw a dragon flying from the west. Its long, slow-beating, vaned wings shone red-gold. A curl of smoke drifted behind it for a moment in the hazy summer air.

"Now," the king said, "what room do I make ready for this guest?"

He spoke as if amused, bemused. But the instant he saw the dragon turn and come wheeling in towards the Tower of the Sword, he ran from the room and down the stairs, startling and outstripping the guards in the halls and at the doors, so that he came out first and alone on the terrace under the white tower.

The terrace was the roof of a banquet hall, a wide expanse of marble with a low balustrade, the Sword Tower rising directly over it and the Queen's Tower nearby. The dragon had alighted on the pavement and was furling its wings with a loud metallic rattle as the king came out. Where it came down its talons had scratched grooves in the marble.

The long, gold-mailed head swung round. The dragon looked at the king.

The king looked down and did not meet its eyes. But he stood straight and spoke clearly. "Orm Irian, welcome. I am Lebannen."

"Agni Lebannen," said the great hissing voice, greeting him as Orm Embar had greeted him long ago, in the farthest west, before he was a king.

Behind him, Onyx and Tehanu had run out onto the terrace along with several guards. One guard had his sword out, and Lebannen saw, in a window of the Queen's Tower, another with drawn bow and notched arrow aimed at the dragon's breast. "Put down your weapons!" he shouted in a voice that made the towers ring, and the guard obeyed in such haste that he nearly dropped his sword, but the archer lowered his bow reluctantly, finding it hard to leave his lord defenseless.

"*Medeu,*" Tehanu whispered, coming up beside Lebannen, her gaze unwavering on the dragon. The great creature's head swung round again and the immense amber eye in a socket of shining, wrinkled scales gazed back, unblinking.

The dragon spoke.

Onyx, understanding, murmured to the king what it said and what Tehanu replied. "Kalessin's daughter, my sister," it said. "You do not fly."

"I cannot change, sister," Tehanu said.

"Shall I?"

"For a while, if you will."

Then those on the terrace and in the windows of the towers saw the strangest thing they might ever see however long they lived in a world of sorceries and wonders. They saw the dragon, the huge creature whose scaled belly and thorny tail dragged and stretched half across the breadth of the terrace, and whose red-horned head reared up twice the height of the king—they saw it lower that big head, and tremble so that its wings rattled like cymbals, and not smoke but a mist breathed out of its deep nostrils, clouding its shape, so that it became cloudy like thin fog or worn glass; and then it was gone. The midday sun beat down on the scored, scarred, white pavement. There was no dragon. There was a woman. She stood some ten paces from Tehanu and the king. She stood where the heart of the dragon might have been.

She was young, tall, and strongly built, dark, dark-haired, wearing a farm woman's shift and trousers, barefoot. She stood motionless, as if bewildered. She looked down at her body. She lifted up her hand and looked at it. "The little thing!" she said, in the common speech, and she laughed. She looked at Tehanu. "It's like putting on the shoes I wore when I was five," she said.

The two women moved towards each other. With a certain stateliness, like that of armed warriors saluting or ships meeting at sea, they embraced. They held each other lightly, but for some moments. They drew apart, and both turned to face the king.

"Lady Irian," he said, and bowed.

She looked a little nonplussed and made a kind of country curtsey. When she looked up he saw her eyes were the color of amber. He looked instantly away.

"I'll do you no harm in this guise," she said, with a broad, white smile. "Your majesty," she added uncomfortably, trying to be polite.

He bowed again. It was he that was nonplussed now. He looked at Tehanu, and round at Tenar, who had come out onto the terrace with Alder. Nobody said anything.

Irian's eyes went to Onyx, standing in his grey cloak just behind the king, and her face lighted up again. "Sir," she said, "are you from Roke Island? Do you know the Lord Patterner?"

Onyx bowed or nodded. He too kept his eyes from hers.

"Is he well? Does he walk among his trees?"

Again the wizard bowed.

"And the Doorkeeper, and the Herbal, and Kurremkarmerruk? They befriended me, they stood by me. If you go back there, greet them with my love and honor, if you please."

"I will," the wizard said.

"My mother is here," Tehanu said softly to Irian. "Tenar of Atuan."

"Tenar of Gont," Lebannen said, with a certain ring to his voice.

Looking with open wonder at Tenar, Irian said, "It was you that brought the Rune Ring from the land of the Hoary Men, along with the Archmage?"

"It was," Tenar said, staring with equal frankness at Irian.

Above them on the balcony that encircled the Tower of the Sword near its summit there was movement: the trumpeters had come out to sound the hour, but at the moment all four of them were gathered on the south side overlooking the terrace, peering down to see the dragon. There were faces in every window of the palace towers, and the thrum of voices down in the streets could be heard like a tide coming in.

"When they sound the first hour," Lebannen said, "the council will gather again. The councillors will have seen you come, my lady, or heard of your coming. So if it please you, I think it best that we go straight among them and let them behold you. And if you'll speak to them I promise you they'll listen."

"Very well," Irian said. For a moment there was a ponderous, reptilian impassivity in her. When she moved, that vanished, and she seemed only a tall young woman who stepped forward quite awkwardly, saying with a smile to Tehanu, "I feel as if I'll float up like a spark, there's no weight to me!"

The four trumpets up in the tower sounded to west, north, east, south in turn, one phrase of the lament a king five hundred years ago had made for the death of his friend.

For a moment the king now remembered the face of that man, Erreth-Akbe, as he stood on the beach of Selidor, dark-eyed, sorrowful, mortally wounded, among the bones of the dragon who had killed him. Lebannen felt it strange that he should think of such faraway things at such a moment; and yet it was not strange, for the living and the dead, men and dragons, all were drawing together to some event he could not see.

He paused until Irian and Tehanu came up to him. As he walked on into the palace with them he said, "Lady Irian, there are many things I would ask you, but what my people fear and what the council will desire to know is whether your people intend to make war on us, and why."

She nodded, a heavy, decisive nod. "I will tell them what I know."

When they came to the curtained doorway behind the dais, the throne room was all in confusion, an uproar of voices, so that the crash of Prince Sege's staff was barely heard at first. Then silence came suddenly on them and they all turned to see the king come in with the dragon.

Lebannen did not sit but stood before the throne, and Irian stood to his left.

"Hear the king," Sege said into that dead silence.

The king said, "Councillors! This is a day that will long be told and sung. Your sons' daughters and your daughters' sons will say, 'I am the grandchild of one who was of the Dragon Council!' So honor her whose presence honors us. Hear Orm Irian."

Some of those who were at the Dragon Council said afterwards that if they looked straight at her she seemed only a tall woman standing there, but if they looked aside what they saw in the corner of their eye was a vast shimmer of smoky gold that dwarfed king and throne. And many of them, knowing a man must not look into a dragon's eye, did look aside; but they stole glimpses too. The women looked at her, some thinking her plain, some beautiful, some pitying her for having to go barefoot in the palace. And a few councillors, not having rightly understood, wondered who the woman was, and when the dragon would be coming.

All the time she spoke, that complete silence endured. Though her voice had the lightness of most women's voices, it filled the high hall easily. She spoke slowly and formally, as if she were translating in her mind from the older speech.

"My name was Irian, of the Domain of Old Iria on Way. I am Orm Irian now. Kalessin, the Eldest, calls me daughter. I am sister to Orm Embar, whom the king knew, and grandchild of Orm, who killed the king's companion Erreth-Akbe and was killed by him. I am here because my sister Tehanu called to me.

"When Orm Embar died on Selidor, destroying the mortal body of the wizard Cob, Kalessin came from beyond the west and brought the king and the great mage to Roke. Then returning to the Dragons' Run, the Eldest called the people of the west, whose speech had been taken from them by Cob, and who were still bewildered. Kalessin said to them, 'You let evil turn you into evil. You have been mad. You are sane again, but so long as the winds blow from the east you can never be what you were, free of both good and evil.'

"Kalessin said: 'Long ago we chose. We chose freedom. Men chose the yoke. We chose fire and the wind. They chose water and the earth. We chose the west, and they the east.'

"And Kalessin said: 'But always among us some envy them their wealth, and always among them some envy us our liberty. So it was that evil came into us and will come into us again, until we choose again, and forever, to be free. Soon I am going beyond the west to fly on the other wind. I will lead you there, or wait for you, if you will come.'

"Then some of the dragons said to Kalessin, 'Men in their envy of us long ago stole half our realm beyond the west from us and made walls of spells to keep us out of it. So now let us drive them into the farthest east, and take back the islands! Men and dragons cannot share the wind.'

"Then Kalessin said, 'Once we were one people. And in sign of that, in every generation of men, one or two are born who are dragons also. And in every generation of our people, longer than the quick lives of men, one of us is born who is also human. Of these one is now living in the Inner Isles. And there is one of them living there now who is a dragon. These two are the messengers, the bringers of choice. There will be no more such born to us or to them. For the balance changes.'

"And Kalessin said to them: 'Choose. Come with me to fly on the far side of the world, on the other wind. Or stay and put on the yoke of good and evil. Or dwindle into dumb beasts.' And at the last Kalessin said: 'The last to make the choice will be Tehanu. After her there will be no choosing. There will be no way west. Only the forest will be, as it is always, at the center.'"

The people of the King's Council were still as stones, listening. Irian stood moveless, gazing as if through them, as she spoke.

"After some years had passed, Kalessin flew beyond the west. Some followed, some did not. When I came to join my people, I followed Kalessin. But I go there and come back, so long as the winds will bear me.

"The disposition of my people is jealous and irate. Those who stayed here on the winds of the world began to fly in bands or singly to the isles of men, saying again, 'They stole half our realm. Now we will take all the west of their realm, and drive them out of it, so they cannot bring their good and evil to us any more. We will not put our necks into their yoke.'

"But they did not try to kill the islanders, because they remembered being mad, when dragon killed dragon. They hate you, but they will not kill you unless you try to kill them.

"So one of these bands has come now to this island, Havnor, that we call the Cold Hill. The dragon who came before them and spoke to Tehanu is my brother Ammaud. They seek to drive you into the east, but Ammaud, like me, enacts the will of Kalessin, seeking to free my people from the yoke you wear. If he and I and the children of Kalessin can prevent harm to your people and ours, we will do so. But dragons have no king, and obey no one, and will fly where they will. For a while they will do as my brother and I ask in Kalessin's name. But not for long. And they fear nothing in the world, except your wizardries of death."

That last word rang heavily in the great hall in the silence that followed Irian's voice.

The king spoke, thanking Irian. He said, "You honor us with your truth-speaking. By my name, we will speak truth to you. I beg you to tell me, daughter of Kalessin who bore me to my kingdom, what it is you say the dragons fear? I thought they feared nothing in the world or out of it."

"We fear your spells of immortality," she said bluntly.

"Of immortality?" Lebannen hesitated. "I am no wizard. Master Onyx, speak for me, if the daughter of Kalessin will permit."

Onyx stood up. Irian looked at him with cold, impartial eyes, and nodded.

"Lady Irian," the wizard said, "we make no spells of immortality. Only the wizard Cob sought to make himself immortal, perverting our art to do so." He spoke slowly and with evident care, searching his mind as he spoke. "Our Archmage, with my lord the king, and with the aid of Orm Embar, destroyed Cob and the evil he had done. And the Archmage gave all his power up to heal the world, restoring the Equilibrium. No other wizard in our lifetime has sought to—" He stopped short.

Irian looked straight at him. He looked down.

"The wizard I destroyed," she said, "the Summoner of Roke, Thorion—what was it he sought?"

Onyx, stricken, said nothing.

"He came back from death," she said. "But not living, as the Archmage and the king did. He was dead, but he came back across the wall by his arts—by your arts—you men of Roke! How are we to trust anything you say? You have unmade the balance of the world. Can you restore it?"

Onyx looked at the king. He was openly distressed. "My

lord, I cannot think that this is the place to discuss such matters—before all men—until we know what we are talking about, and what we must do..."

"Roke keeps its secrets," Irian said with calm scorn.

"But on Roke—" Tehanu said, not standing; her weak voice died away. Prince Sege and the king both looked at her and motioned her to speak.

She stood up. At first she kept the left side of her face to the councillors, all sitting motionless on their benches, like stones with eyes.

"On Roke is the Immanent Grove," she said. "Isn't that what Kalessin meant, sister, speaking of the forest that is at the center?" Turning to Irian, she showed the people watching her the whole ruin of her face; but she had forgotten them. "Maybe we need to go there," she said. "To the center of things."

Irian smiled. "I'll go there," she said.

They both looked at the king.

"Before I send you to Roke, or go with you," he said slowly, "I must know what is at stake. Master Onyx, I'm sorry that matters so grave and chancy force us to debate our course so openly. But I trust my councillors to support me as I find and hold the course. What the council needs to know is that our islands need not fear attack from the People of the West—that the truce, at least, holds."

"It holds," Irian said.

"Can you say how long?"

"A half year?" she offered, carelessly, as if she had said, "A day or two."

"We will hold the truce a half year, in hope of peace to

follow. Am I right to say, Lady Irian, that to have peace with us, your people want to know that our wizards' meddling with the...laws of life and death will not endanger them?"

"Endanger all of us," Irian said. "Yes."

Lebannen considered this and then said, in his most royal, affable, urbane manner, "Then I believe I should come to Roke with you." He turned to the benches. "Councillors, with the truce declared, we must seek the peace. I'll go wherever I must on that quest, ruling as I do in the Sign of Elfarran's Ring. If you see any hindrance to this journey, speak here and now. For it may be that the balance of power within the Archipelago, as well as the Equilibrium of the whole, is in question. And if I go, I must go now. Autumn is near, and it's not a short voyage to Roke Island."

The stones with eyes sat there for a long minute, all staring, none speaking. Then Prince Sege said, "Go, my lord king, go with our hope and trust, and the magewind in your sails." There was a little murmur of assent from the councillors: Yes, yes, hear him.

Sege asked for further questions or debate; nobody spoke. He closed the session.

Leaving the throne room with him, Lebannen said, "Thank you, Sege," and the old prince said, "Between you and the dragon, Lebannen, what could the poor souls say?"

CHAPTER IV

Dolphin

M ANY MATTERS HAD TO BE settled and arrangements
made before the king could leave his capital; there
was also the question of who should go with him to Roke.
Irian and Tehanu, of course, and Tehanu wanted her mother
with her. Onyx said that Alder should by all means go with
them, and also the Pelnish wizard Seppel, for the Lore of
Paln had much to do with these matters of crossing between
life and death. The king chose Tosla to captain the *Dolphin*,
as he had done before. Prince Sege would look after affairs of
state in the king's absence, with a selected group of councillors, as he also had done before.

So it was all settled, or so Lebannen thought, until Tenar
came to him two days before they were to sail and said, "You'll
be talking of war and peace with the dragons, and of matters
even beyond that, Irian says, matters that concern the balance
of all things in Earthsea. The people of the Kargad Lands
should hear these discussions and have a voice in them."

"You will be their representative."

"Not I. I am not a subject of the High King. The only person here who can represent his people is his daughter."

Lebannen took a step away from her, turned partly from her, and at last said in a voice stifled by the effort to speak without anger, "You know that she is completely unfitted for such a journey."

"I know nothing of the kind."

"She has no education."

"She's intelligent, practical, and courageous. She's aware of what her station requires of her. She hasn't been trained to rule, but then what can she learn boxed up there in the River House with her servants and some court ladies?"

"To speak the language, in the first place!"

"She's doing that. I'll interpret for her when she needs it."

After a brief pause Lebannen spoke carefully: "I understand your concern for her people. I will consider what can be done. But the princess has no place on this voyage."

"Tehanu and Irian both say she should come with us. Master Onyx says that, like Alder of Taon, her being sent here at this time cannot be an accident."

Lebannen walked farther away. His tone remained stiffly patient and polite: "I cannot permit it. Her ignorance and inexperience would make her a serious burden. And I can't put her at risk. Relationships with her father—"

"In her ignorance, as you call it, she showed us how to answer Ged's questions. You are as disrespectful of her as her father is. You speak of her as of a mindless thing." Tenar's face was pale with anger. "If you're afraid to put her at risk, ask her to take it herself."

Again there was a silence. Lebannen spoke with the same wooden calmness, not looking directly at her. "If you and Tehanu and Orm Irian believe this woman should come with us to Roke, and Onyx agrees with you, I accept your judgment, though I believe it is mistaken. Please tell her that if she wishes to come, she may do so."

"It is you who should tell her that."

He stood silent. Then he walked out of the room without a word.

He passed close by Tenar, and though he did not look at her he saw her clearly. She looked old and strained, and her hands trembled. He was sorry for her, ashamed of his rudeness to her, relieved that no one else had witnessed the scene; but these feelings were mere sparks in the huge darkness of his anger at her, at the princess, at everyone and everything that laid this false obligation, this grotesque duty on him. As he went out of the room he tugged open the collar of his shirt as if it were choking him.

His majordomo, a slow and steady man called Thoroughgood, was not expecting him to return so soon or through that door and jumped up, staring and startled. Lebannen returned his stare icily and said, "Send for the High Princess to attend me here in the afternoon."

"The High Princess?"

"Is there more than one of them? Are you unaware that the High King's daughter is our guest?"

Amazed, Thoroughgood stammered an apology, which Lebannen interrupted: "I shall go to the River House myself." And he strode on out, pursued, impeded, and gradually controlled by the majordomo's attempts to slow him down long enough for a suitable retinue to be gathered, horses to be brought from the stables, the petitioners waiting for audience in the Long Room to be put off till afternoon, and so on. All his obligations, all his duties, all the trappery and trammel, rites and hypocrisies that made him king pulled at him, sucking and tugging him down like quicksand into suffocation.

When his horse was brought across the stable yard to him, he swung up into the saddle so abruptly that the horse caught his mood and backed and reared, driving back the hostlers and attendants. To see the circle widen out around him gave Lebannen a harsh satisfaction. He set the horse straight for the gateway without waiting for the men in his retinue to mount. He led them at a sharp trot through the streets of the city, far ahead of them, aware of the dilemma of the young officer who was supposed to precede him calling, "Way for the king!" but who had been left behind him and now did not dare ride past him.

It was near noon; the streets and squares of Havnor were hot and bright and mostly deserted. Hearing the clatter of hooves, people hurried to the doorways of little dark shops to stare and recognise and salute the king. Women sitting in their windows fanning themselves and gossiping across the way looked down and waved, and one of them threw a flower down at him. His horse's hooves rang on the bricks of a broad, sunbaked square that lay empty except for a curly-tailed dog trotting away on three legs, unconcerned with royalty. Out of the square the king took a narrow passage that led to the paved way beside the Serrenen, and followed it in the shadow of the willows under the old city wall to River House.

The ride had changed his temper somewhat. The heat

and silence and beauty of the city, the sense of multitudinous life behind walls and shutters, the smile of the woman who had tossed a flower, the petty satisfaction of keeping ahead of all his guardians and pomp makers, then finally the scent and coolness of the river ride and the shady courtyard of the house where he had known days and nights of peace and pleasure, all took him a little distance from his anger. He felt estranged from himself, no longer possessed but emptied.

The first riders of his retinue were just coming into the courtyard as he swung off his horse, which was glad to stand in the shade. He went into the house, dropping among dozing footmen like a stone into a glassy pond, causing quick-widening circles of dismay and panic. He said, "Tell the princess that I am here."

Lady Opal of the Old Demesne of Ilien, currently in charge of the princess's ladies-in-waiting, appeared promptly, greeted him graciously, offered him refreshment, behaved quite as if his visit were no surprise at all. This suavity half placated, half irritated him. Endless hypocrisy! But what was Lady Opal to do—gawp like a stranded fish (as a very young lady-in-waiting was doing) because the king had finally and unexpectedly come to see the princess?

"I'm so sorry Mistress Tenar isn't here at present," she said. "It's so much easier to converse with the princess with her help. But the princess is making admirable progress in the language."

Lebannen had forgotten the problem of language. He accepted the cool drink offered him and said nothing. Lady Opal made small talk with the assistance of the other ladies, getting very little from the king. He had begun to realise that he would probably be expected to speak with the princess in the company of all her ladies, as was only proper. Whatever he had intended to say to her, it had become impossible to say anything. He was just about to get up and excuse himself, when a woman whose head and shoulders were hidden by a red circular veil appeared in the doorway, fell plop on her knees, and said, "Please? King? Princess? Please?"

"The princess will receive you in her chambers, sire," Lady Opal interpreted. She waved to a footman, who escorted him upstairs, along a hall, through an anteroom, through a large, dark room that seemed to be crammed absolutely full of women in red veils, and out onto a balcony over the river. There stood the figure he remembered: the immobile cylinder of red and gold.

The breeze from the water made the veils tremble and shimmer, so that the figure did not appear solid but delicate, moving, shivering, like the willow foliage. It seemed to shrink, to shorten. She was making her courtesy to him. He bowed to her. They both straightened up and stood in silence.

"Princess," Lebannen said, with a feeling of unreality, hearing his own voice, "I am here to ask you to come with us to Roke Island."

She said nothing. He saw the fine red veils part in an oval as she spread them with her hands. Long-fingered, golden-skinned hands, held apart to reveal her face in the red shadow. He could not see her features clearly. She was nearly as tall as he, and her eyes looked straight at him.

"My friend Tenar," she said, "say: king to see king, face and face. I say: yes. I will."

Half understanding, Lebannen bowed again. "You honor me, my lady."

"Yes," she said. "I honor you."

He hesitated. This was a different ground entirely. Her ground.

She stood there straight and still, the gold edging of her veils shivering, her eyes looking at him out of the shadow.

"Tenar, and Tehanu, and Orm Irian, agree that it would be well if the Princess of the Kargad Lands were with us on Roke Island. So I ask you to come with us."

"To come."

"To Roke Island."

"On ship," she said, and suddenly made a little moaning plaintive noise. Then she said, "I will. I will to come."

He did not know what to say. He said, "Thank you, my lady."

She nodded once, equal to equal.

He bowed. He left her as he had been taught to leave the presence of his father the prince at formal occasions in the court of Enlad, not turning his back but stepping backwards.

She stood facing him, still holding her veil parted till he reached the doorway. Then she dropped her hands, and the veils closed, and he heard her gasp and breathe out hard as if in release from an act of will sustained almost past endurance.

Courageous, Tenar had called her. He did not understand, but he knew that he been in the presence of courage. All the anger that had filled him, brought him here, was gone, vanished. He had not been sucked down and suffocated, but brought up short in front of a rock, a high place in clear air, a truth.

He went out through the room full of murmuring, perfumed, veiled women who shrank back from him into the darkness. Downstairs, he chatted a little with Lady Opal and the others, and had a kind word for the gawping twelve-year-old lady-in-waiting. He spoke pleasantly to the men of his retinue waiting for him in the courtyard. He quietly mounted his tall grey horse. He rode quietly, thoughtfully, back to the Palace of Maharion.

ALDER HEARD WITH fatalistic acceptance that he was to sail back to Roke. His waking life had become so strange to him, more dreamlike than his dreams, that he had little will to question or protest. If he was fated to sail from island to island the rest of his life, so be it; he knew there was no such thing as going home for him now. At least he would be in the company of the ladies Tenar and Tehanu, who put his heart at ease. And the wizard Onyx had also shown him kindness.

Alder was a shy man and Onyx a deeply reserved one, and there was all the difference of their knowledge and status to be bridged; but Onyx had come to him several times simply to talk as one man of the art to another, showing a respect for Alder's opinion that puzzled his modesty. But Alder could not withhold his trust; and so when the time to depart was near at hand, he took to Onyx the question that had been worrying him.

"It's the little cat," he said with embarrassment. "I don't feel right about taking him. Keeping him cooped up so long. It's unnatural for a young creature. And I think, what would become of him..."

Onyx did not ask what he meant. He asked only, "He still helps you keep from the wall of stones?"

"Well, often he does."

Onyx pondered. "You need some protection, till we get to Roke. I have thought . . . Have you spoken with the wizard Seppel here?"

"The man from Paln," Alder said, with a slight unease in his voice.

Paln, the greatest island west of Havnor, had the reputation of being an uncanny place. The Pelnish spoke Hardic with a peculiar accent, using many words of their own. Their lords had in ancient times refused fealty to the kings of Enlad and Havnor. Their wizards did not go to Roke for their training. The Pelnish Lore, which called upon the Old Powers of the Earth, was widely believed to be dangerous if not sinister. Long ago the Grey Mage of Paln had brought ruin on his island by summoning the souls of the dead to advise him and his lords, and that tale was part of the education of every sorcerer: "The living should not take counsel of the dead." There had been more than one duel in wizardry between a man of Roke and a man of Paln; in one such combat two centuries ago a plague had been loosed on the people of Paln and Semel that had left half the towns and farmlands desolate. And fifteen years ago, when the wizard Cob had used the Pelnish Lore to cross between life and death, the Archmage Sparrowhawk had spent all his own power to defeat him and heal the evil he had done.

Alder, like almost everyone else at court and in the King's Council, had politely avoided the wizard Seppel.

"I've asked the king to bring him with us to Roke," said Onyx.

Alder blinked.

"They know more than we do about these matters," Onyx said. "Most of our art of Summoning comes from the Pelnish Lore. Thorion was a master of it... The Summoner of Roke now, Brand of Venway, won't use any part of his craft that draws from that lore. Misused, it has brought only harm. But it may be only our ignorance that's led us to use it wrongly. It goes back to very ancient times; there may be knowledge in it we've lost. Seppel is a wise man and mage. I think he should be with us. And I think he might help you, if you can trust him."

"If he has your trust," Alder said, "he has mine."

When Alder spoke with the silver tongue of Taon, Onyx was likely to smile a little drily. "Your judgment's as good as mine, Alder, in this business," he said. "Or better. I hope you use it. But I'll take you to him."

So they went down into the city together. Seppel's lodging was in an old part of town near the shipyards, just off Boatwright Street; there was a little colony of Pelnish folk there, brought in to work in the king's yards, for they were great shipbuilders. The houses were ancient, crowded close, with the bridges between roof and roof that gave Havnor Great Port a second, airy web of streets high above its paved ones.

Seppel's rooms, up three flights of stairs, were dark and close in the heat of this late summer. He took them up one more steep flight onto the roof. It was joined to other roofs by a bridge on each side, so that there was a regular crossroads and thoroughfare across it. Awnings were set up by the low parapets, and the breeze from the harbor cooled the shaded air. There they sat on striped canvas mats in the corner that was Seppel's bit of the roof, and he gave them a cool, slightly bitter tea to drink.

He was a short man of about fifty, round-bodied, with small hands and feet, hair that was a little curly and unruly, and what was rare among men of the Archipelago, a beard, clipped short, on his dark cheeks and jaw. His manners were pleasant. He spoke in a clipped, singing accent, softly.

He and Onyx talked, and Alder listened for a good while to them. His mind drifted when they spoke about people and matters of which he knew nothing. He looked out over the roofs and awnings, the roof gardens and the arched and carven bridges, northward to Mount Onn, a great pale-grey dome above the hazy hills of summer. He came back to himself hearing the Pelnish wizard say, "It may be that even the Archmage could not wholly heal the wound in the world."

The wound in the world, Alder thought: yes. He looked more intently at Seppel, and Seppel glanced at him. For all the soft look of the man his eyes were sharp.

"Maybe it's not only our desire to live forever that has kept the wound open," Seppel said, "but the desire of the dead to die."

Again Alder heard the strange words and felt that he recognised them without understanding them. Again Seppel glanced at him as if seeking a response.

Alder said nothing, nor did Onyx speak. Seppel said at last, "When you stand at the bourne, Master Alder, what is it they ask of you?"

"To be free," Alder replied, his voice only a whisper.

"Free," Onyx murmured.

Silence again. Two girls and a boy ran past across the roofway, laughing and calling, "Down at the next!"—playing one of the endless games of chase children made with their city's maze of streets and canals and stairs and bridges.

"Maybe it was a bad bargain from the beginning," Seppel said, and when Onyx looked a question at him he said, *"Verw nadan."*

Alder knew the words were in the Old Speech, but he did not know their meaning.

He looked at Onyx, whose face was very grave. Onyx said only, "Well, I hope we can come to the truth of these things, and soon."

"On the hill where truth is," Seppel said.

"I'm glad you'll be with us there. Meanwhile, here is Alder summoned to the bourne night after night and seeking some reprieve. I said that you might know a way to help him."

"And you would accept the touch of the wizardry of Paln?" Seppel asked Alder. His tone was softly ironic. His eyes were bright and hard as jet.

Alder's lips were dry. "Master," he said, "we say on my island, the man drowning doesn't ask what the rope cost. If you can keep me from that place even for a night, you'll have my heart's thanks, little as that is worth in return for such a gift."

Onyx looked at him with a slight, amused, unreproving smile.

Seppel did not smile at all. "Thanks are rare, in my trade," he said. "I would do a good deal for them. I think I can help you, Master Alder. But I have to tell you the rope is a costly one."

Alder bowed his head.

"You come to the bourne in dream, not by your own will, that is so?"

"So I believe."

"Wisely said." Seppel's keen glance approved him. "Who knows his own will clearly? But if it is in dream you go there, I can keep you from that dream—for a while. And at a cost, as I said."

Alder looked his question.

"Your power."

Alder did not understand him at first. Then he said, "My gift, you mean? My art?"

Seppel nodded.

"I'm only a mender," Alder said after a little time. "It's not a great power to give up."

Onyx made as if to protest, but looked at Alder's face and said nothing.

"It is your living," Seppel said.

"It was my life, once. But that's gone."

"Maybe your gift will come back to you, when what must happen has happened. I cannot promise that. I will try to restore what I can of what I take from you. But we're all walking in the night, now, on ground we don't know. When the day comes we may know where we are, or we may not. Now, if I spare you your dream, at that price, will you thank me?"

"I will," Alder said. "What's the little good of my gift, against the great evil my ignorance could do? If you spare me the fear I live in now, the fear that I may do that evil, I'll thank you till the end of my life."

Seppel drew a deep breath. "I've always heard that the harps of Taon play true," he said. He looked at Onyx. "And Roke has no objection?" he asked, with a return to his mild ironic tone.

Onyx shook his head, but he now looked very grave.

"Then we will go to the cave at Aurun. Tonight if you like."

"Why there?" Onyx asked.

"Because it's not I but the Earth that will help Alder. Aurun is a sacred place, full of power. Although the people of Havnor have forgotten that, and use it only to defile it."

Onyx managed to have a private word with Alder before they followed Seppel downstairs. "You need not go through with this, Alder," he said. "I thought I trusted Seppel, but I don't know, now."

"I'll trust him," Alder said. He understood Onyx's doubts, but he had meant what he said, that he would do anything to be free of the fear of doing some dreadful wrong. Each time he had been drawn back in dream to that wall of stones, he felt that something was trying to come into the world through him, that it would do so if he listened to the dead calling to him, and each time he heard them, he was weaker and it was harder to resist their call.

The three men went a long way through the city streets in the heat of the late afternoon. They came out into the countryside south of the city, where rough ridgy hills ran down to the bay, a poor bit of country for this rich island: swampy lowland between the ridges, a little arable land on their rocky backs. The wall of the city here was very old, built of great unmortared rocks taken from the hills, and beyond it were no suburbs and few farms.

They walked along a rough road that zigzagged up the first ridge and followed its crest eastward towards the higher hills. Up there, where they could see all the city lying in a golden haze northward, to their left, the road widened out into a maze of footpaths. Going straight forward they came suddenly to a great crack in the ground, a black gap twenty feet wide or more, right across their way.

It was as if the spine of rock had been cracked apart by a wrenching of the earth and had never healed again. The western sunlight streaming over the lips of the cave lighted the vertical rock faces a little way down, but below that was darkness.

There was a tannery in the valley under the ridge, south of it. The tanners had brought their wastes up here and dumped them into the crack, carelessly, so that all around it was a litter of rancid scraps of half-cured leather and a stink of rot and urine. There was another smell from the depths of the cave as they approached the sheer edge: a cold, sharp, earthy air that made Alder draw back.

"I grieve for this, I grieve for this!" the wizard of Paln said aloud, looking around at the rubbish and down at the roofs of the tannery with a strange expression. But he spoke to Alder after a while in his usual mild way: "This is the cave or cleft called Aurun, that we know from our most ancient maps in Paln, where it is also called the Lips of Paor. It used to speak to the people here, when they first came here from the west. A long time ago. Men have changed. But it is what it was then. Here you can lay down your burden, if that is what you want."

"What must I do?" Alder said.

Seppel led him to the south end of the great split in the ground, where it narrowed back together in fissured ridges of rock. He told him to lie facedown where he could gaze into the depth of darkness stretching down and down away from him. "Hold to the earth," he said. "That is all you must do. Even if it moves, hold to it."

Alder lay there staring down between the walls of stone. He felt rocks jabbing his chest and hip as he lay on them; he heard Seppel begin to chant in a high voice in words he knew were the Language of the Making; he felt the warmth of the sun across his shoulders, and smelled the carrion stink of the tannery. Then the breath of the cave blew up out of the depths with a hollow sharpness that took his own breath away and made his head spin. The darkness moved up towards him. The ground moved under him, rocked and shook, and he held on to it, hearing the high voice sing, breathing the breath of the earth. The darkness rose up and took him. He lost the sun.

When he came back, the sun was low in the west, a red ball in the haze over the western shores of the bay. He saw that. He saw Seppel sitting nearby on the ground, looking tired and forlorn, his black shadow long on the rocky ground among the long shadows of the rocks.

"There you are," Onyx said.

Alder realised that he was lying on his back, his head on Onyx's knees, a rock digging into his backbone. He sat up, dizzy, apologising.

They set off as soon as he could walk, for they had some miles to go and it was clear that neither he nor Seppel would be able to keep a fast pace. Full night had fallen when they came by Boatwright Street. Seppel bade them farewell, looking searchingly at Alder as they stood in the light from a tavern door nearby. "I did as you asked me," he said, with that same unhappy look.

"I thank you for it," Alder said, and put out his right hand to the wizard in the manner of the people of the Enlades. After a moment Seppel touched it with his hand; and so they parted.

Alder was so tired he could barely make his legs move. The sharp, strange taste of the air from the cave was still in his mouth and throat, making him feel light, light-headed, hollow. When at last they came to the palace, Onyx wanted to see him to his room, but Alder said he was well and only needed to rest.

He came into his room and Tug came dancing and tail-waving to greet him. "Ah, I don't need you now," Alder said, bending down to stroke the sleek grey back. Tears came into his eyes. It was only that he was very tired. He lay down on the bed, and the cat jumped up and curled up purring on his shoulder.

And he slept: black, blank sleep with no dream he could remember, no voice calling his name, no hill of dry grass, no dim wall of stones, nothing.

WALKING IN THE GARDENS of the palace in the evening before they were to sail south, Tenar was heavyhearted and anxious. She did not want to be setting off to Roke, the Isle of the Wise, the Isle of the Wizards. (*Accursed-sorcerers*, a voice in her mind said in Kargish.) What had she to do there? What possible use could she be? She wanted to go home to Gont, to Ged. To her own house, her own work, her own dear man.

She had estranged Lebannen. She had lost him. He was polite, affable, and unforgiving.

How men feared women! she thought, walking among the late-flowering roses. Not as individuals, but women when they talked together, worked together, spoke up for one another— then men saw plots, cabals, constraints, traps being laid.

Of course they were right. Women were likely, as women, to take the next generation's part, not this one's; they wove the links men saw as chains, the bonds men saw as bondage. She and Seserakh were indeed in league against him and ready to betray him, if he truly was nothing unless he was independent. If he was only air and fire, no weight of earth to him, no patient water...

But that was not Lebannen so much as Tehanu. Unearthly, her Therru, the winged soul that had come to stay with her a while and was soon, she knew, to leave her. From fire to fire.

And Irian, with whom Tehanu would go. What had that bright, fierce creature to do with an old house that needed sweeping, an old man who needed looking after? How could Irian understand such things? What was it to her, a dragon, that a man should undertake his duty, marry, have children, wear the yoke of earth?

Seeing herself alone and useless among beings of high, inhuman destiny, Tenar gave in altogether to homesickness.

Homesickness not for Gont only. Why should she not be in league with Seserakh, who might be a princess as she herself had been a priestess, but who was not going to go flying off on fiery wings, being deeply and entirely a woman of the earth? And she spoke Tenar's own language! Tenar had dutifully tutored her in Hardic, had been delighted with her quickness to learn, and realised only now that the true delight had been just to speak Kargish with her, hearing and saying words that held in them all her lost childhood.

As she came to the walk that led to the fish ponds beneath the willows, she saw Alder. With him was a small boy. They were talking quietly, soberly. She was always glad to see Alder. She pitied him for the pain and fear he was in and honored his patience in bearing it. She liked his honest, handsome face, and his silver tongue. What was the harm in adding a grace note or two to ordinary speech? Ged had trusted him.

Pausing at a distance so as not to disturb the conversation, she saw him and the child kneel down on the path, looking into the bushes. Presently Alder's little grey cat emerged from under a bush. It paid no attention to them, but set off across the grass, paw by paw, belly low and eyes alight, hunting a moth.

"You can let him stay out all night, if you like," Alder said to the child. "He can't stray or come to harm here. He has a great taste for the open air. But this is like all Havnor to him, you see, these great gardens. Or you can give him his freedom in the mornings. And then, if you like, he can sleep with you."

"I would like that," the boy said, shyly decisive.

"Then he needs his box of sand in your room, you know. And a bowl of drinking water, never to go dry."

"And food."

"Yes, indeed; once a day. Not too much of it. He's a bit greedy. Inclined to think Segoy made the islands so that Tug could fill his belly."

"Does he catch fish in the pond?" The cat was now near one of the carp pools, sitting on the grass looking about; the moth had flown.

"He likes to watch them."

"I do too," the boy said. They got up and walked together towards the pools.

Tenar was moved to tenderness. There was an innocence to Alder, but it was a man's innocence, not childish. He should have had children of his own. He would have been a good father to them.

She thought of her own children, and of the little grand-children—though Apple's eldest, Pippin, was it possible? was Pippin about to be twelve? She would be named this year or next! Oh, it was time to go home. It was time to visit Middle Valley, take a nameday present to her granddaughter and toys to the babies, make sure Spark in his restlessness wasn't overpruning the pear trees again, sit a while and talk with her kind daughter Apple...Apple's true name was Hayohe, the name Ogion had given her...The thought of Ogion came as always with a pang of love and longing. She saw the hearthplace of the house at Re Albi. She saw Ged sitting there at the hearth. She saw him turn his dark face to ask her a question. She answered it, aloud, in the gardens of the New Palace of Havnor hundreds of miles from that hearth: "As soon as I can!"

IN THE MORNING, the bright summer morning, they all went down from the palace to go aboard the *Dolphin.* The people of the City of Havnor made it a festival, swarming afoot in the streets and on the wharves, choking the canals with the little poled boats they called chips, dotting the great bay with sailboats and dinghies all flying bright flags; and flags and pennants flew from the towers of the great houses and the banner poles on bridges high and low. Passing among these cheerful crowds, Tenar thought of the day long ago she and Ged came sailing into Havnor, bringing home the Rune of Peace, Elfarran's Ring. That Ring had been on her arm, and she had held it up so the silver would flash in the sunlight and the people could see it, and they had cheered and held out their arms to her as if they all wanted to embrace her. It made her smile to think of that. She was smiling as she went up the gangplank and bowed to Lebannen.

He greeted her with the traditional formality of a ship's master: "Mistress Tenar, be welcome aboard." She replied, moved by she knew not what impulse, "I thank you, son of Elfarran."

He looked at her for a moment, startled by that name. But Tehanu followed close after her, and he repeated the formal greeting: "Mistress Tehanu, be welcome aboard."

Tenar went on towards the prow of the ship, remembering a corner there near a capstan where a passenger could be out of the way of the hardworking sailors and yet see all that happened on the crowded deck and outside the ship too.

There was a commotion in the main street leading to the dock: the High Princess was arriving. Tenar saw with satisfaction that Lebannen, or perhaps his majordomo, had arranged for the princess's arrival to be fittingly magnificent. Mounted escorts opened a way through the crowds, their horses snorting and clattering in fine style. Tall red plumes, such as Kargish warriors wore on their helmets, waved from the top of the closed, gilt-bedizened carriage that had brought the princess across the city and on the headstalls of the four grey horses that drew it. A band of musicians waiting on the waterside struck up with trumpet, tambour, and tambourine. And the people, discovering that they had a princess to cheer and peer at, cheered loudly, and pressed as close as the horsemen and foot guards would allow them, gaping and full of praises and somewhat random greetings. "Hail the Queen of the Kargs!" some of them shouted, and others, "She ain't," and others, "Look at 'em all in red, fine as rubies, which one is her?" and others, "Long live the Princess!"

Tenar saw Seserakh—veiled of course from hat to foot, but unmistakable by her height and bearing—descend from the carriage and sail, stately as a ship herself, towards the gangplank. Two of her shorter-veiled attendants trotted close behind her, followed by Lady Opal of Ilien. Tenar's heart sank. Lebannen had decreed that no servants or followers were to be taken on this journey. It was not a cruise or pleasure trip, he had said sternly, and those aboard must have good reason to be aboard. Had Seserakh not understood that? Or did she so cling to her silly countrywomen that she meant to defy the king? That would be a most unfortunate beginning of the voyage.

But at the foot of the gangplank the gold-rippling red cylinder stopped and turned. It put forth hands, gold-skinned hands shining with gold rings. The princess embraced her handmaidens, clearly bidding them farewell. She also embraced Lady Opal in the approved stately manner of royalty and nobility in public. Then Lady Opal herded the handmaidens back towards the carriage, while the princess turned again to the gangplank.

There was a pause. Tenar could see that featureless column of red and gold take a deep breath. It drew itself up taller.

It proceeded up the gangplank, slowly, for the tide had been rising and the angle was steep, but with an unhesitant dignity that kept the crowds ashore silent, fascinated, watching.

It attained the deck and stopped there, facing the king.

"High Princess of the Kargad Lands, be welcome aboard," Lebannen said in a ringing voice. At that the crowds burst out—"Hurrah for the Princess! Long live the Queen! Well walked, Reddy!"

Lebannen said something to the princess which the cheering made inaudible to others. The red column turned to the crowd on the waterside and bowed, stiff-backed but gracious.

Tehanu had waited for her near where the king stood, and now came forward and spoke to her and led her to the aft cabin of the ship, where the heavy, soft-flowing red and golden veils disappeared. The crowd cheered and called more wildly than ever. "Come back, Princess! Where's Reddy? Where's our lady? Where's the Queen?"

Tenar looked down the length of the ship at the king. Through her misgivings and heaviness of heart, unruly laughter welled up in her. She thought, Poor boy, what will you do now? They've fallen in love with her the first chance they got to see her, even though they can't see her... Oh, Lebannen, we're all in league against you!

DOLPHIN WAS A FAIR-SIZED ship, fitted out to carry a king in some state and comfort; but first and foremost she was made to sail, to fly with the wind, to take him where he needed to go as quickly as could be. Accommodations were cramped enough when it was only the crew and officers, the king and a few companions aboard. On this voyage to Roke, accommodations were jammed. The crew, to be sure, were in no more than usual discomfort, sleeping down in the three-foot-high kennel of the foreward hold; but the officers had to share one wretched black closet under the forecastle. As for the passengers, all four women were in what was normally the king's cabin, which ran the narrow width of the sterncastle of the ship, while the cabin beneath it, usually occupied by the ship's master and one or two other officers, was shared by the king, the two wizards, the sorcerer, and Tosla. The probability of misery and bad temper was, Tenar thought, limitless. The first and most urgent probability, however, was that the High Princess was going to be sick.

They were sailing down the Great Bay with the mildest following wind, the water calm, the ship gliding along like a swan on a pond; but Seserakh cowered on her bunk, crying out in despair whenever she looked out through her veils and caught sight of the sunny, peaceful vista of unexcited water, the mild white wake of the ship, through the broad stern windows. "It will go up and down," she moaned in Kargish.

"It is not going up and down at all," Tenar said. "Use your head, princess!"

"It is my stomach not my head," Seserakh whimpered.

"Nobody could possibly be seasick in this weather. You are simply afraid."

"Mother," Tehanu protested, understanding the tone if not the words. "Don't scold her. It's miserable to be sick."

"She is not sick!" Tenar said. She was absolutely convinced of the truth of what she said. "Seserakh, you are not sick. You are afraid of being sick. Get hold of yourself. Come out on deck. Fresh air will make all the difference. Fresh air and courage."

"Oh my friend," Seserakh murmured in Hardic. "Make me courage!"

Tenar was a little taken aback. "You have to make it yourself, princess," she said. Then, relenting, "Come on, just try it out on deck for a minute. Tehanu, see if you can persuade her. Think what she'll suffer if we do meet some weather!"

Between them they got Seserakh to her feet and into her cylinder of red veiling, without which she could not of course appear before the eyes of men; they coaxed and wheedled her to creep out of the cabin, onto the bit of deck to the side of it, in the shade, where they could all sit in a row on the bone-white, impeccable decking and look out at the blue and shining sea.

Seserakh parted her veils enough that she could see

straight in front of her; but she mostly looked at her lap, with an occasional, brief, terrified glance at the water, after which she shut her eyes and then looked down at her lap again.

Tenar and Tehanu talked a little, pointing out ships that passed, birds, an island. "It's lovely. I forgot how I like to sail!" Tenar said.

"I like it if I can forget the water," said Tehanu. "It's like flying."

"Ah, you dragons," Tenar said.

It was spoken lightly, but it was not lightly said. It was the first time she had ever said anything of the kind to her adopted daughter. She was aware that Tehanu had turned her head to look at her with her seeing eye. Tenar's heart beat heavily. "Air and fire," she said.

Tehanu said nothing. But her hand, the brown slender hand, not the claw, reached out and took hold of Tenar's hand and held it tightly.

"I don't know what I am, mother," she whispered in her voice that was seldom more than a whisper.

"I do," Tenar said. And her heart beat heavier and harder than before.

"I'm not like Irian," Tehanu said. She was trying to comfort her mother, to reassure her, but there was longing in her voice, yearning jealousy, profound desire.

"Wait, wait and find out," her mother replied, finding it hard to speak. "You'll know what to do . . . what you are . . . when the time comes."

They were talking so softly that the princess could not hear what they said, if she could understand it. They had forgotten her. But she had caught the name Irian, and parting her veils with her long hands and turning to them, her eyes looking out bright from the warm red shadow, she asked, "Irian, she is?"

"Somewhere forward—up there—" Tenar waved at the rest of the ship.

"She makes herself courage. Ah?"

After a moment Tenar said, "She doesn't need to make it, I think. She's fearless."

"Ah," said the princess.

Her bright eyes were gazing out of shadow all the length of the ship, to the prow, where Irian stood beside Lebannen. The king was pointing ahead, gesturing, talking with animation. He laughed, and Irian, standing by him, as tall as he, laughed too.

"Barefaced," Seserakh muttered in Kargish. And then in Hardic, thoughtfully, almost inaudibly, "Fearless."

She closed her veils and sat featureless, unmoving.

THE LONG SHORES OF Havnor were blue behind them. Mount Onn floated faint and high in the north. The black basalt columns of the Isle of Omer towered off the ship's right side as she worked across the Ebavnor Straits towards the Inmost Sea. The sun was bright, the wind fresh, another fine day. All the women were sitting under the sailcloth awning the sailors had rigged for them beside the aftercabin. Women brought good luck to a ship, and the sailors couldn't do enough for them in the way of ingenious little comforts and amenities. Because wizards could bring good luck or, equally, bad luck to a ship, the sailors also treated the wizards very well; their awning was rigged in a corner of the quarterdeck, where they had a good view forward. The women had velvet cushions to sit on (provided by the king's forethought, or his majordomo's); the wizards had packets of sailcloth, which did very well.

Alder found himself treated as and considered to be one of the wizards. He could do nothing about it, though it embarrassed him lest Onyx and Seppel should think he was claiming equality with them, and it also troubled him because he was now not even a sorcerer. His gift was gone. He had no power at all. He knew it as surely as he would have known the loss of his sight, the paralysis of his hand. He could not have mended a broken pitcher now, unless with glue; and he would have done it badly, because he had never had to do it.

And beyond the craft he had lost was something else, something larger than the craft, that was gone. Its loss left him, as his wife's death had, in a blankness in which no joy, no new thing was or would ever be. Nothing could happen, nothing could change.

Not having known of this larger aspect of his gift till he lost it, he pondered on it, wondering about its nature. It was like knowing the way to go, he thought, like knowing the direction of home. Not a thing one could identify or even say much about, but a connection on which everything else depended. Without it he was desolate. He was useless.

But at least he did no harm. His dreams were fleeting, meaningless. They never took him to those dreary moorlands, the hill of dead grass, the wall. No voices called him to the dark.

He thought often of Sparrowhawk, wishing he could talk with him: the Archmage who had spent all his power, and having been great among the great, now lived his life out poor and disregarded. Yet the king longed to show him honor; so Sparrowhawk's poverty was by choice. Perhaps, Alder thought, riches or high estate would have been only shameful to a man who had lost his true wealth, his way.

Onyx clearly regretted having led Alder to make this trade or bargain. He had always been entirely civil to Alder, but he now treated him with regard and compunction, while his manner to the wizard of Paln had become a little distant. Alder himself felt no resentment towards Seppel and no distrust of his intentions. The Old Powers were the Old Powers. You used them at your risk. Seppel had told him what he must pay, and he had paid it. He had not understood quite how much there was to pay; but that was not Seppel's fault. It was his own, for never having valued his gift at its true worth.

So he sat with the two wizards, thinking of himself as false coin to their gold, but listening to them with all his mind; for they trusted him and spoke freely, and their talk was an education he had never dreamed of as a sorcerer.

Sitting there in the bright pale shade of the canvas awning, they talked of a bargain, a greater bargain than the one he had made to stop his dreams. Onyx said more than once the words of the Old Speech Seppel had spoken on the rooftop: *Verw nadan.* As they talked, little by little Alder gathered that the meaning of those words was something like a choice, a division, making two things of one. Far, far back in time, before the Kings of Enlad, before the writing of Hardic, maybe before there was a Hardic tongue, when there was only the Language of the Making, it seemed that people had made some kind of choice, given up one great power or possession to gain another.

The wizards' talk of this was hard to follow, not so much because they hid anything but because they themselves were groping after things lost in the cloudy past, the time before memory. Words of the Old Speech came into their talk of necessity, and sometimes Onyx spoke entirely in that tongue. But Seppel would answer him in Hardic. Seppel was sparing with the words of the Making. Once he held up his hand to stop Onyx from going on, and at the Roke wizard's look of surprise and question, said mildly, "Spellwords act."

Alder's teacher Gannet, too, had called the words of the Old Speech spellwords. "Each is a deed of power," he had said. "True word makes truth be." Gannet had been stingy with the spellwords he knew, speaking them only at need, and when he wrote any rune but the common ones that were used to write Hardic, he erased it almost as he finished it. Most sorcerers were similarly careful, either to guard their knowledge for themselves or because they respected the power of the Language of the Making. Even Seppel, wizard as he was, with a far wider knowledge and understanding of those words, preferred not to use them in conversation, but to keep to ordinary language which, if it allowed lies and errors, also permitted uncertainty and retraction.

Perhaps that had been part of the great choice men made in ancient times: to give up the innate knowledge of the Old Speech, which they once shared with the dragons. Had they done so, Alder wondered, in order to have a language of their own, a language suited to mankind, in which they could lie, cheat, swindle, and invent wonders that never had been and would never be?

The dragons spoke no speech but the Old Speech. Yet it was always said that dragons lied. Was it so? he wondered. If spellwords were true, how could even a dragon use them to lie?

Seppel and Onyx had come to one of the long, easy, thoughtful pauses in their conversation. Seeing that Onyx was, in fact, at least half asleep, Alder asked the Pelnish wizard softly, "Is it true that dragons can tell untruth in the true words?"

The Pelnishman smiled. "That—so we say on Paln—is the very question Ath asked Orm a thousand years ago, in the ruins of Ontuego. 'Can a dragon lie?' the mage asked. And Orm replied, 'No,' and then breathed on him, burning him to ashes... But are we to believe the story, since it was only Orm who could have told it?"

Infinite are the arguments of mages, Alder said to himself, but not aloud.

Onyx had gone definitely to sleep, his head tilted back against the bulkhead, his grave, tense face relaxed.

Seppel spoke, his voice even quieter than usual. "Alder, I hope you do not regret what we did at Aurun. I know our friend thinks I did not warn you clearly enough."

Alder said without hesitation, "I am content."

Seppel inclined his dark head.

Alder said presently, "I know that we try to keep the Equilibrium. But the Powers of the Earth keep their own account."

"And theirs is a justice that is hard for men to understand."

"That's it. I try to see why it was just that, my craft, I mean, that I must give up to free myself from that dream. What has the one to do with the other?"

Seppel did not answer for a while, and then it was with a question. "It was not by your craft that you came to the wall of stones?"

"Never," Alder said with certainty. "I had no more power to go there if I willed it than I had to prevent myself from going."

"So how did you come there?"

"My wife called me, and my heart went to her."

A longer pause. The wizard said, "Other men have lost beloved wives."

"So I said to my Lord Sparrowhawk. And he said: that's true, and yet the bond between true lovers is as close as we come to what endures forever."

"Across the wall of stones, no bond endures."

Alder looked at the wizard, the swarthy, soft, keen-eyed face. "Why is it so?" he said.

"Death is the bond breaker."

"Then why do the dead not die?"

Seppel stared at him, taken aback.

"I'm sorry," Alder said. "I misspeak in my ignorance. What I mean is this: death breaks the bond of soul with body, and the body dies. It goes back to the earth. But the spirit must go to that dark place, and wear a semblance of the body, and endure there—for how long? Forever? In the dust and dusk there, without light, or love, or cheer at all? I cannot bear to think of Lily in that place. Why must she be there? Why can she not be—" his voice stumbled—"be free?"

"Because the wind does not blow there," Seppel said. His look was very strange, his voice harsh. "It was stopped from blowing, by the art of man."

He continued to stare at Alder but only gradually did he begin to see him. The expression in his eyes and face changed. He looked away, up the beautiful white curve of the foresail, full of the breath of the northwest wind. He glanced back at Alder. "You know as much as I do of this matter, my friend," he said with almost his usual softness. "But you know it in your body, your blood, in the pulse of your heart. And I know only words. Old words . . . So we had better get to Roke, where maybe the wise men will be able to tell us what we need to know. Or if they cannot, the dragons will, perhaps. Or maybe it will be you who shows us the way."

"That would be the blind man who led the seers to the cliff's edge, indeed!" Alder said with a laugh.

"Ah, but we're at the cliff's edge already, with our eyes shut," said the wizard of Paln.

LEBANNEN FOUND THE SHIP too small to contain the enormous restlessness that filled him. The women sat under their little awning and the wizards sat under theirs like ducks in a row, but he paced up and down, impatient with the narrow confines of the deck. He felt it was his impatience and not the wind that sent *Dolphin* running so fast to the south, but never fast enough. He wanted the journey over.

"Remember the fleet on the way to Wathort?" Tosla said, joining him while he stood near the steersman, studying the chart and the clear sea before them. "That was a grand sight. Thirty ships aline!"

"I wish it was Wathort we were bound for," Lebannen said.

"I never did like Roke," Tosla agreed. "Not an honest wind or current for twenty miles off that shore, but only wizards' brew. And the rocks north of it never in the same place twice. And the town full of cheats and shape-shifters." He spat, competently, to leeward. "I'd rather meet old Gore and his slavers again!"

Lebannen nodded, but said nothing. That was often the pleasure of Tosla's company: he said what Lebannen felt it was better that he himself not say.

"Who was the dumb man, the mute," Tosla asked, "the one that killed Falcon on the wall?"

"Egre. Pirate turned slave taker."

"That's it. He knew you, there at Sorra. Went right for you. I always wondered how."

"Because he took me as a slave once."

It was not easy to surprise Tosla, but the seaman looked at him with his mouth open, evidently not believing him but not able to say so, and so with nothing to say. Lebannen enjoyed the effect for a minute and then took pity on him.

"When the Archmage took me hunting after Cob, we went south, first. A man in Hort Town betrayed us to the slave takers. They knocked the Archmage on the head, and I ran off thinking I could lead them away from him. But it was me they were after—I was salable. I woke up chained in a galley bound for Sowl. He rescued me before the next night passed. The irons fell off us all like bits of dead leaves. And he told Egre not to speak again until he found something worth saying... He came to that galley like a great light over the water... I never knew what he was till then."

Tosla mulled this over a while. "He unchained all the slaves? Why didn't the others kill Egre?"

"Maybe they took him on to Sowl and sold him," Lebannen said.

Tosla mulled a while longer. "So that's why you were so keen to do away with the slave trade."

"One reason."

"Doesn't improve the character, as a rule," Tosla observed. He studied the chart of the Inmost Sea tacked on the board to the steersman's left. "Island of Way," he remarked. "Where the dragon woman's from."

"You keep clear of her, I notice."

Tosla pursed his lips, though he did not whistle, being aboard ship. "You know that song I mentioned, about the Lass of Belilo? Well, I never thought of it as anything but a tale. Until I saw her."

"I doubt she'd eat you, Tosla."

"It would be a glorious death," the sailor said, rather sourly.

The king laughed.

"Don't push your own luck," said Tosla.

"No fear."

"You and she were talking there so free and easy. Like making yourself easy with a volcano, to my mind... But I'll tell you, I wouldn't mind seeing a bit more of that present the

Kargs sent you. There's a sight worth seeing in there, to judge by the feet. But how do you get it out of the tent? The feet are grand, but I'd like a bit more ankle, to begin with."

Lebannen felt his face turn grim, and turned aside to keep Tosla from seeing it.

"If anybody gave me a package like that," Tosla said, staring out over the sea, "I'd open it."

Lebannen could not restrain a slight movement of impatience. Tosla saw it; he was quick. He grinned his wry grin and said no more.

The ship's master had come out on deck, and Lebannen engaged him in talk. "Looks a bit thick ahead?" he said, and the master nodded: "Thunder squalls to the south and west there. We'll be in them tonight."

The sea grew choppier as the afternoon drew on, the benign sunlight took on a brassy tinge, and gusts of wind blew from one quarter then another. Tenar had told Lebannen that the princess was afraid of the sea and of seasickness, and he glanced back once or twice at the aftercabin, expecting to see no red-veiled form among the ducks in a row. But it was Tenar and Tehanu who had gone in; the princess was still there, and Irian was sitting beside her. They were talking earnestly. What on earth did a dragon woman from Way have to talk about with a harem woman from Hur-at-Hur? What language had they in common? The question seemed so much in need of answering to Lebannen that he walked aft.

When he got there Irian looked up at him and smiled. She had a strong, open face, a broad smile; she went barefoot by choice, was careless about her dress, let the wind tangle her hair; altogether she seemed no more than a handsome, hot-hearted, intelligent, untaught countrywoman, till you saw her eyes. They were the color of smoky amber, and when she looked straight at Lebannen, as she was doing now, he could not meet them. He looked down.

He had made it clear that there was to be no courtly ceremony on the ship, no bows and courtesies, nobody was to leap up when he came near; but the princess had got to her feet. They were, as Tosla had observed, beautiful feet, not small, but high-arched, strong, and fine. He looked at them, the two slender feet on the white wood of the deck. He looked up from them and saw that the princess was doing as she had done the last time he faced her: parting her veils so that he, though no one else, could see her face. He was a little staggered by the stern, almost tragic beauty of the face in that red shadow.

"Is—is everything all right, princess?" he asked, stammering, a thing he very seldom did.

She said, "My friend Tenar said, breathe wind."

"Yes," he said, rather at random.

"Is there anything your wizards could do for her, do you think, maybe?" said Irian, unfolding her long limbs and standing up too. She and the princess were both tall women.

Lebannen was trying to make out what color the princess's eyes were, since he was able to look at them. They were blue, he thought, but like blue opals they held other colors in them, or maybe it was the sunlight coming through the red of her veils. —"Do for her?"

"She wants very much not to be seasick. She had a terrible time of it coming from the Kargish places."

"I will not to fear," the princess said. She gazed straight at him as if challenging him to—what?

"Of course," he said, "of course. I'll ask Onyx. I'm sure there's something he can do." He made a sketchy bow to them both and went off hurriedly to find the wizard.

Onyx and Seppel conferred and then consulted Alder. A spell against seasickness was more in the province of sorcerers, menders, healers, than of learned and powerful wizards. Alder could not do anything himself at present, of course, but he might remember a charm...? He did not, having never dreamed of going to sea until his troubles began. Seppel confessed that he himself always got seasick in small boats or rough weather. Onyx finally went to the aftercabin and begged the princess's pardon: he himself had no skill to help her, and nothing to offer her but—apologetically—a charm or talisman one of the sailors hearing of her plight—the sailors heard everything—had pressed upon him to give her.

The princess's long-fingered hand emerged from the red and gold veils. The wizard placed in it a queer little black-and-white object: dried seaweed braided round a bird's breastbone. "A petrel, because they ride the storm," Onyx said, shamefaced.

The princess bowed her unseen head and murmured thanks in Kargish. The fetish disappeared within her veils. She withdrew to the cabin. Onyx, meeting the king quite nearby, apologised to him. The ship was pitching energetically now in hard, erratic gusts on a choppy sea, and he said, "I could, you know, sire, say a word to the winds..."

Lebannen knew well that there were two schools of

thought concerning weatherworking: the old-fashioned one, that of the Bagmen who ordered the winds to serve their ships as shepherds order their dogs to run here and there, and the newfangled notion—a few centuries old at most—of the Roke School, that the magewind might be raised at real need, but it was best to let the world's winds blow. He knew that Onyx was a devout upholder of the way of Roke. "Use your own judgment, Onyx," he said. "If it seems we're in for a really bad night...But if it's no more than a few squalls..."

Onyx looked up at the masthead, where already a wisp or two of fallow fire had flickered in the cloud-darkened dusk. Thunder rumbled grandly in the blackness before them, all across the south. Behind them the last of the daylight fell wan, tremulous across the waves. "Very well," he said, rather dismally, and went below to the small and crowded cabin.

Lebannen stayed out of that cabin almost entirely, sleeping on deck when he slept at all. Tonight was not one for sleep for anybody on the *Dolphin*. It was not a single squall, but a chain of violent late-summer storms boiling up out of the southwest, and between the terrific commotion of the lightning-dazzled sea, the thunder crashes that seemed about to knock the ship apart, and the crazy storm gusts that kept her pitching and rolling and taking queer jumps, it was a long night and a loud one.

Onyx consulted Lebannen once: Should he say a word to the wind? Lebannen looked to the master, who shrugged. He and his crew were busy enough, but unconcerned. The ship was in no trouble. As for the womenfolk, they were reported to be sitting up in their cabin, gambling. Irian and the princess had come out on deck earlier, but it was hard to stay afoot at times and they had seen they were in the crew's way, so they had retired. The report that they were gambling came from the cook's boy, who had been sent to see if they wanted anything to eat. They had wanted whatever he could bring.

Lebannen found himself possessed by the same intense curiosity he had felt in the afternoon. There was no doubt the lamps were all alight in the stern cabin, for the glow of them streamed out golden on the foam and race of the ship's wake. About midnight, he went aft and knocked.

Irian opened the door. After the dazzle and blackness of the storm the lamplight in the cabin seemed warm and steady, though the swinging lamps cast swinging shadows; and he was confusedly aware of colors, the soft, various colors of the women's clothes, their skin, brown or pale or gold, their hair, black or grey or tawny, their eyes—the princess's eyes staring at him, startled, as she snatched up a scarf or some cloth to hold before her face.

"Oh! We thought it was the cook's boy!" Irian said with a laugh.

Tehanu looked at him and said in her shy, comradely way, "Is there trouble?"

He realised that he was standing in the doorway staring at them like some speechless messenger of doom.

"No— None at all— Are you getting on all right? I'm sorry it's been so rough—"

"We don't hold you answerable for the weather," Tenar

said. "Nobody could sleep, so the princess and I have been teaching the others Kargish gambling."

He saw five-sided ivory dice-sticks scattered over the table, probably Tosla's.

"We've been betting islands," Irian said. "But Tehanu and I are losing. The Kargs have already won Ark and Ilien."

The princess had lowered the scarf; she sat facing Lebannen resolutely, extremely tense, as a young swordsman might face him before a fencing match. In the warmth of the cabin they were all bare-armed and barefoot, but her consciousness of her uncovered face drew his consciousness as a magnet draws a pin.

"I'm sorry it's been so rough," he said again, idiotically, and closed the door. As he turned away he heard them all laughing.

He went to stand by the steersman. Looking into the gusty, rainy darkness lit by fitful, distant lightning, he could still see everything in the stern cabin, the black fall of Tehanu's hair, Tenar's affectionate, teasing smile, the dice on the table, the princess's round arms, honey-colored like the lamplight, her throat in the shadow of her hair, though he did not remember looking at her arms and throat but only at her face, at her eyes full of defiance, despair. What was the girl afraid of? Did she think he wanted to hurt her?

A star or two was shining out high in the south. He went to his crowded cabin, slung a hammock, for the bunks were full, and slept for a few hours. He woke before dawn, restless as ever, and went up on deck.

The day came as bright and calm as if no storm had ever been. Lebannen stood at the forward rail and saw the first sunlight strike across the water, and an old song came into his mind:

O my joy!
Before bright Éa was, before Segoy
Bade the islands be,
The morning wind blew on the sea.
O my joy, be free!

It was a fragment of a ballad or lullaby from his childhood. He could remember no more of it. The tune was sweet. He sang it softly and let the wind take the words from his lips.

Tenar emerged from the cabin and, seeing him, came to him. "Good morning, my dear lord," she said, and he greeted her fondly, with some memory that he had been angry at her but not knowing why he had been or how he could have been.

"Did you Kargs win Havnor last night?" he asked.

"No, you may keep Havnor. We went to bed. All the young ones are still there, lolling. Shall we—what is it? lift Roke today?"

"Raise Roke? No, not till early tomorrow. But before noon we should be in Thwil Harbor. If they let us come to the island."

"What do you mean?"

"Roke defends itself from unwelcome visitors."

"Oh: Ged told me about that. He was on a ship trying to

sail back there, and they sent the wind against him, the Roke wind he called it."

"Against *him*?"

"It was a long time ago." She smiled with pleasure at his incredulity, his unwillingness that any affront should ever have been offered to Ged. "When he was a boy who had meddled with the darkness. That's what he said."

"When he was a man he still meddled with it."

"He doesn't now," Tenar said, serene.

"No, it's we who have to." His face had grown somber. "I wish I knew what we're meddling with. I am certain that things are drawing to some great chance or change—as Ogion foretold—as Ged told Alder. And I am certain that Roke is where we need to be to meet it. But beyond that, no certainty, nothing. I don't know what it is we face. When Ged took me into the dark land, we knew our enemy. When I took the fleet to Sorra, I knew what the evil was I wanted to undo. But now— Are the dragons our enemies or our allies? What has gone wrong? What is it we must do or undo? Will the Masters of Roke be able to tell us? Or will they turn their wind against us?"

"Fearing—?"

"Fearing the dragon. The one they know. Or the one they don't know..."

Tenar's face was sober too, but gradually it broke into a smile. "What a ragbag you are bringing them, to be sure!" she said. "A sorcerer with nightmares, a wizard from Paln, two dragons, and two Kargs. The only respectable passengers on this ship are you and Onyx."

Lebannen could not laugh. "If only *he* were with us," he said.

Tenar put her hand on his arm. She started to speak and then did not.

He laid his hand over hers. They stood silent thus for some time, side by side, looking out at the dancing sea.

"The princess has something she wants to tell you before we come to Roke," Tenar said. "It's a story from Hur-at-Hur. Off there in their desert they remember things. I think this goes back before anything I ever heard except the story of the Woman of Kemay. It has to do with dragons... It would be kind of you to invite her, so that she doesn't have to ask."

Aware of the care and caution with which she spoke, he felt a moment of impatience, a flick of shame. He watched, far south across the sea, the course of a galley bound for Kamery or Way, the faint, tiny flash of the lifted sweeps. He said, "Of course. About noon?"

"Thank you."

ABOUT NOON, HE SENT a young seaman to the stern cabin to request the princess to join the king on the foredeck. She emerged at once, and the ship being only about fifty feet long, he could observe her entire progress towards him: not a long walk, though perhaps for her it was a long one. For it was not a featureless red cylinder that approached him but a tall young woman. She wore soft white trousers, a long shirt of dull red, a gold circlet that held a very thin red veil over her face and head. The veil fluttered in the sea wind. The young sailor led her round the various obstacles and up and down the descents and ascents of the crowded, cumbered, narrow deck. She walked slowly and proudly. She was barefoot. Every eye in the ship was on her.

She arrived on the foredeck and stood still.

Lebannen bowed. "Your presence honors us, princess."

She performed a deep, straight-backed courtesy and said, "Thank you."

"You were not ill last night, I hope?"

She put her hand on the charm she wore on the cord round her neck, a small bone tied with black, showing it to him. *"Kerez akath akatharwa erevi,"* she said. He knew the word *akath* in Kargish meant sorcerer or sorcery.

There were eyes everywhere, eyes in hatchways, eyes up in the rigging, eyes that were like augurs, like gimlets.

"Come forward, if you will. We may see Roke Island soon," he said, though there was not the remotest chance of seeing a glimmer of Roke till dawn. With a hand under her elbow though not actually touching her, he guided her up the steep slant of the deck to the forepeak, where between a capstan, the slant of the bowsprit, and the port rail was a little triangle of decking that—when a sailor had scurried away with the cable he was mending—they had quite to themselves. They were as visible as ever to the rest of the ship, but they could turn their backs on it: as much privacy as royalty can hope for.

When they had gained this tiny haven, the princess turned to him and pushed back the veil from her face. He had intended to ask what he could do for her, but the question seemed both inadequate and irrelevant. He said nothing.

She said, "Lord King. In Hur-at-Hur I am *feyagat.* In

Roke Island I am to be king's daughter of Kargad. To be this, I am not *feyagat*. I am bare face. If it please you."

After a moment he said, "Yes. Yes, princess. This is— this is well done."

"It please you?"

"Very much. Yes. I thank you, princess."

"*Barrezú*," she said, a regal acceptance of his thanks. Her dignity abashed him. Her face had been flaming red when she first put back the veil; there was no color in it now. But she stood straight and still, and gathered up her forces for another speech.

"Too," she said. "Also. My friend Tenar."

"Our friend Tenar," he said with a smile.

"Our friend Tenar. She says I am to tell King Lebannen of the Vedurnan."

He repeated the word.

"Long ago long ago—Karg people, sorcery people, dragon people, hah? Yes?— All people one, all speak one— one— Oh! *Wuluah mekrevt!*"

"One language?"

"Hah! Yes! One language!" In her passionate attempt to speak Hardic, to tell him what she wanted to tell him, she was losing her self-consciousness; her face and eyes shone. "But then, dragon people say: Let go, let go all things. Fly!— But we people, we say: No, keep. Keep all things. Dwell!— So we go apart, hah? dragon people and we people? So they make the Vedurnan. These to let go—these to keep. Yes? But to keep all things, we must to let go that language. That dragon people language."

"The Old Speech?"

"Yes! So we people, we let go that Old Speech language, and keep all things. And dragon people let go all things, but keep that, keep that language. Hah? *Seyneha?* This is the Vedurnan." Her beautiful, large, long hands gestured eloquently and she watched his face with eager hope of understanding. "We go east, east, east. Dragon people go west, west. We dwell, they fly. Some dragon come east with us, but not keep the language, forget, and forget to fly. Like Karg people. Karg people speak Karg language, not dragon language. All keep the Vedurnan, east, west. *Seyneha?* But in—"

At a loss, she brought her hands together from her "east" and "west," and Lebannen said, "In the middle?"

"Hah, yes! In the middle!" She laughed with the pleasure of getting the word. "In the middle—you! Sorcery people! Hah? You, middle people, speak Hardic language but too, also, keep to speak Old Speech language. You *learn* it. Like I learn Hardic, hah? Learn to speak. Then, then—this is the bad. The bad thing. Then you say, in that sorcery language, in that Old Speech language, you say: *We will not to die.* And it is so. And the Vedurnan is broken."

Her eyes were like blue fire.

After a moment she asked, *"Seyneha?"*

"I'm not sure I understand."

"You keep life. You keep. Too long. You never to let go. But to die—" She threw her hands out in a great opening gesture as if she threw something away, into the air, across the water.

He shook his head regretfully.

"Ah," she said. She thought a minute, but no words came. Defeated, she moved her hands palms down in a graceful pantomime of relinquishment. "I must to learn more words," she said.

"Princess, the Master Patterner of Roke, the Master of the Grove—" He watched her for comprehension, and began again. "On Roke Island, there is a man, a great mage, who is a Karg. You can tell him what you have told me—in your own language."

She listened intently and nodded. She said, "The friend of Irian. I will in my heart to talk to this man." Her face was bright with the thought.

That touched Lebannen. He said, "I'm sorry you have been lonely here, princess."

She looked at him, alert and luminous, but did not reply.

"I hope, as time goes on—as you learn the language—"

"I learn quick," she said. He did not know if it was a statement or a prediction.

They were looking straight at each other.

She resumed her stately attitude and spoke formally, as she had at the beginning: "I thank you to listen, Lord King." She dipped her head and shielded her eyes in a formal sign of respect and made the deep knee-bend courtesy again, speaking some formula in Kargish.

"Please," he said, "tell me what you said."

She paused, hesitated, thought, and replied, "Your— your, ah—small kings?—sons! Sons, your sons, let them to be dragons and kings of dragons. Hah?" She smiled radiantly, let the veil fall over her face, backed away four steps, turned and departed, lithe and sure-footed down the length of the ship. Lebannen stood as if last night's lightning had struck him at last.

CHAPTER V

Rejoining

⌒

THE LAST NIGHT OF THE sea voyage was calm, warm, starless. *Dolphin* moved with a long, easy rocking over the smooth swells southward. It was easy to sleep, and the people slept, and sleeping dreamed.

Alder dreamed of a little animal that came in the dark and touched his hand. He could not see what it was, and when he reached out to it, it was gone, lost. Again he felt the small, velvet muzzle touch his hand. He half roused, and the dream slipped from him, but the piercing ache of loss was in his heart.

In the bunk below him, Seppel dreamed that he was in his own house in Ferao on Paln, reading an old lore-book from the Dark Time, content with his work; but he was interrupted. Someone wanted to see him. "It will only take a minute," he told himself, and went to speak to the caller. It was a woman; her hair was dark with a glint of red in it, her face was beautiful and full of trouble. "You must send him to me," she said. "You will send him to me, won't you?" He thought: I don't know who she means, but I must pretend I do, and he said, "That will not be easy, you know." At that the woman drew her hand back and he saw that she held a stone, a heavy stone. Startled, he thought she meant to throw it at him or strike him down with it, and recoiling from her, he woke in the darkness of the cabin. He lay listening to the breathing of the other sleepers and the whisper of the sea along the ship's side.

In his bunk on the other side of the small cabin, Onyx lay on his back gazing into the dark; he thought his eyes were open, he thought he was awake, but he thought that many small, thin cords had been tied around his arms and legs and hands and head, and that all these cords ran out into the darkness, over land and sea, over the curve of the world: and the cords were drawing him, tugging him, so that he and the ship he was in and all its passengers were being pulled gently, gently to the place where the sea dried up, where the ship would go aground silently on blind sands. But he could not speak or do anything because the cords tied shut his jaws, his eyelids.

Lebannen had come down to the cabin to sleep for a while, wanting to be fresh at dawn when they might raise Roke Island. He slept quickly and deeply, and his dreams fleeted and changed: a high green hill above the sea—a woman who smiled and, lifting her hand, showed him she could make the sun rise—a claimant in his court of justice in Havnor from whom he learned to his horror and shame that half the people of the kingdom were starving to death in locked rooms beneath houses—a child who cried out to him, "Come to me!" but he could not find the child— As he slept, his right hand held the rock in the little amulet bag at his throat, clenched it tight.

In the deck cabin above these dreamers, the women dreamed. Seserakh walked up into the mountains, the beautiful dear desert mountains of her home. But she was walking on the forbidden way, the dragon path. Human feet must not walk that path, must not even cross it. The dust of it was smooth and warm under her bare soles, and though she knew she must not walk on it, she walked on, until she looked up and saw that the mountains were not those she knew, but were black, jagged precipices which she could never climb. Yet she must climb them.

Irian flew joyous on the storm wind, but the storm sent loops of lightning up over her wings, drawing her down and down towards the clouds, and as she was pulled nearer and nearer she saw they were not clouds but black rocks, a black and jagged mountain range. Her wings were tied to her sides by cords of lightning, and she fell.

Tehanu crawled through a tunnel deep underground. There was not enough air to breathe and the tunnel grew narrower as she crawled. She could not turn back. But the glimmering roots of trees, growing down through the dirt into the tunnel, gave her handholds sometimes by which she could pull herself on into the dark.

Tenar climbed up the steps of the Throne of the Nameless Ones in the sacred Place of Atuan. She was very small and the steps were very high, so that she could climb them only laboriously. But when she reached the fourth step she did not pause and turn around, as the priestesses had told her she must do. She went on. She climbed the next step, and the next, and the next, in dust so thick it had obliterated the steps and she must feel for the levels where no foot had ever trodden. She went hastily, because behind the empty throne Ged had left something or lost something, something of great importance to myriads of people, and she had to find it. Only she did not know what it was. "A stone, a stone," she told herself. But behind the throne, when she crawled there at last, was only dust, owls' droppings and dust.

In the alcove of the Old Mage's house on the Overfell of Gont, Ged dreamed that he was Archmage. He was talking with his friend Thorion as they walked the corridor of runes towards the meeting room of the Masters of the School. "I had no power at all," he told Thorion earnestly, "for years and years." The Summoner smiled and said, "That was only a dream, you know." But Ged was troubled by the long black wings that trailed behind him through the corridor; he shrugged his shoulders, trying to lift the wings, but they dragged on the floor like empty sacks. "Do you have wings?" he asked Thorion, who said, "Oh, yes," complacently, showing him how his wings were tied tight against his back and legs by many small, thin cords. "I am well yoked," he said.

Among the trees of the Immanent Grove on Roke Island, Azver the Patterner slept as he often did in summer in an open glade near the eastern edge of the wood, where he could look up and see the stars through the leaves. There his sleep was light, transparent, his mind moving from thought to dream and back, guided by the movements of the stars and leaves as they changed places in their dance. But tonight there were no stars, and the leaves hung still. He looked up into the lightless sky and saw through the clouds. In the high black sky were stars: small, bright, and still. They did not move. He knew there would be no sunrise.— He sat up then, awake, gazing into the faint, soft light that always hung in the aisles of the trees. His heart beat slow and hard.

In the Great House the young men, sleeping, turned and cried out, dreaming that they must go fight an army on a plain of dust, but the warriors they must fight were old men, old women, weak, sick people, weeping children.

The Masters of Roke dreamed that a ship was sailing towards them over the sea, heavy laden, low in the water. One dreamed that the freight of the ship was black rocks. Another dreamed she carried burning fire. Another dreamed that her cargo was dreams.

The seven masters who slept in the Great House woke, one and then another, in their stone sleeping cells, made a little werelight, and got up. They found the Doorkeeper already afoot and waiting at the door. "The king will come," he said with a smile, "at daybreak."

"Roke Knoll," Tosla said, gazing forward at the far, faint, unmoving wave in the southwest above the twilit waves. Lebannen, standing beside him, said nothing. The cloud cover had dispersed, and the sky arched its pure uncolored dome over the great circle of the waters.

The ship's master joined them. "A fair dawn," he said, whispering in the silence.

The east brightened slowly to yellow. Lebannen glanced aft. Two of the women were afoot, standing at the rail outside their cabin; tall women, barefoot, silent, gazing east.

The top of the round green hill caught the sunlight first. It was broad daylight when they sailed in between the headlands of Thwil Bay. Everyone aboard was on deck, watching. But still they spoke little and softly.

The wind died down within the harbor. It was so still the water reflected the little town that rose above the bay and the walls of the Great House that rose above the town. The ship glided on slower, still slower.

Lebannen glanced at the ship's master and at Onyx. The master nodded. The wizard moved his hands up and outward slowly in a spell and murmured a word.

The ship glided on softly, not slowing until she came alongside the longest of the docks. Then the master spoke, and the great sail was furled while men aboard tossed the lines to men on the dock, shouting, and the silence was broken.

There were people on the quay to welcome them, townsfolk gathering, and a group of young men from the School, among them a big, deep-chested, dark-skinned man who held a heavy staff that matched his own height. "Welcome to Roke, King of the Western Lands," he said, coming forward as the gangplank was run out and made fast. "And welcome to all your company."

The young men with him and all the townsfolk called out hail and greeting to the king, and Lebannen answered them merrily as he came down the gangplank. He greeted the Master Summoner, and they spoke a while.

Those watching could see that despite his words of welcome, the Master Summoner's frowning gaze went to the ship again and again, to the women who stood at the rail, and that his answers did not satisfy the king.

When Lebannen left him and came back up into the ship, Irian came forward to meet him. "Lord King," she said, "you may tell the masters that I don't want to enter their house—this time. I wouldn't enter it if they asked me."

Lebannen's face was extremely stern. "It is the Master Patterner who asks you to come to him, to the Grove," he said.

At that Irian laughed, radiant. "I knew he would," she said. "And Tehanu will come with me."

"And my mother," Tehanu whispered.

He looked at Tenar; she nodded.

"So be it," he said. "And the rest of us will be lodged in the Great House, unless any of us prefer another place."

"By your leave, my lord," Seppel said, "I too will ask the hospitality of the Master Patterner."

"Seppel, that's not necessary," Onyx said harshly. "Come with me to my house."

The Pelnish wizard made a little placating gesture. "No reflection on your friends, my friend," he said. "But I have longed all my life to walk in the Immanent Grove. And I would be easier there."

"It may be that the doors of the Great House are shut to me, as they were before," Alder said, hesitant; and now Onyx's sallow face was red with shame.

The princess's veiled head had turned from face to face as she eagerly listened, trying to understand what was said. Now she spoke: "Please, my Lord King, I will to be with my friend Tenar? My friend Tehanu? And Irian? And to speak to that Karg?"

Lebannen looked at them all, glanced back to the Master Summoner standing massively at the foot of the gangplank, and laughed. He spoke from the rail, in his clear, affable voice: "My people have been cooped up in ship's cabins, Summoner, and it would seem they long for grass underfoot and leaves above their heads. If we all beg the Patterner to take us in, and he agrees, will you forgive our seeming slight to the hospitality of the Great House for a time at least?"

After a pause the Summoner bowed stiffly.

A short, stocky man had come up beside him on the dock, and was looking up smiling at Lebannen. He lifted his staff of silvery wood.

"Sire," he said, "I took you about the Great House once, a long time ago, and told you lies about everything."

"Gamble!" said Lebannen. They met midway on the gangplank and embraced, and talking, went down onto the dock.

Onyx was the first to follow; he greeted the Summoner gravely and with ceremony, then turned to the man called Gamble. "Are you Windkey now?" he demanded, and when Gamble laughed and said yes, he also embraced him, saying, "A master well made!" Taking Gamble a little aside, he talked with him, eager and frowning.

Lebannen looked up to the ship to signal the others to come ashore, and as they came down one by one he introduced them to the two Masters of Roke, Brand the Summoner and Gamble the Windkey.

On most islands of the Archipelago people did not touch palms in greeting as was the way of Enlad, but only bowed the head or held both palms open before the heart, as if in offering. When Irian and the Summoner met, neither bowed or made any gesture. They stood stiff with their hands at their sides.

The princess made her deep, straight-backed courtesy.

Tenar made the conventional gesture, and the Summoner returned it.

"The Woman of Gont, the daughter of the Archmage, Tehanu," Lebannen said. Tehanu dipped her head and made the conventional gesture. But the Master Summoner stared at her, gasped, and stepped back as if he had been struck.

"Mistress Tehanu," said Gamble quickly, coming forward between her and the Summoner, "we welcome you to Roke—for your father's sake, and your mother's, and your own. I hope your voyage was a pleasant one?"

She looked at him in confusion, and ducked, hiding her face, rather than bowed; but she managed to whisper some kind of answer.

Lebannen, his face a bronze mask of calm composure, said, "Yes, it was a good voyage, Gamble, though the end of it is still in doubt. Shall we walk up through the town, now, Tenar—Tehanu—Princess—Orm Irian?" He looked at each as he spoke, saying the last name with particular clarity.

He set off with Tenar, and the others followed. As Seserakh came down the gangplank, she resolutely swept back the red veils from her face.

Gamble walked with Onyx, Alder with Seppel. Tosla stayed with the ship. The last to leave the quay was Brand the Summoner, walking alone and heavily.

TENAR HAD ASKED GED about the Grove more than once, liking to hear him describe it. "It seems like any grove of trees, when you see it first. Not very large. The fields come right up to it on the north and east, and there are hills to the south and usually to the west... It looks like nothing much. But it draws your eye. And sometimes, from up on Roke Knoll, you can see that it's a forest, going on and on. You try to make out where it ends, but you can't. It goes off into the west... And when you walk in it, it seems ordinary again, though the trees are mostly a kind that grows only there. Tall, with brown trunks, something like an oak, something like a chestnut."

"What are they called?"

Ged laughed. "*Arhada*, in the Old Speech. Trees... The trees of the Grove, in Hardic... Their leaves don't all turn in autumn, but some at every season, so the foliage is always green with a gold light in it. Even on a dark day those trees seem to hold some sunlight. And in the night, it's never quite dark under them. There's a kind of glimmer in the leaves, like moonlight or starlight. Willows grow there, and oak, and fir, other kinds; but as you go deeper in, it's more and more only the trees of the Grove. And the roots of those go down deeper than the island. Some are huge trees, some slender, but you don't see many fallen, nor many saplings. They live a long, long time." His voice had grown soft, dreamy. "You can walk and walk in their shadow, in their light, and never come to the end of them."

"But is Roke so large an island?"

He looked at her peacefully, smiling. "The forests here on Gont Mountain are that forest," he said. "All forests are."

And now she saw the Grove. Following Lebannen, they had come up through the devious streets of Thwil Town, gathering a flock of townsfolk and children come out to see and greet their king. These cheerful followers dropped away little by little as the travelers left the town on a lane between hedges and farms, which petered out into a footpath past the high, round hill, Roke Knoll.

Ged had told her of the Knoll, too. There, he said, all magic is strong; there all things take their true nature. "There," he said, "our wizardry and the Old Powers of the Earth meet, and are one."

The wind blew in the high, half-dry grass on the hill. A donkey colt galloped off stiff-legged across a stubble field, flicking and flirting its tail. Cattle walked in slow procession along a fence that crossed a little stream. And there were trees ahead, dark trees, shadowy.

They followed Lebannen through a stile and over a footbridge to a sunlit meadow at the edge of the wood. A small, decrepit house stood near the stream. Irian broke from their group, ran across the grass to the house, and patted the door frame as one would pat and greet a beloved horse or dog after long absence. "Dear house!" she said. And turning to the others, smiling, "I lived here," she said, "when I was Dragonfly."

She looked round, searching the eaves of the wood, and then ran forward again. "Azver!" she called.

A man had come out of the shadow of the trees into the sunlight. His hair shone in it like silver gilt. He stood still as Irian ran to him. He lifted his hands to her, and she caught them in hers. "I won't burn you, I won't burn you this time," she was saying, laughing and crying, though without tears. "I'm keeping my fires out!"

They drew each other close and stood face to face, and he said to her, "Daughter of Kalessin, welcome home."

"My sister is with me, Azver," she said.

He turned his face—a light-skinned, hard, Kargish face, Tenar saw—and looked straight at Tehanu. He came to her. He dropped on both his knees before her. *"Hama Gondun!"* he said, and again, "Daughter of Kalessin."

Tehanu stood motionless for a moment. Slowly she put out her hand to him—her right hand, the burnt hand, the claw. He took it, bowed his head, and kissed it.

"My honor is that I was your prophet, Woman of Gont," he said, with a kind of exulting tenderness.

Then, rising, he turned at last to Lebannen, made his bow, and said, "My king, be welcome."

"It's a joy to me to see you again, Patterner! But I bring a crowd into your solitude."

"My solitude is crowded already," said the Patterner. "A few live souls might keep the balance."

His eyes, pale grey-blue-green, glanced round among them. He suddenly smiled, a smile of great warmth, surprising on his hard face. "But here are women of my own people," he said in Kargish, and came to Tenar and Seserakh, who stood side by side.

"I am Tenar of Atuan—of Gont," she said. "With me is the High Princess of the Kargad Lands."

He made a proper bow. Seserakh made her stiff courtesy, but her words poured out, tumultuous, in Kargish—"Oh, Lord Priest, I'm glad you're here! If it weren't for my friend Tenar I would have gone mad, thinking nobody was left in the world that could talk like a human being except the idiot women they sent with me from Awabath—but I am learning to speak as they do—and I am learning courage, Tenar is my friend and teacher— But last night I broke taboo! I broke taboo! Oh, Lord Priest, please tell me what I must do to atone! I walked on the Dragons' Way!"

"But you were aboard the ship, princess," said Tenar ("I dreamed," Seserakh said, impatient), "and the Lord Patterner is not a priest but an—a sorcerer—"

"Princess," said Azver the Patterner, "I think we're all walking on the Dragons' Way. And all taboos may well be shaken or broken. Not only in dream. We'll speak of this later, under the trees. Have no fear. But let me greet my friends, if you will?"

Seserakh nodded regally, and he turned away to greet Alder and Onyx.

The princess watched him. "He is a warrior," she said to Tenar in Kargish, with satisfaction. "Not a priest. Priests have no friends."

They all moved on slowly and came under the shadow of the trees.

Tenar looked up into the arcades and ogives of branches, the layers and galleries of leaves. She saw oaks and a big hemmen tree, but most were the trees of the Grove. Their oval leaves moved easily in the air, like the leaves of aspen and poplar; some had yellowed, and there was a dapple of gold and brown on the ground at their roots, but the foliage in the morning light was the green of summer, full of shadows and deep light.

The Patterner led them along a path among the trees. As they went, Tenar thought again about Ged, remembering his voice as he told her about this place. She felt nearer him than she had been since she and Tehanu left him in the dooryard of their house in the early summer and walked down to Gont Port to take the king's ship to Havnor. She knew Ged had lived here with the Patterner of long ago, and had walked here with Azver. She knew the Grove was to him the central and sacred place, the heart of peace. She felt that she might look up and see him at the end of one of the long, sun-dappled glades. And that notion eased her heart.

For her dream of the night before had troubled her, and when Seserakh burst out with her dream of breaking taboo, Tenar had been deeply startled. She too had broken taboo in her dream, transgressed. She had climbed the last three stairs of the Empty Throne, the forbidden steps. The Place of the Tombs on Atuan was long ago and far away, and maybe the earthquake had left no throne or steps there at all in the temple where her name had been taken from her: but the Old Powers of the Earth were there, and they were here. They were not changed or moved. They were the earth-quake, and the earth. Their justice was not man's justice. As she had walked by the round hill, Roke Knoll, she knew she walked where all the powers met.

She had defied them, long ago, breaking free of the Tombs, stealing the treasure, fleeing here to the West. But they were here. Under her feet. In the roots of these trees, in the roots of the hill.

So, here in the center where earth's powers met, the human powers had also met together: a king, a princess, the masters of wizardry. And the dragons.

And a priestess-thief turned farmwife, and a village sor-cerer with a broken heart...

She looked round at Alder. He was walking beside

Tehanu. They were talking quietly. Tehanu talked more readily with him than with anyone, even Irian, and looked at ease when she was with him. It cheered Tenar to see them, and she walked on under the great trees, letting her awareness slip into a half trance of green light and moving leaves. She was sorry when, after only a short way, the Patterner halted. She felt she could walk forever in the Grove.

They gathered in a grassy glade, open to the sky in the center where the branches did not reach to meet. A tributary of the Thwilburn ran across one side of it, willow and alder growing along its course. Not far from the stream was a low, lumpy house built of stone and sod, with a taller lean-to against its wall made of withies and mats of woven reed. "My winter palace, my summer palace," Azver said.

Both Onyx and Lebannen stared at these small structures in surprise, and Irian said, "I never knew you had a house at all!"

"I didn't," said the Patterner. "But bones get old."

With a little fetching and carrying from the ship, the house was soon furnished with bedding for the women, and the lean-to for the men. Boys ran back and forth to the eaves of the Grove with plentiful provisions from the kitchens of the Great House. And late in the afternoon, the Masters of Roke came at the invitation of the Patterner to meet with the king's party.

"Is this where they gather to choose the new Archmage?" Tenar asked Onyx, for Ged had told her of that secret glade.

Onyx shook his head. "I think not," he said. "The king would know, for he was there when they last met. But maybe only the Patterner could tell you. Because things change in this wood, you know. 'It is not always where it is.' Nor are the ways through it ever quite the same, I think."

"It should be frightening," she said, "but I can't seem to be afraid."

Onyx smiled. "So it is, here," he said.

She watched the masters come into the glade, led by the big, bearlike Summoner and Gamble the young weather-master. Onyx told her who the others were: the Changer, the Chanter, the Herbal, the Hand: all grey-haired, the Changer frail with age, using his wizard's staff as a walking stick. The Doorkeeper, smooth-faced and almond-eyed, seemed neither young nor old. The Namer, who came last, looked forty or so. His face was calm and closed. He presented himself to the king, naming himself Kurremkarmerruk.

At that Irian burst out, indignant, "But you are not!"

He looked at her and said evenly, "It is the Namer's name."

"Then my Kurremkarmerruk is dead?"

He nodded.

"Oh," she cried, "that's hard news to bear! He was my friend, when I had few friends here!" She turned away and would not look at the Namer, angry and tearless in her grief. She had greeted the Master Herbal with affection, and the Doorkeeper, but she did not speak to the others.

Tenar saw that they watched Irian under their grey brows with uneasy looks.

From her they looked at Tehanu; and looked away again; and glanced back, sidelong. And Tenar began to wonder what they saw when they looked at Tehanu and Irian. For these were men who saw with wizard's eyes.

So she bade herself forgive the Summoner for his uncouth and unconcealed horror when he first saw Tehanu. Maybe it had not been horror. Maybe it had been awe.

When they were all made known to one another and were seated in a circle, with cushions and stump seats for those who needed them, the grass for carpet, and sky and leaves for ceiling, the Patterner said in his voice that still had some Kargish accent in it, "If it please him, my fellow masters, we will hear the king."

Lebannen stood up. As he spoke, Tenar watched him with irrepressible pride. He was so beautiful, so wise in his youth! She did not follow all his words at first, only the sense and passion of them.

He told the masters, briefly and clearly, all the matter that had brought him to Roke: the dragons and the dreams.

He ended, "It seemed to us that night by night all these things draw together, always more certainly, to some event, some end. It seemed to us that here, on this ground, with your knowledge and power aiding us, we might foresee and meet that event, not letting it overwhelm our understanding. The wisest of our mages have foretold: a great change is upon us. We must join together to learn what that change is, its causes, its course, and how we may hope to turn it from conflict and ruin to harmony and peace, in whose sign I rule."

Brand the Summoner stood to answer him. After some stately politenesses, with a special welcome to the High Princess, he said, "That the dreams of men, and more than their dreams, forewarn us of dire changes, all the masters and wizards of Roke agree. That there is a disturbance of the deepset boundaries between death and life—transgressions of those boundaries, and the threat of worse—we confirm. But that these disturbances can be understood or controlled by any but the masters of the art magic, we doubt. And very deeply do we doubt that dragons, whose lives and death are wholly different from that of man, can ever be trusted to submit their wild wrath and jealousy to serve human good."

"Summoner," Lebannen said, before Irian could speak, "Orm Embar died for me on Selidor. Kalessin bore me to my throne.— Here in this circle are three peoples: the Kargish, the Hardic, and the People of the West."

"They were all one people, once," said the Namer in his level, toneless voice.

"But they are not now," said the Summoner, each word heavy and separate. "Do not misunderstand me because I speak hard truth, my Lord King! I honor the truce you have sworn with the dragons. When the danger we are in is past, Roke will aid Havnor in seeking lasting peace with them. But the dragons have nothing to do with this crisis that is upon us. Nor have the eastern peoples, who foreswore their immortal souls when they forgot the Language of the Making."

"Es eyemra," said a soft, hissing voice: Tehanu, standing. The Summoner stared at her.

"Our language," she repeated in Hardic, staring back at him.

Irian laughed. *"Es eyemra,"* she said.

"You are not immortal," Tenar said to the Summoner. She had had no intention of speaking. She did not stand up. The words broke from her like fire from struck rock. *"We* are!

We die to rejoin the undying world. It was you who foreswore immortality."

Then they were all still. The Patterner had made a small movement of his hands, a gentle movement.

His face was preoccupied, untroubled, as he studied a design of a few twigs and leaves he had made on the grass where he sat, just in front of his crossed legs. He looked up, looked round at them all. "I think we will have to go there soon," he said.

After another silence, Lebannen asked, "Go where, my lord?"

"Into the dark," said the Patterner.

As ALDER SAT LISTENING to them speak, slowly the voices grew faint, fading, and the warm late sunlight of late summer dimmed into darkness. Nothing was left but the trees: tall blind presences between the blind earth and the sky. The oldest living children of the earth. *O Segoy,* he said in his heart: *made and maker, let me come to you.*

The darkness went on and on, past the trees, past everything.

Against that emptiness he saw the hill, the high hill that had been on their right as they walked up out of the town. He saw the dust of the road, the stones of the path, that led past that hill.

He turned now aside from the path, leaving the others, and walked up the slope.

The grasses were tall. The spent flower cases of sparkweed nodded among them. He came on a narrow path and followed it up the steep hillside. Now I am myself, he said in his heart. *Segoy, the world is beautiful. Let me come through it to you.*

I can do again what I was meant to do, he thought as he walked. I can mend what was broken. I can rejoin.

He reached the top of the hill. Standing there in the sun and wind among the nodding grasses he saw on his right the fields, the roofs of the little town and the big house, the bright bay and the sea beyond it. If he turned he would see behind him in the west the trees of the endless forest, fading on and on into blue distances. Before him the hill slope was dim and grey, going down to the wall of stones and the darkness beyond the wall, and the crowding, calling shadows at the wall. *I will come,* he said to them. *I will come!*

Warmth fell across his shoulders and his hands. Wind stirred in the leaves above his head. Voices spoke, speaking, not calling, not crying out his name. The Patterner's eyes were watching him across the circle of grass. The Summoner too was watching him. He looked down, bewildered. He tried to listen. He gathered his mind and listened.

The king was speaking, using all his skill and strength to hold these fierce, willful men and women to one purpose. "Let me try to tell you, Masters of Roke, what I learned from the High Princess as we sailed here. Princess, may I speak for you?"

Unveiled, she gazed across the circle at him, and bowed grave permission.

"This is her tale, then: long ago, the human and the dragon peoples were one kind, speaking one language. But they sought different things, and so they agreed to part—to go different ways. That agreement was called the Vedurnan."

Onyx's head went up, and Seppel's bright dark eyes widened. *"Verw nadan,"* he whispered.

"The human beings went east, the dragons west. The humans gave up their knowledge of the Language of the Making, and in exchange received all skill and craft of hand, and ownership of all that hands can make. The dragons let go all such things. But they kept the Old Speech."

"And their wings," said Irian.

"And their wings," Lebannen said. He had caught Azver's eye. "Patterner, perhaps you can continue the story better than I?"

"The villagers of Gont and Hur-at-Hur remember what the wise men of Roke and the priests of Karego forget," Azver said. "Yes, as a child I was told this tale, I think, or something like it. But the dragons had been forgotten in it. It told how the Dark Folk of the Archipelago broke their oath. We had all promised to forgo sorcery and the language of sorcery, speaking only our common tongue. We would name no names, and make no spells. We would trust to Segoy, to the powers of the Earth our mother, mother of the Warrior Gods. But the Dark Folk broke the covenant. They caught the Language of the Making in their craft, writing it in runes. They kept it, taught it, used it. They made spells with it, with the skill of their hands, with false tongues speaking the true words. So the Kargish people can never trust them. So says the tale."

Irian spoke: "Men fear death as dragons do not. Men want to own life, possess it, as if it were a jewel in a box. Those ancient mages craved everlasting life. They learned to use true names to keep men from dying. But those who cannot die can never be reborn."

"The name and the dragon are one," said Kurremkarmerruk the Namer. "We men lost our names at the *verw nadan,* but we learned how to regain them. Name is self. Why should death change that?"

He looked at the Summoner; but Brand sat heavy and grim, listening, not speaking.

"Say more of this, Namer, if you will," the king said.

"I say what I have half learned, half guessed, not from village tales but from the most ancient records in the Isolate Tower. A thousand years before the first kings of Enlad, there were men in Éa and Soléa, the first and greatest of the mages, the Rune Makers. It was they who learned to write the Language of the Making. They made the runes, which the dragons never learned. They taught us to give each soul its true name: which is its truth, its self. And with their power they granted to those who bear their true name life beyond the body's death."

"Life immortal," Seppel's soft voice took the word. He spoke smiling a little. "In a great land of rivers and mountains and beautiful cities, where there is no suffering or pain, and where the self endures, unchanged, unchanging, forever... That is the dream of the ancient Lore of Paln."

"Where," the Summoner said, "where is that land?"

"On the other wind," said Irian. "The west beyond the west." She looked round at them all, scornful, irate. "Do you think we dragons fly only on the winds of this world? Do you think our freedom, for which we gave up all possessions, is no greater than that of the mindless seagulls? That our realm is a few rocks at the edge of your rich islands? You own the earth, you own the sea. But we are the fire of sunlight, we fly the wind! You wanted land to own. You wanted things to make and keep. And you have that. That was the division, the *verw nadan*. But you were not content with your share. You wanted not only your cares, but our freedom. You wanted the wind! And by the spells and wizardries of those oath-breakers, you stole half our realm from us, walled it away from life and light, so that you could live there forever. Thieves, traitors!"

"Sister," Tehanu said. "These are not the men who stole from us. They are those who pay the price."

A silence followed her harsh, whispering voice.

"What was the price?" said the Namer.

Tehanu looked at Irian. Irian hesitated, and then said in a much subdued voice, "*Greed puts out the sun.* These are Kalessin's words."

Azver the Patterner spoke. As he spoke, he looked into the aisles of the trees across the clearing, as if following the slight movements of the leaves. "The ancients saw that the dragons' realm was not of the body only. That they could fly...outside of time, it may be...And envying that freedom, they followed the dragons' way into the west beyond the west. There they claimed part of that realm as their own. A timeless realm, where the self might be forever. But not in the body, as the dragons were. Only in spirit could men be there...So they made a wall which no living body could cross, neither man nor dragon. For they feared the anger of the dragons. And their arts of naming laid a great net of spells upon all the western lands, so that when the people of the islands die, they would come to the west beyond the west and live there in the spirit forever.

"But as the wall was built and the spell laid, the wind ceased to blow, within the wall. The sea withdrew. The springs ceased to run. The mountains of sunrise became the mountains of the night. Those that died came to a dark land, a dry land."

"I have walked in that land," Lebannen said, low and unwillingly. "I do not fear death, but I fear it."

There was a silence among them.

"Cob, and Thorion," the Summoner said in his rough, reluctant voice, "they tried to break down that wall. To bring the dead back into life."

"Not into life, master," Seppel said. "Still, like the Rune Makers, they sought the bodiless, immortal self."

"Yet their spells disturbed that place," the Summoner said, brooding. "So the dragons began to remember the ancient wrong... And so the souls of the dead come reaching now across the wall, yearning back to life."

Alder stood up. He said, "It is not life they yearn for. It is death. To be one with the earth again. To rejoin it."

They all looked at him, but he hardly knew it; his awareness was half with them, half in the dry land. The grass beneath his feet was green and sunlit, was dead and dim. The leaves of the trees trembled above him and the low stone wall lay only a little distance from him, down the dark hill. Of them all he saw only Tehanu; he could not see her clearly, but he knew her, standing between him and the wall. He spoke to her. "They built it, but they cannot unbuild it," he said. "Will you help me, Tehanu?"

"I will, Hara," she said.

A shadow rushed between them, a great dark bulky strength, hiding her, seizing him, holding him; he struggled, gasped for breath, could not draw breath, saw red fire in the darkness, and saw nothing more.

THEY MET IN THE STARLIGHT at the edge of the glade, the king of the western lands and the Master of Roke, the two powers of Earthsea.

"Will he live?" the Summoner asked, and Lebannen answered, "The healer says he is in no danger now."

"I did wrong," said the Summoner. "I am sorry for it."

"Why did you summon him back?" the king asked, not reproving but wanting an answer.

After a long time the Summoner said, grimly, "Because I had the power to do it."

They paced along in silence down an open path among the great trees. It was very dark to either hand, but the starlight shone grey where they walked.

"I was wrong. But it is not right to want to die," the Summoner said. The burr of the East Reach was in his voice. He spoke low, almost pleadingly. "For the very old, the very ill, it may be. But life is given us. Surely it's wrong not to hold and treasure that great gift!"

"Death also is given us," said the king.

ALDER LAY ON A PALLET on the grass. He should lie out under the stars, the Patterner had said, and the old Master Herbal had agreed to that. He lay asleep, and Tehanu sat still beside him.

Tenar sat in the doorway of the low stone house and watched her. The great stars of late summer shone above the clearing: highest of them the star called Tehanu, the Swan's Heart, the linchpin of the sky.

Seserakh came quietly out of the house and sat down on the threshold beside her. She had taken off the circlet that held her veil, leaving her mass of tawny hair unbound.

"Oh my friend," she murmured, "what will happen to us? The dead are coming here. Do you feel them? Like the tide rising. Across that wall. I think nobody can stop them. All the dead people, from the graves of all the islands of the west, all the centuries..."

Tenar felt the beating, the calling, in her head and in her blood. She knew now, they all knew, what Alder had known. But she held to what she trusted, even if trust had become mere hope. She said, "They are only the dead, Seserakh. We built a false wall. It must be unbuilt. But there is a true one."

Tehanu got up and came softly over to them. She sat on the doorstep below them.

"He's all right, he's sleeping," she whispered.

"Were you there with him?" Tenar asked.

Tehanu nodded. "We were at the wall."

"What did the Summoner do?"

"Summoned him—brought him back by force."

"Into life."

"Into life."

"I don't know which I should fear more," Tenar said, "death or life. I wish I could be done with fear."

Seserakh's face, the wave of her warm hair, bent down to Tenar's shoulder for a moment in a light caress. "You are brave, brave," she murmured. "But oh! I fear the sea! and I fear death!"

Tehanu sat quietly. In the faint soft light that hung among the trees, Tenar could see how her daughter's slender hand lay crossed over her burnt and twisted hand.

"I think," Tehanu said in her soft, strange voice, "that when I die, I can breathe back the breath that made me live. I can give back to the world all that I didn't do. All that I might have been and couldn't be. All the choices I didn't make. All the things I lost and spent and wasted. I can give them back to the world. To the lives that haven't been lived yet. That will be my gift back to the world that gave me the life I did live, the love I loved, the breath I breathed."

She looked up at the stars and sighed. "Not for a long time yet," she whispered. Then she looked round at Tenar.

Seserakh stroked Tenar's hair gently, rose, and went silently into the house.

"Before long, I think, mother . . ."

"I know."

"I don't want to leave you."

"You have to leave me."

"I know."

They sat on in the glimmering darkness of the Grove, silent.

"Look," Tehanu murmured. A shooting star crossed the sky, a quick, slow-fading trail of light.

FIVE WIZARDS SAT IN starlight. "Look," one said, his hand following the trail of the shooting star.

"The soul of a dragon dying," said Azver the Patterner. "So they say in Karego-At."

"Do dragons die?" asked Onyx, musing. "Not as we do, I think."

"They don't live as we do. They move between the worlds. So says Orm Irian. From the world's wind to the other wind."

"As we sought to do," said Seppel. "And failed."

Gamble looked at him curiously. "Have you on Paln always known this tale, this lore we have learned today—of the parting of dragon and mankind, and the making of the dry land?"

"Not as we heard it today. I was taught that the *verw nadan* was the first great triumph of the art magic. And that the goal of wizardry was to triumph over time and live forever... Hence the evils the Pelnish Lore has done."

"At least you kept the Mother knowledge we despised," Onyx said. "As your people did, Azver."

"Well, you had the sense to build your Great House here," the Patterner said, smiling.

"But we built it wrong," Onyx said. "All we build, we build wrong."

"So we must knock it down," said Seppel.

"No," said Gamble. "We're not dragons. We do live in houses. We have to have some walls, at least."

"So long as the wind can blow through the windows," said Azver.

"And who will come in the doors?" asked the Doorkeeper in his mild voice.

There was a pause. A cricket trilled industriously somewhere across the glade, fell silent, trilled again.

"Dragons?" said Azver.

The Doorkeeper shook his head. "I think maybe the division that was begun, and then betrayed, will be completed at last," he said. "The dragons will go free, and leave us here to the choice we made."

"The knowledge of good and evil," said Onyx.

"The joy of making, shaping," said Seppel. "Our mastery."

"And our greed, our weakness, our fear," said Azver.

The cricket was answered by another, closer to the stream. The two trills pulsed, crossed, in and out of rhythm.

"What I fear," said Gamble, "so much that I fear to say it—is this: that when the dragons go, our mastery will go with them. Our art. Our magic."

The silence of the others showed that they feared what he did. But the Doorkeeper spoke at last, gently, but with some certainty. "No, I think not. They are the Making, yes. But we learned the Making. We made it ours. It can't be taken from us. To lose it we must forget it, throw it away."

"As my people did," said Azver.

"Yet your people remembered what the earth is, what life everlasting is," said Seppel. "While we forgot."

There was another long silence among them.

"I could reach my hand out to the wall," Gamble said in a very low voice, and Seppel said, "They are near, they are very near."

"How are we to know what we should do?" Onyx said.

Azver spoke into the silence that followed the question. "Once when my lord the Archmage was here with me in the Grove, he said to me he had spent his life learning how to choose to do what he had no choice but to do."

"I wish he were here now," said Onyx.

"He's done with doing," the Doorkeeper murmured, smiling.

"But we're not. We sit here talking on the edge of the precipice—we all know it." Onyx looked round at their star-lit faces. "What do the dead want of us?"

"What do the dragons want of us?" said Gamble. "These women who are dragons, dragons who are women—why are they here? Can we trust them?"

"Have we a choice?" said the Doorkeeper.

"I think not," said the Patterner. An edge of hardness, a sword's edge, had come into his voice. "We can only follow."

"Follow the dragons?" Gamble asked.

Azver shook his head. "Alder."

"But he's no guide, Patterner!" said Gamble. "A village mender?"

Onyx said, "Alder has wisdom, but in his hands, not in his head. He follows his heart. Certainly he doesn't seek to lead us."

"Yet he was chosen from among us all."

"Who chose him?" Seppel asked softly.

The Patterner answered him: "The dead."

They sat silent. The crickets' trill had ceased. Two tall figures came towards them through the grass lit grey by starlight. "May Brand and I sit with you a while?" Lebannen said. "There is no sleep tonight."

ON THE DOORSTEP OF the house on the Overfell, Ged sat watching the stars above the sea. He had gone in to sleep an hour or more ago, but as he closed his eyes he saw the hillside and heard the voices rising like a wave. He got up at once and went outside, where he could see the stars move.

He was tired. His eyes would close, and then he would be there by the wall of stones, his heart cold with dread that he would be there forever, not knowing the way back. At last, impatient and sick of fear, he got up again, fetched a lantern from the house and lit it, and set off on the path to Moss's house. Moss might or might not be frightened; she lived pretty near the wall, these days. But Heather would be in a panic, and Moss would not be able to soothe her. And since whatever had to be done, it wasn't he who could do it this time, he could at least go comfort the poor half-wit. He could tell her it was only dreams.

It was hard going in the dark, the lantern throwing great shadows of small things across the path. He walked slower than he would have liked to walk, and stumbled sometimes.

He saw a light in the widower's house, late as it was. A child wailed, over in the village. *Mother, mother, why are the people crying? Who are the people crying, mother?* There was no sleep there, either. There was not much sleep anywhere in Earthsea, tonight, Ged thought. He grinned a little as he thought it; for he had always liked that pause, that fearful pause, the moment before things changed.

ALDER WOKE. HE LAY ON earth and felt its depth beneath him. Above him the bright stars burned, the stars of summer, moving between leaf and leaf with the wind's blowing, moving from east to west with the world's turning. He watched them a while before he let them go.

Tehanu was waiting for him on the hill.

"What must we do, Hara?" she asked him.

"We have to mend the world," he said. He smiled, because his heart had grown light at last. "We have to break the wall."

"Can they help us?" she asked, for the dead were gathered waiting down in the darkness as countless as grass or sand or stars, silent now, a great, dim beach of souls.

"No," he said, "but maybe others can." He walked down the hill to the wall. It was little more than waist-high here. He put his hands on one of the stones of the coping row and tried to move it. It was fixed fast, or was heavier than a stone should be; he could not lift it, could not make it move at all.

Tehanu came beside him. "Help me," he said. She put her hands on the stone, the human hand and the burnt claw, gripping it as well as she could, and gave a lifting tug as he did. The stone moved a little, then a little more. "Push it!" she said, and together they pushed it slowly out of place, grating hard on the rock beneath it, till it fell on the far side of the wall with a dull heavy thump.

The next stone was smaller; together they could lift it up out of its place. They let it drop into the dust on the near side.

A tremor ran through the ground under their feet then. Small chinking stones in the wall rattled. And with a long sigh, the multitudes of the dead came closer to the wall.

THE PATTERNER STOOD UP suddenly and stood listening. Leaves stormed all about the glade, the trees of the Grove bowed and trembled as if under a great wind, but there was no wind.

"Now it changes," he said, and he walked away from them, into the darkness under the trees.

The Summoner, the Doorkeeper, and Seppel rose and followed him, quick and silent. Gamble and Onyx followed more slowly after them.

Lebannen stood up; he took a few steps after the others, hesitated, and hurried across the glade to the low house of stone and sod. "Irian," he said, stooping to the dark doorway. "Irian, will you take me with you?"

She came out of the house; she was smiling, and there was a kind of fiery brightness all about her. "Come then, come quick," she said, and took his hand. Her hand burned like a coal of fire as she lifted him into the other wind.

After a little time Seserakh came out of the house into the starlight, and after her came Tenar. They stood and looked about them. Nothing moved; the trees were still again.

"They are all gone," Seserakh whispered. "On the Dragons' Way."

She took a step forward, gazing into the dark.

"What are we to do, Tenar?"

"We are to keep the house," Tenar said.

"Oh!" Seserakh whispered, dropping to her knees. She had seen Lebannen lying near the doorway, stretched face-down in the grass. "He isn't dead—I think— Oh, my dear Lord King, don't go, don't die!"

"He's with them. Stay with him. Keep him warm. Keep the house, Seserakh," Tenar said. She went to where Alder lay, his unseeing eyes turned to the stars. She sat down by him, her hand on his. She waited.

ALDER COULD SCARCELY move the great stone his hands were on, but the Summoner was beside him, stooping with his shoulder against it, and said, "Now!" Together they pushed it till it overbalanced and dropped down with that same heavy, final thump on the far side of the wall.

Others were there now with him and Tehanu, wrenching at the stones, casting them down beside the wall. Alder saw his own hands cast shadows for an instant from a red gleam. Orm Irian, as he had seen her first, a great dragon shape, had let out her fiery breath as she struggled to move a boulder from the lowest rank of stones, deepset in the earth. Her talons struck sparks and her thorned back arched, and the rock rolled ponderously free, breaching the wall entirely in that place.

There was a vast, soft cry among the shadows on the other side, like the sound of the sea on a hollow shore. Their darkness surged up against the wall. But Alder looked up and saw that it was no longer dark. Light moved in that sky where the stars had never moved, quick sparks of fire far in the dark west.

"Kalessin!"

That was Tehanu's voice. He looked at her. She was gazing upward, westward. She had no eye for earth.

She reached up her arms. Fire ran along her hands, her arms, into her hair, into her face and body, flamed up into great wings above her head, and lifted her into the air, a creature all fire, blazing, beautiful.

She cried out aloud, a clear, wordless cry. She flew high, headlong, fast, up into the sky where the light was growing and a white wind had erased the unmeaning stars.

From among the hosts of the dead a few here and there,

like her, rose up flickering into dragons, and mounted on the wind.

Most came forward afoot. They were not pressing, not crying out now, but walking with unhurried certainty to-wards the fallen places in the wall: great multitudes of men and women, who as they came to the broken wall did not hesitate but stepped across it and were gone: a wisp of dust, a breath that shone an instant in the ever-brightening light.

Alder watched them. He still held in his hands, forgot-ten, a chinking stone he had wrenched from the wall to loosen a larger rock. He watched the dead go free. At last he saw her among them. He tossed the stone aside then and stepped forward. "Lily," he said. She saw him and smiled and held out her hand to him. He took her hand, and they crossed together into the sunlight.

LEBANNEN STOOD BY the ruined wall and watched the dawn brighten in the east. There was an east now, where there had been no direction, no way to go. There was east and west, and light and motion. The very ground moved, shook, shiv-ering like a great animal, so that the wall of stones beyond where they had broken it shuddered and slid into rubble. Fire broke from the far, black peaks of the mountains called Pain, the fire that burns in the heart of the world, the fire that feeds dragons.

He looked into the sky over those mountains and saw, as he and Ged had seen them once above the western sea, the dragons flying on the wind of morning.

Three came wheeling towards him where he stood

among the others near the crest of the hill, above the ruined wall. Two he knew, Orm Irian and Kalessin. The third had bright mail, gold, with wings of gold. That one flew highest and did not stoop down to them. Orm Irian played about her in the air and they flew together, one chasing the other higher and higher, till all at once the highest rays of the rising sun struck Tehanu and she burned like her name, a great bright star.

Kalessin circled again, flew low, and alighted hugely amid the ruins of the wall.

"Agni Lebannen," said the dragon to the king.

"Eldest," the king said to the dragon.

"Aissadan verw nadannan," said the vast, hissing voice, like a sea of cymbals.

Beside Lebannen, Brand the Summoner of Roke stood planted solidly. He repeated the dragon's words in the Speech of the Making, and then said them in Hardic: "What was divided is divided."

The Patterner stood near them, his hair bright in the brightening light. He said, "What was built is broken. What was broken is made whole."

Then he looked up yearning into the sky, at the gold dragon and the red-bronze one; but they had flown almost out of sight, wheeling now in vast gyres over the long, falling land, where empty shadow cities faded to nothing in the light of day.

"Eldest," he said, and the long head swung slowly back to him.

"Will she follow the way back through the forest, sometimes?" Azver asked in the speech of dragons.

Kalessin's long, fathomless, yellow eye regarded him. The enormous mouth seemed, like the mouths of lizards, closed upon a smile. It did not speak.

Then ponderously dragging its length along the wall so that stones still standing slid and fell grating beneath its iron belly, Kalessin writhed away from them, and with a rush and rattle of upraised wings pushed off from the hillside and flew low over the land towards the mountains, whose peaks now were bright with smoke and white steam, fire and sunlight.

"Come, friends," said Seppel in his soft voice. "It's not yet our time to go free."

SUNLIGHT WAS IN THE sky above the crowns of the highest trees, but the glade still held the chill grey of dawn. Tenar sat with her hand on Alder's hand, her face bowed down. She looked at the cold dew beading a grass blade, how it hung in tiny, delicate drops along the blade, each drop reflecting all the world.

Someone spoke her name. She did not look up.

"He's gone," she said.

The Patterner knelt by her. He touched Alder's face with a gentle hand.

He knelt there silent a while. Then he said to Tenar in her language, "My lady, I saw Tehanu. She flies golden on the other wind."

Tenar glanced up at him. His face was white and worn, but there was a shadow of glory in his eyes.

She struggled and then said, speaking roughly and almost inaudibly, "Whole?"

He nodded.

She stroked Alder's hand, the mender's hand, fine, skillful. Tears came into her eyes.

"Let me be with him a while," she said, and she began to cry. She put her hands to her face and cried hard, bitterly, silently.

AZVER WENT TO THE little group by the door of the house. Onyx and Gamble were near the Summoner, who stood, heavy and anxious, near the princess. She crouched beside Lebannen, her arms across him, protecting him, daring any wizard to touch him. Her eyes flashed. She held Lebannen's short steel dagger naked in her hand.

"I came back with him," Brand said to Azver. "I tried to stay with him. I wasn't sure of the way. She won't let me near him."

"*Ganaí,*" Azver said, her title in Kargish, princess.

Her eyes flashed up to him. "Oh may Atwah-Wuluah be thanked and the Mother praised for ever!" she cried. "Lord Azver! Make these accursed-sorcerers go away. Kill them! They have killed my king." She held out the dagger to him by its slender steel blade.

"No, princess. He went with the dragon Irian. But this sorcerer brought him back to us. Let me see him," and he knelt and turned Lebannen's face a little to see it better, and laid his hands on his chest. "He's cold," he said. "It was a hard way back. Take him in your arms, princess. Keep him warm."

"I have tried to," she said, biting her lip. She flung down the dagger and bent to the unconscious man. "O poor king!" she said softly in Hardic, "dear king, poor king!"

Azver got up and said to the Summoner, "I think he will be all right, Brand. She is much more use than we are, now."

The Summoner put out his big hand and took hold of Azver's arm. "Steady now," he said.

"The Doorkeeper," Azver said, going whiter than before and looking around the glade.

"He came back with the Pelnishman," Brand said. "Sit down, Azver."

Azver obeyed him, sitting down on the log seat the old Changer had sat on in their circle the afternoon before. A thousand years ago it seemed. The old men had gone back to the School in the evening...And then the long night had begun, the night that brought the wall of stones so close that to sleep was to be there, and to be there was terror, so no one had slept. No one, maybe, in all Roke, in all the isles...Only Alder, who went to guide them...Azver found he was dozing and shivering.

Gamble tried to make him go inside the winter house, but Azver insisted that he should be near the princess to interpret for her. And near Tenar, he thought without saying it, to protect her. To let her grieve. But Alder was done with grieving. He had passed his grief to her. To them all. His joy...

The Herbal came from the School and fussed about Azver, put a winter cloak over his shoulders. He sat on in a weary, feverish half doze, not heeding the others, dimly irritated by the presence of so many people in his sweet silent glade, watching the sunlight creep down among the leaves. His vigil was rewarded when the princess came to him, knelt before him looking with solicitous respect into his face, and said, "Lord Azver, the king would speak with you."

She helped him stand up, as if he were an old man. He did not mind. "Thank you, *gaínha*," he said.

"I am not queen," she said with a laugh.

"You will be," said the Patterner.

IT WAS THE STRONG TIDE of the full moon, and *Dolphin* had to wait for the slack to run between the Armed Cliffs. Tenar did not disembark in Gont Port till midmorning, and then there was the long walk uphill. It was near sunset when she came through Re Albi and took the cliff path to the house.

Ged was watering the cabbages, well grown by now.

He straightened up and looked at her coming to him, that hawk look, frowning. "Ah," he said.

"Oh my dear," she said. She hurried, the last few steps, as he came to her.

SHE WAS TIRED. She was very glad to sit with him with a glass of Spark's good red wine and watch the evening of early autumn flare into gold over all the western sea.

"How can I tell you everything?" she said.

"Tell it backward," he said.

"All right. I will. They wanted me to stay, but I said I wanted to go home. But there was a council meeting, the King's Council, you know, for the betrothal. There'll be a grand wedding and all, of course, but I don't think I have to go. Because that was truly when they married. With Elfarran's Ring. Our ring."

He looked at her and smiled, the broad, sweet smile that

she thought, perhaps wrongly, perhaps rightly, nobody but her had ever seen on his face.

"Yes?" he said.

"Lebannen came and stood here, see, on my left, and then Seserakh came and stood here on my right. In front of Morred's throne. And I held up the Ring. The way I did when we brought it to Havnor, remember? in *Lookfar*, in the sunlight? Lebannen took it in his hands and kissed it and gave it back to me. And I put it on her arm, it just went over her hand—she's not a little woman, Seserakh— Oh, you should see her, Ged! What a beauty she is, what a lion! He's met his match. —And everybody shouted. And there were festivals and so on. And so I could get away."

"Go on."

"Backward?"

"Backward."

"Well. Before that was Roke."

"Roke's never simple."

"No."

They drank their red wine in silence.

"Tell me of the Patterner."

She smiled. "Seserakh calls him the Warrior. She says only a warrior would fall in love with a dragon."

"Who followed him to the dry land—that night?"

"He followed Alder."

"Ah," Ged said, with surprise and a certain satisfaction.

"So did others of the masters. And Lebannen, and Irian..."

"And Tehanu."

A silence.

"She went out of the house. When I came out she was gone." A long silence. "Azver saw her. In the sunrise. On the other wind."

A silence.

"They're all gone. There are no dragons left in Havnor or the western islands. Onyx said: as that shadow place and all the shadows in it rejoined the world of light, so they regained their true realm."

"We broke the world to make it whole," Ged said.

After a long time Tenar said in a soft, thin voice, "The Patterner believes Irian will come to the Grove if he calls to her."

Ged said nothing, till, after a while: "Look there, Tenar."

She looked where he was looking, into the dim gulf of air above the western sea.

"If she comes, she'll come from there," he said. "And if she doesn't come, she is there."

She nodded. "I know." Her eyes were full of tears. "Lebannen sang me a song, on the ship, when we were going back to Havnor." She could not sing; she whispered the words. "*O my joy, be free . . .*"

He looked away, up at the forests, at the mountain, the darkening heights.

"Tell me," she said, "tell me what you did while I was gone."

"Kept the house."

"Did you walk in the forest?"

"Not yet," he said.

246